Big Lies in Small Town

Karen Kennedy Samoranos

Gallatin Peak Productions

Warning

This book contains adult language and scenes. This story is meant only for adults as defined by the laws of the country where you made your purchase. Store your books carefully where they cannot be accessed by younger readers.

Other Books by Karen Kennedy Samoranos

Red Rock North
The Secret Life of Richard McCoy
Road Apples
The Curious Number
Death by Bitter Waters

To Clifford C. Samoranos,
who has kept the fictional mavericks,
crackpots and beatniks
of Lassen County alive and flourishing

Chapter One
Make Hay

In a world of disappointment and heartache, the defiant acts of a few are often mistaken for courage. On a bleak March morning in Lassen County, a teenager's pissy nature helped determine the final outcome of a school shooting.

At the critical moment Ian Calhoun sat with blood tricking onto the concrete floor of the Susanville High auditorium, he had little energy left to reflect on the personal catastrophe that carried him straight into the path of a bullet. In his haste to rescue the girl, he was summarily reduced to a headline in the *Great Basin Register*.

* * * *

Ian blamed his difficulties on raging hormones coupled with social anxiety, a chemical stew that heightened his awareness of the opposite sex.

The only girl that didn't reduce him to a sweaty mess was Kristina Sumner. Neither friends nor colleagues, they shared fifth period English, though Ian noted they rode the same bus.

Kristina's self-possessed objectivity was often attributed to a cold, lifeless heart. Outspoken and frank with opinion, she was recognized by teachers as a rare intellect.

A shadowy bystander, Ian had developed a secret attraction to the girl. His secret infatuation began around the time the *Great Basin Register* published an article written by the Reverend Gilbert Kinnion, the prison's chaplain.

In "America's Final Decree," the Reverend sternly quoted from Leviticus, encouraging a theocratic government with an eye for an eye constitution, assuring all sinners they were incapable of change, and therefore destined for the fires of hell.

Kinnion focused on the Biblical exclusion of freethinking women and homosexuals from society, asserting that God's mighty wrath translated into natural disaster. The article claimed to have scientific

1

evidence the Old Testament anger of God was displayed through severe weather patterns and plate tectonics, wiping sacrilegious nonsense off the face of the earth:

The dire predictions of St. Paul are coming to fruition in these, the final days of humanity, marked by the moral decline of America. These signs are manifested by the decay of society in the great female uprising, known as "feminism," against the Godly and rightful place of men. We must add in the perversions of homosexuality, which together with feminism are abominations of nature, to be destroyed by the righteous hand of God through earthquake, flood, hurricane and tidal wave.

* * * *

On a Thursday, and just a few days after the article's publication, Ian found himself sitting at the bus stop right next to Kristina Sumner. He thought, w*hat the hell, I got nothing to lose,* and broke the silence.

"Well, hey," he said. "You're Kristina."

She turned her head and scrutinized him with the same lack of interest a biologist would in studying a mundane and long-discovered life form.

"You should know. You're *in* my English class."

"Right."

"I didn't think you were capable of speech."

"What do you mean?"

"You never express your opinion. You just let life wash over you and drain away."

"That's not exactly true. I *can* talk. I'd just rather not. I like to keep my thoughts to myself."

"So, tell me again why you're talking to me right now?"

"I just figured." He shrugged. "You know, I see you almost every day."

"I see that bush over there almost every day, but I'm not having a conversation with it."

"I see your point." He dithered, and then reminded himself he was already damned. "Ms. Rojas seems to think you're going to be a famous writer someday."

"Not a writer, specifically a journalist," she corrected.

"You going to stay in Susanville? Maybe, work for the *Register*?"

She snorted, and he knew he'd been successful in hitting a sore spot. This was proof that Kristina Sumner had emotions, and the realization made the blood rush to his head.

"Are you kidding me?" she scoffed. "Any paper that lets a hack like Gilbert Kinnion write religious garbage, and then publishes it, doesn't deserve to have a real journalist working for it."

2

"Maybe they think the Reverend Kinnion can really write. He must've gone to college, or something, to become a minister."

"Kinnion's daughter is the editor of the *Register*. That's how he got his shoe in the door. As far as I'm concerned, Kara Kinnion's a Christian propagandist, who doesn't belong in the editor's seat. She wouldn't last a second in a real paper, even one like the *Reno Gazette*."

Ian was intrigued with Kristina's deadpan delivery. She'd managed to detach from her brief moment of passion. Her words were ardent, yet her tone flat, and demonstrated unusual self-control.

He scratched his head. "Why don't you like the article?"

"That article is bigoted and sexist, but that's no surprise from a hardline religious zealot like Kinnion."

"So, I guess that means you wouldn't work for the *Register*."

"Look, Ian, is it? When you get home, you go ask your mommy what she thinks about that junk Kinnion wrote."

"Why would I ask my mom about it?"

"Because, your mother and my mother are in the same quilting group, which means they're like-minded. Kinnion's article already got my mom pissed off."

Ian briefly considered Kate Sumner, a middle-aged hottie. Evidently Kristina had taken after her mother in physical appearance.

The bus rounded the back of the school, belching a cloud of diesel exhaust. Students who'd been griping about waiting in the cold were now scrambling to gather backpacks and schoolbooks and line up for a decent seat. Hurrying was pointless, because some had to endure another forty minute ride just to reach their rural bus stop.

Kristina swung her satchel over one shoulder, paying no further attention to Ian. Being chivalrous, Ian took his place behind her, as the line of students slowly loaded onto the bus.

"I'll ask my mother what she thinks about Reverend Kinnion," he finally spoke to the back of Kristina's head.

She'd apparently been listening, half-turning with a wicked smile twisting her mouth.

"*That* should be interesting."

When it was her turn, she climbed the bus steps, and found a seat in the back, so he couldn't ask her why his mother's opinion should matter.

* * * *

That evening, Ian had a taste of his mother's sentiment well before supper, and around the time three members of the Gateway Baptist church came to call.

Rebecca Calhoun was Jewish, and had married Ian's father, Timothy, a disgruntled Irish-Catholic, without remorse. Both parents raised Ian with a sense of secular fairness, disconnected from a particular religious source, though they still maintained deep-rooted reminders of their forebears.

Though Judaism was an alien faith in northeastern California, reflected by the lack of a synagogue in Lassen County, Rebecca followed the Hebrew custom of affixing a *mezuzah* to the lintel of the front door. The *mezuzah* contained a hand-written parchment with the Jewish prayer, "Shema Yisrael," modestly announcing the presence of a Jewish household to the community.

The *mezuzah* had the added misfortune of attracting evangelical Christians to the Calhoun home. If the Protestant crusaders were ever successful in passing through the front door, there would be further confusion in an oversized carved wooden crucifix hanging above the fireplace mantel.

Ian was in his room, struggling through algebra homework, when the doorbell rang.

"I'll get it, darling," his mother called out, and then, "Crap!" after she opened the door, and realized just who was standing on the step.

Her mild profanity brought Ian from his room, just in time to witness Rebecca Calhoun chasing the Baptists off the front porch. The Bible-thumpers beelined for the sidewalk, and scattered in opposite directions, while Rebecca stood at the curb for a few minutes, hands on her hips, to make sure they wouldn't sneak back up the porch stairs when her back was turned.

Later, at supper, Ian mentioned the visit from the missionaries, and his mother snorted.

"Those idiots, always panhandling for what they believe to be godless souls," Rebecca said sharply. "They don't realize Jesus was a Jew, not a Christian."

Timothy perked up. "Were those damn Gateway Baptists here again?"

Before Rebecca could answer, Ian said, with admiration, "You should've seen Mom. She ran them off."

"Maybe I should start bringing the Torah into their homes," Rebecca proposed, with a glint in her eye. "I'd love to see how brotherly they'd act if I tried to shove my religion down their throats."

"Huh!" Timothy grunted, nodding. "That'd be some great entertainment."

Ian could sense momentum between his parents and thought about Kristina Sumner.

"Say, Mom, uh, what did you think about Kinnion's article in the *Register* the other day?"

Before Rebecca could answer, Timothy shouted, "Kinnion's a bloodsucking atheist!"

"Tolerance, my love," Rebecca warned. "You don't want Ian to get the wrong idea. He might end up thinking we're as warped as Kinnion." She'd apparently forgotten her notion of proselytizing to the Baptists.

Timothy only muttered something too low for Ian's ears, and the dinner conversation came to an abrupt end.

* * * *

The following day at school, Ian ducked his normal reserve, and approached Kristina Sumner while they waited in the chilly wind for the bus.

"I did it," he said.

"And?" She didn't even turn her head, her eyes riveted on the distant mountains.

"But first these people came from Gateway."

"I'm sure your mother conducted herself like the liberal she is."

"Uh…well, she chased them away."

"Props to Mom." Now she turned her head, and stared at him with huge eyes, a dark blue that tended toward the color gray, like granite rock. "What did she say about the article?"

"Nothing, but my dad didn't like it very much."

"I'm guessing he wouldn't. Your father works the bar at the White Dog."

"Well, yeah, he's part owner, so why not?"

"And I'm betting the Reverend Kinnion looks down his virtuously narrow nose at your father because he handles alcohol. Serves it out in filthy little glasses to a row of lushes."

"Now, just you wait! My dad—"

"Don't get bent out of shape, it's a metaphor. I'm a Catholic, so I get to sip the Blood of Christ every Sunday, and I don't have a problem with alcohol."

"Oh."

"My family's coming to your house for supper on Sunday," Kristina announced.

"Oh."

"What are you, back to your speech impediment again?"

"What do you want from me?"

"I just want you to watch what happens when the adults start talking about Kinnion."

"They're not going to talk about Kinnion. He's old news."

"Really." She folded her arms.

The bus made the turn around the back of the school, trailing its cloud of noxious diesel exhaust. Everyone except for Kristina and Ian got

5

into the line for load in. Kristina just sat waiting patiently, while Ian brooded.

Ian finally stood, picked up his backpack, and slung it over one shoulder.

"Aren't you coming?" he asked, getting antsy, because less than a dozen kids were left on the ground.

Kristina primly rose to her feet and adjusted her satchel.

"They'll talk about Kinnion," she said firmly, and he watched in silence as she climbed into the bus.

"You getting on the bus, Calhoun?" asked the driver. Ms. Russell was a middle-aged woman, with skinny arms and big tits, an unlit cigarette dangling from her mouth. Ian knew from conversation at home that Ms. Russell was a regular at the White Dog bar. No wonder his father never fooled around, with that sort of customer base.

"Yeah. Sure."

He sighed, and climbed aboard, searching for Kristina in the horde, finding her way in the back, seated by a window, where she studied her own reflection all the way to Ian's stop on the outskirts of town, without glancing at him once.

* * * *

The supper party was Sunday evening, hosted at the Calhoun home, with the Sumner family in attendance—Paul, Kate, their two youngest sons, and the object of Ian's private affections, Kristina.

Ian sat at the table across from Kristina, staring back and forth between mother and daughter, his hormones quietly simmering. He was so caught up in pubescent discomfort, he missed the moment when Kristina softly mentioned Reverend Kinnion's article in the *Register*.

Kate Sumner spoke up immediately, before Ian's father could even open his mouth. The edge to her voice instantly cleared the clouds of unregulated testosterone from Ian's head.

"I'll say it again." Kate's voice seemed to reverberate in the dimly lit dining room. "Gilbert Kinnion neither understands nor loves God. Kinnion understands hate, and anyone who believes his drivel is just as guilty."

Ian happened to glance up, and see Kristina staring directly at him with an expression of gleeful sarcasm.

"What're you going to do?" Rebecca asked quickly, because Timothy was heating to a boil.

"Somebody needs to write a letter to the newspaper to condemn Kinnion's reasoning, and the editor, too, for publishing that crap."

"Huh!" Timothy bared his teeth. "Who's gonna do that? Nobody's got the balls to do that."

"I do," Kate said, with satisfaction.

6

"Oh, no," said Paul Sumner, shining forehead an indicator that he was breaking into a sweat.

"What are you going to say?" Timothy prodded, but Rebecca cut the conversation short, pushed back her chair, and cleared the dishes, despite the fact that supper wasn't finished.

"You'll see, Mr. Calhoun," said Kristina, still eyeing Ian. "Mom's got a way with words."

"That she does," her father agreed, removing his spectacles, and rubbing the steam off with a napkin. Paul met Kate's eyes, and smiled wanly. "That she does."

* * * *

There followed a period of one-sided romantic pain, wherein Kristina ignored Ian completely without allowing discussion of the can of worms she'd opened at Sunday supper.

For the entire week, she waited for the bus, seated on top of a cinder block wall, immersed in *The Grapes of Wrath*, far from Ian's position at the bus stop. He assumed she was faking her way through the paperback to block his approach, and any subsequent conversation, except that by Friday, the book was gone, replaced by a copy of *The New Yorker* magazine.

She was on his mind all weekend, like a delinquent bill, or an ambiguous skin disease, eating away at his thoughts. Finally, on Monday afternoon, a week past her unsociable wall sitting, Kristina approached Ian at the bus stop, and presented him with a copy of the *Great Basin Register*.

"What's this?" he asked, the paper crinkling in his hand.

"It's the *Register*, duh." She pointed to the date. "It's this week's issue."

"How did you get this? The *Register* doesn't come out until tomorrow."

"I've got my sources." When he sat there, staring at her with a dumbfounded expression, she scowled. "It's a preemptive copy, from Ms. Rojas. The *Register* always sends over a couple of advance copies for the school newspaper to have a day before publication."

"So, what about it?"

She grabbed the paper, and opened the *Lassen Living* section to the editorial page. "My mother wrote that promised letter. I think you should read it." She pressed the paper into his hands, and put a finger on the text, signed *Kate Sumner, Spotted Horse Ranch:*

It is an interesting fact that Gil Kinnion advocates hatred rather than following the heartfelt recommendations of Christ, which state, "Love your neighbor as yourself," and "Love God with all your heart." Let's add in "Thou shall not bear false witness," as a noteworthy passage from the Ten Commandments. I am very curious if Gil Kinnion has even read the teachings of Christ, the Son of the Commandment Giver, since Chaplain Kinnion's doctrine is a prime example of the dithering of an incomprehensible illiterate. So, folks, when you see Gil Kinnion on the street, it would be best to treat him with compassion, this clergy whose parochial cloth is too stingy to cover all of his obvious shortcomings.

Ian let the paper drop and cleared his throat. "I wonder what will come of it."

"That's all you have to say, 'I wonder what will come of it'?"

The bus was making its turn around the back of the school, and both Ian and Kristina gauged the time remaining for their conversation. Her cheeks were flushed, but her eyes were as cold as ever.

"I'll tell you what will come of it, Ian. There's going to be a day of reckoning for everyone."

"What's a day of reckoning?"

"It's what the fundamentalist Christians refer to as 'Judgment Day.' But it won't be the kind of Judgment Day that Reverend Kinnion wrote about."

With that, she snatched the paper from his hand, and marched off to the bus, while Ian dawdled at the back of the line, a sick feeling in the pit of his stomach.

* * * *

After Kristina's brusque Monday dismissal and her chilling prophesy, she again avoided Ian. She spent the time seated each day beneath the bus shelter with a crowd of shivering students escaping three days of intermittent snowfall. By Friday, the snow was gone, replaced with a bitter wind. Now her escapism involved a battered hardcover copy of *God's Little Acre.*

Ian had wearied of her power over their conversations. He felt as though she were toying with him. Having lack of control was worse than the ugly psychological rubble created through her words. By Friday, he decided to plunk himself down between Kristina and some pimply underclassman and tap the cover of the book to get her attention.

She raised her eyes and studied him impassively.

"Whatcha got there?" he asked.

"It's a *book.*"

"I know it's a book." He sighed. "It looks real old. Where'd you get it?"

She closed the book carefully and slid it into her satchel. "It used to belong to my grandfather. He was…let's just say, a beatnik."

"Really?"

"You have no idea what a beatnik is, do you?"

"No." He grimaced. "What's so…er, beatnik about the book you're reading?"

"It was written in the nineteen-thirties by Erskine Caldwell."

"Who?"

"Never mind *who* he was. Just remember that you won't find any Erskine Caldwell in this town. He's a banned author. See, here in Whistle-Stop, they promote *Adventures of Tom Sawyer* for its racist elements, but they don't approve of Caldwell, because the old order thinks Caldwell wrote pornography."

Ian lost all direction. The only clear points were that she was dangerous, manipulative, and way out of his league.

"Anyway, forget it." She dropped the matter, a relief for Ian, because they spoke in different tongues, with few common terms. Her eyes, when they considered him briefly, were two pieces of ice.

The bus was on its approach, and she, like the crowd, began to leave the comfort of the herd to form a line.

"What you said on Monday," he spoke.

"What *did* I say on Monday?"

"That it's going to be Judgment Day."

"It'll come. You'll see." She smiled, and her teeth caught the light, before she loaded in with the rest.

Inside of the bus, the driver, Ms. Russell had the heater roaring. The woman stank of smoke, though a pungent heated bus was better than walking all the way home with that north wind in his face.

Encouraged by her smile, and regardless of its menace, he'd wanted to engage Kristina further, but she'd found an empty seat in the back, and avoided his gaze. She had this manner of watching from the side of her eye, without making it obvious. Reluctantly, he took a chair in the front, and that was the last he saw of her, until the following Monday.

* * * *

"I thought you should know," was the first thing Kristina said after school on Monday, as she slapped the early edition of the *Register* onto Ian's lap.

The afternoon was crisp and sunny, and Ian was sitting in the bus shelter, enjoying the mild weather after a weekend of snow and rain.

"What?" Hesitantly, he picked up the paper, and shuffled through the *Lassen Living* section while Kristina observed closely.

"A letter in the *Register* from P.D. Pervis, in response to my mother's letter about Kinnion's article."

"P.D. Pervis." Ian rubbed snot from the end of his nose. "Isn't Pervis that guy who pretends to be all religious and stuff, and then acts like a total whore?"

Kristina yanked the paper from Ian's hands. "Wrong! 'Whore' suggests he's worth his weight in gold. I think the professionals would be offended at your misrepresentation. The fact is Pervis is nothing but a scheming degenerate."

She found the letter and began to read aloud.

"Mrs. Sumner is a well-known loon, an Indian, and as such, a supporter of the Indian Casino ('gambling'). Mrs. Sumner is married to Paul Sumner, who strangely won a seat on the city council, despite not actually living within Susanville city limits. This loud, mixed-race family are Catholics and LIBERALS, a dangerous mix. We all know that the Catholic Church is a filthy breeding ground for pedophiles and thieves. Should we take seriously the words of a person such as Mrs. Sumner, who peddles her un-Christ-like wares? I think not. Should we listen to a person such as Mrs. Sumner, who supports Indian Gaming, a form of gambling, which is a dirty sin? I think not. Therefore, Mrs. Sumner, go back to the squalid reservation where you belong, and leave our proud and clean city to the Christian elders who know where their place is according to the Bible."

"I'm no lawyer, but I could swear that's wrong," said Ian. "Isn't the paper supposed to filter out the yucky stuff that people send them?"

"Remember, Ian, this is the *Register* we're talking about. Libel isn't in their vocabulary."

"Still…"

"Don't you get it? I *told* you, Ian, soon it's going to be Judgment Day. Not just for people like Kinnion or Pervis, but for everyone who takes a crooked path while pretending to be something better than they really are."

And then, she laughed, the tone of which made his blood run cold.

When the bus came, he was only too relieved that she once again chose to ignore him. For a moment, he would have preferred the two-mile walk home, because there was a menacing nuance to everything she said. Ultimately, hormones and laziness won over, and Ian decided Kristina Sumner was beginning to creep him out.

* * * *

On Saturday, Ian's mother brought him to the Sumners' Spotted Horse Ranch for a quilting party, as though he were still five years old, and required adult supervision. Not that he minded, because Ian was a voyeur of conversation and enjoyed hovering in the background.

The only hitch was that Kristina was in the room, and he still felt a little uneasy after the sum of their multiple conversations. Cautiously, he took a chair close to where she sat at the dining room table, engrossed in a large book of quilt patterns.

10

Right off the bat, Kate Sumner expressed her ridicule for P.D. Pervis's letter.

"Pervis told me to go 'back to the squalid reservation.' How do I reconcile 'squalid' with the Quinault Indian Nation? It gets twelve feet of rain. That much water would make a bag lady come up smelling like roses."

"Now, Kate," said Rebecca Calhoun. "Don't get too worked up over all of this P.D. Pervis hubbub."

Kate smiled tolerantly. "Poor Mr. Pervis is lacking in the most basic jerkwater school education. I'm sure if his intelligence quotient were measured, it would prove my point."

"And what's this Pervis wrote about Paul's city council seat?" Rebecca went on.

"You remember, we own some property inside the Susanville town limits," Kate said calmly. "Paul could have registered for the council seat using that address, but there isn't anything in the regulations which state that city council seats must be exclusive to city residents. Look at Richard Jenks. He and Sue live way out in Milford."

"I didn't know being a liberal Catholic was a dangerous mix," said Dove Foster, as she fiddled with her prosthetic leg that leaned against her chair like an attentive pet. Mrs. Foster had once been a professional bull rider and was missing part of leg from knee down as a result of being stomped. The artificial leg often pained her, and so she had a habit of removing it, the way other people would casually slip off their shoes.

"I'm certain Pope J.P. would forgive me," Kate murmured, "even if the poor fool of a man doesn't think very highly of women."

"That's just it," offered Dove, patting the prosthesis with one hand. "You act out, you feel guilty, say you're sorry, and Father Sanger absolves you in God's name. You don't have to worry about what the Pope thinks. He's light years away."

"Well, Father Sanger happens to like women, so I agree," Kate said bravely. "And you know us Catholics: it's wine, Bingo, and dinner-dance fundraisers. We love to drink, gamble, and dance till dawn."

"Still, I don't know what you're going to do about P.D. Pervis," said Rebecca, and she shook her dignified head.

Amy May Sterling ripped out a seam with a vicious yank. As the former Mrs. P.D. Pervis, she understood firsthand the depths of the man's depravity, and his warped religious fraud.

"You know, screw that bastard, Kate!" countered Amy May. "No one takes him seriously anyway, nobody who counts for anything."

Exhausted by the conversation and its crude drift, Ian turned his attention toward Kristina, who was still bent over the pattern book. She displayed no awareness of his presence. Thoroughly distracted, Ian was unprepared for conversation. When she spoke, he almost jumped out of his chair in shock.

"Why did you come to this thing?" Kristina asked, still focused on the page.

"I'm...writing a paper on the traditional skill of quilting." Ian figured he'd be able to lie smoothly, and anyway, she probably wouldn't care what came out of his mouth.

She raised her head from the book and leveled a suspicious gaze at him. "In which class, Ian?"

"You know. English. That special project we're supposed to do." He was shot down instantly by her expression of disgust.

"You are a lying sack of shit!" she whispered loudly, her words framed like shining pearls of wisdom.

Her choice of words stunned him. She might speak in terminologies designed to go way over his head, but she'd always maintained a distance from expletives. He fell back in his chair, while Kristina, cool and collected, turned away to continue her study of the quilt patterns.

"Where'd you learn all that?" he finally worked up the nerve to ask. The question was laughable, as they both attended the same high school, where teenaged banter thrived off profanity.

She clucked her tongue condescendingly. "It's not as though I live in isolation. We *do* get into town every now and then." She looked at him with ice-cold eyes. "And then, there's those banned books I love to read."

Ian was still trying to regain mental equilibrium. "I never heard your mother cuss." In his own ears, that sounded just about as stupid as asking quick-witted Kristina where she'd learned to swear. He had no clue about the content of any of the books she regularly consumed to treat her literary starvation as though it were an official disease.

She batted her eyes. "Just because you've never heard those exact words from my mother, doesn't mean it hasn't been said at one time or another. Besides, Mom says enough in that tone of hers."

He hunkered down in the chair. Beyond them, the quilting group had reverted to proper business, their conversation on color choices and block motifs, abandoning discussion of P.D. Pervis's moral degeneracy.

"So...uh, what else don't I know about you?"

"Don't dwell on what you don't know; tell me what you do know about me, Ian. I mean, *really* know. Or what you *think* you may know about me."

"Well." He shrugged. "You're a genius, too smart for average people. And a prude." He scratched the end of his nose, recalling the nickname that circulated around Susanville High. "Tucker Parker calls you 'The Ice Queen.'"

At the mention of Tucker Parker, Kristina's face grew red, and she swiftly inhaled a lungful of air with an undertone of loathing. This was the first time Ian witnessed Kristina truly losing her glacial poise, and having difficulty reclaiming it.

"That's because Tucker Parker is a documentable asshole!" she replied in a fierce whisper. "Didn't you hear what happened? I broke his arm because he tried to grope me."

"Tucker said he broke his arm in a hay baler."

She curled her lip as though detecting a rotten smell. "Hay baling in January? You believe what you want to believe. But I *am* my mother's daughter."

Which referred to that maxim used by local law-enforcement: "Never monkey around with Kate McLain." Prior to becoming Mrs. Sumner, Kate killed a man in self-defense.

"Well. I'm not scared of your mom," said Ian.

"You *should* be afraid," she warned.

"Afraid of who?"

"Maybe you're afraid of my brother, Daniel."

Ian laughed nervously, considering Daniel Sumner, a college freshman, and Susanville High honors student. Rumor had it that he'd secured a third-degree black belt at age nine. By the appearance of Daniel's streamlined, agile physique, the hearsay could well be true.

Ian swallowed. "I'm not afraid of Daniel, not exactly. I just wouldn't get on his bad side."

"Then maybe you're afraid of me."

He was unsettled how often she hit the nail on the head. Those cold gray eyes boring into him didn't alleviate his discomfort.

"Yeah, that's true, I am afraid of you," he admitted.

After weeks of trying to get to know her, he understood her tools in provocative novels and razor-sharp wit designed to keep the world at bay, as though Kristina Sumner was superior to common folk.

"Good!" she crowed, triumphant. "That's how it's supposed to be. I want the whole world to fear me."

Ian would remember that pivotal day at the Spotted Horse Ranch, and her sincerity, like a mad scientist bent on world domination.

What attracted him to Kristina, with those fearful qualities stacked against her, such as her ability to intimidate? She wasn't a heartbreaker like their flirtatious classmate, Janelle Call, who knew how to flaunt the curves. Kristina was obscurely pretty in an elegant sense, but neither would she figure into a Miss Lassen County, nor be voted onto the Homecoming court.

She was wise and smart, and coldly unafraid, important qualities that deflected boys of the garden-variety, who were accustomed to using their libidos as a barometer of femininity.

* * * *

"Face it, Calhoun," said Claremont Whitehead, in a post-P.E. locker room conversation. Claremont was a jock, fixated on rodeo rather than conventional school sports. A man's-man, Claremont could barely conceal his disdain of Ian's idiotic sentiment about Kristina Sumner, and her complex intellect.

"Face *what?*" For a cynic, Ian was unwittingly clueless, except that he was reminded of Kristina's mention of the approach of Judgment Day.

"Look, here's the deal. Kristina Sumner is an elite. There's nobody in a thousand square miles who can measure up to that bitch." The bold statement astounded Ian, as Claremont was one of Kristina's closest male allies.

"Bitch?" Ian tested the word on his tongue, appalled. "No, I just don't see her as a bitch. She's actually very nice. And besides, aren't you supposed to be her friend?"

Which brought raw laughter from Claremont, and a cryptic warning—"You'll see just *how* nice she can be!"

* * * *

On the raw and snowy morning of March ninth, a school-wide assembly was held at Susanville High School. Hundreds of students itching to horseplay were herded through veils of windblown flakes into a crisply heated auditorium, only to be subjected to an uninspiring presentation.

The guest lecturer was Gregory Redman, a retired warden from State Fish & Game. Today's demonstration featured gun safety, tendered in Gregory's plainspoken style, and coupled with a slide show from an ancient Kodak projector—two ingredients guaranteed to lull a theater filled with fidgety adolescents into mindless trances.

The tedium of Mr. Redman's monologue was an excuse for Ian to slouch down in his seat and get some shut-eye. His classmates used the time to giggle and pass notes, interfering with Ian's opportunity for sleep. The half-hearted whispered reprimands of teachers were ignored, as the staff was as equally anesthetized by Mr. Redman's boring talk.

In the midst of half the student body reduced to slumbering beneath the drone of Gregory's speech, Tucker Parker and Kristina Sumner lurched up from the front row. Locked in a strange embrace, the tops of their heads were drilled by the streaming light from the projector.

Kristina was seized in the grip of the much taller Tucker, who stood behind her, one of his arms clamped tightly around her throat. Tucker turned his body, so they faced the audience, blinking painfully in the dazzling beam from the projector.

Ian initially thought it a prank, a sudden finale to Mr. Redman's dreary presentation. The crowd assumed likewise, as a nervous twitter washed through the audience like The Wave at a sporting event. The glaring light revealed a large revolver held in Tucker's fist to Kristina's temple, proof their awkward dance was no joke.

The principal, Mr. Davies, who had been standing sentry at the double doors, immediately leaped into action and threw on the house lights. Mr. Redman assessed the situation, and shut down the projector, the two men gaining realization they were about to witness the execution-style slaying of a female student right before their eyes, and those of about two hundred fifty dumbstruck students.

"Excuse me, young man!" Mr. Redman called out.

Tucker responded by thumbing back the hammer, an unnecessary procedure in a double-action revolver, and meant as theatrics.

The click of the barrel goaded the entire population of the theater into fleeing for the exit. The faculty was comprised of assorted teachers and administrators, who milled like cattle at a feed bin. They crowded up against the rear wall of the auditorium, their pleas for calm useless in the panic and chaos. All were likely consumed by ensuring the safety of their juvenile charges and raw terror in their own mortality.

Mr. Davies fumbled with his cell phone. His intention had been to call the school resources officer, but David Lane had called in sick earlier in the day. Frustrated, Mr. Davies tried to press out 9-1-1, but his fingers, slippery with fear sweat, lost grip on the phone, which skittered beneath the pounding feet of stampeding students.

Ian saw all of this, his mind working quickly, ticking away the seconds in slow motion. There was Tucker's arm pressed against the slender stalk of Kristina's neck, an irony, if it were true she'd broken his other arm. The cast stood out like a chunk of chalk against her bronze flesh, and surely beginning to tremble at the effort. The cocked revolver, its blue shine bright as the muzzle was pressed into Kristina's cheek.

Why, she can't do anything, Ian surmised.

She couldn't move, nor protest. She couldn't incapacitate Tucker with a foot, or hit his face with the back of her skull. The moment rendered her with paralytic stillness that was unnatural to Kristina Sumner.

That boldness, the lack of fear she draped around herself, couldn't protect her vulnerability to death. She'd served them a ruse, and Ian knew she was just a teenaged girl, with frailties like his own. This strange understanding compelled him to save her, no matter his cost.

15

The student body was parting around Ian while he braced himself against the seats. As he was pushed back and forth, and pummeled by the knees and elbows of his terrorized compatriots, he saw his chance at about the same time Mr. Redman decided to mount a charge, the heavy Kodak projector hoisted over his head as a makeshift weapon. Even Mr. Davies had freed himself from the throng, and was running toward the front of the auditorium, a struggling man weighed with lead feet.

But Ian beat them all to the punch. There was no way he would let Kristina Sumner die without a fight. With a cat's agility, he pushed off of the back of an upperclassman, danced along the tops of the metal seats, nearly slipping, and then expertly caught his balance.

Tucker, his concentration frayed in keeping Kristina under control while maintaining his footing as the auditorium emptied, caught sight of Ian peripherally.

Ian launched his body; Tucker swung the revolver; Kristina hooked Tucker in the balls with one foot.

The gun went off, and Ian's body rushed to meet the bullet as it tore through the thick air. Tucker, relieved of vigilance by his throbbing testicles, fell to the hard floor between the rows of seats, while Kristina pounded his head viciously against the concrete with the heel of her booted foot. The smoking gun lay mere inches beyond Tucker's outstretched fingers, while Kristina continued her merciless assault, uttering a fierce grunt with every beat.

By the time Mr. Redman pulled a snarling Kristina out of boot range, Tucker was far too late to find his redemption on earth.

Ian, holding the slug close to his heart, sat casually in an opened, velvet-covered auditorium seat as though waiting for the next event, blood spilling onto the floor, while the wailing of sirens gained in the distance.

* * * *

Ian sometimes imagined being famous, surrounded by adulation and envy. The headline announcing his feat in the Great Basin Register was an uninspired "Boy Saves Local Girl." Not even an adjective to attach him to this place the way it embraced Kristina. No words could properly describe how he'd stopped a bullet for the sake of romantic devotion.

The truth was Ian certainly didn't need a near-crippling wound to measure his loyalty. He'd been a Nobody, until he liberated the most lethal girl in school. No matter the love affair was one-sided, a universe of possibility described only in his imagination, a veracity measured by the mind.

At the Susanville Cemetery, graves were covered in a blanket of snow, a cautionary tale of stillness and finality. A single opening in the earth yawned darkly for its fill, rewarded with a casket lowered into the freezing ground.

Before the burial, and following the height of small-town gossip, an official police inquest was mounted. The police determined Tucker Parker had contributed to his own demise by concealing the revolver inside his jacket, and smuggling it into the assembly. Further, Tucker's father, ever mindful of home protection—and even a teensy bit paranoid—had left the loaded thirty-eight in a niche in their vintage hall tree. If anyone could be assigned blame for Tucker's death, the finger would have to point at the ultimate victim.

Kristina's resiliency precluded her from being anyone's fall guy. Ian was the only person who seemed to understand her secret toughness.

"You're more like your mom every day," said Ian, from his hospital bed at Renown Medical Center in Reno.

Kristina was perched on the edge of his mattress, reminding him of one of those steely-eyed hawks that chase down little birds with bloody vengeance. He wasn't sure if guilt were on her face, or smugness. Even after all her talk, he didn't know her well enough to make the call.

She tilted her head. "Why do you think I'm like my mother?"

"You killed someone," Ian said through the tubes, the pain, and the weakness, thankful for being able to feel, because sensation of any kind meant he was not only going to survive, but he also wasn't paralyzed.

Here she smiled, but privately. The grin was a lapse in character, and not meant for him, part of a sanctimonious attitude she artfully concealed behind dangerous books and carefully plotted words.

"Ian." She raised one eyebrow. "It was only a matter of time."

17

Chapter Two
Elvis Goes Down in Flames

The singlewide mobile home perched on a precarious slope of Thompson Peak, overlooking the Honey Lake Valley. Standing on the lip of the porch, P.D. Pervis pretended to lord over the desert expanse. Far from royalty, he in fact easily qualified as stereotyped trailer trash for being poor, white, and belligerently Christian fundamentalist.

His initials, "P.D." were an abbreviation of his given name, Parley Dunford. The acronym was P.D.'s innovation, to regulate his active dislike of the numerous Dunford relatives populating Lassen County. Dunfords seemed to cram their multitude of squalling litters into the most derelict shacks from Doyle to Ravendale, sow-bellied, toothless, and deliberately ignorant.

To validate the low-class niche, some Dunfords actually lived in decaying wheeled trailers with disintegrated frameworks, no longer able to be safely transported behind a moving vehicle. During the summer, one could find inbred, gum-brained Dunfords lined up along Bureau of Land Management campsites on the Susan River, freeloading off the federal government by ignoring the self-pay envelopes.

Just the thought of the Dunford clan was enough to make P.D. deny his lineage with relentless vigor.

P.D. woke up to either the Christian radio station belching dogma, or the conservative populist talk-show hosts on KSUE. He was leery of anything actively disputing the King James Version, such as natural sciences or advanced technology. His early morning regimen was measured by the weight of the Bible that he would jam into his naked chest as a means of self-flagellation.

His morning habit, aside from Bible-hugging, was to scan the Honey Lake Valley daily, searching for what the Reverend Kinnion had defined last year as "Signs," indications from God to keep inconsequential man on track with His all-encompassing wishes. P.D.'s entire being rested upon the interpretation of these Signs, which he considered more important than his duties as handyman with Lassen Sunset House, a retirement community in Janesville.

His blatant rejection of empirical science, combined with hyper-religious lunacy, dissolved P.D.'s marriage twelve years ago. The result was a deeply disturbed man with plenty of downtime on his hands.

The greatest joke was P.D. Pervis's entire facade, his supposedly devout nature, which served as a perfect shield to hide his true debauchery. People who had not been sucked into the Born Again theme could see right through the pious cloak P.D. pulled around himself, like a vast mirage. Those women blindly at odds with the indecency of the past were in his direct line of fire.

P.D. was the master of self-spin. He owned a voice of conviction that gathered witless sheep to his demon's lair. He would take advantage of their secular confusions to gratify his sexual pleasures, and then toss them into the fire to burn with yet more unwarranted guilt.

He was known by the ignorant folk at the local Church of the Glen, as a Tongue to the Almighty. The only tongue P.D. had aligned with God was the figurative one that hung out of his mouth when a discombobulated woman plodded past.

P.D. was too filled with self-importance to care whether he lacked pure intent. He was P.D. Pervis, by golly, as glorious as his favorite entertainer of all time, Elvis Presley, and just as gifted with twitchy hips. Elvis may have hypnotized middle-aged women at the acme of greatness, but P.D. had the moves to get what he deserved before a befuddled female even knew what had hit her.

Only once had P.D. been in jeopardy of losing his freedom by engaging in sexual relations with an underaged girl. But of course, the denigration had been *her* fault. She'd sworn herself to be over eighteen, and foolish in her boy talk. For her vanity, P.D. forced penance in the basement of the Church of the Glen, down where those old, bearded church ladies stored the Nativity scene and the hundreds of tinkling communion glasses with their tint of grape juice stain. At least she hadn't been a virgin, so after the act, P.D. could taunt her for promiscuity, and remove any foundation of self-respect from beneath her teetering heels.

"You make men do this with you because of your slutty clothes and your slutty ways," he'd drilled, zipping his pants.

His favored sensation, besides the forbidden act itself, was walking around sticky on the inside of his underwear, a guilty secret with no one the wiser.

"May God forgive you, though he probably won't," he'd added.

The girl was sobbing pathetically, because all P.D. had offered to do was show her where the Sunday school pamphlets were stockpiled. In the dim of the fusty basement, P.D. recognized the innocence of this particular sheep. He admonished her sinful garments, and then forced her to remove them as a form of atonement. The blame for his behavior was all hers, and he carefully took pains to reinforce her guilt.

P.D. may have been Protestant, but he was adept at one-upping the Catholic mode of thinking. He discovered that shaming worked well on those who had become Born Again after leaving the foundation of the Roman flock, unconsciously indoctrinated with a boundless hunger for clemency. Combined with P.D.'s unquenchable thirst for sex and its illusory power, he had a perfect method of control and expression.

At dawn, with the Bible creasing his chest, the sun gained the top of a desert horizon slightly rumpled with naked rock and sun blasted hills. P.D. had very little to say to God at the moment of sunrise, for if he earnestly believed what doctrine suggested, P.D. was on a downward shot straight to Hell.

* * * *

P.D. pulled into the dusty lot of the Church of the Glen in his rattletrap Ford truck, brakes squealing, as he hurried to park at the base of the stairs.

Gathered at the top of the steps, and observing P.D. with teenaged glares of suspicion was the fourteen-member Youth Group, come to paint the hall on Saturday. They'd been awaiting P.D.'s arrival with the entry key and paint.

"Gotta watch that son of a bitch," warned Steven Haskins, hands jammed deeply into the pockets of his jacket. "Len Cross says Pervis likes to grab girls in the privates, though I ain't never seen him do it."

"He has slim pickings here," said Gina Hannigan. Of the fourteen, a mere four were female.

Janelle Call, wearing designer jeans for weekend painting, tossed her wavy mane of hair over her shoulders, and laughed. She had a way about her, with the hair gesture and tight pants accentuating every curve.

"Mr. Pervert wouldn't dare touch us," she claimed, using the colorful insult they covertly reserved for P.D. "We're jailbait."

"I've heard rumors," said Jessica Espinoza, shaking her head. "But Mr. Pervert likes lonely single women, not little girls."

Janelle shook her endowments quite clearly, the boys in the group snapping to attention. "I'll just bet you, if any girl came on to that pervert, he'd gladly have a piece, regardless of age."

Wanda Ray hit Janelle's shoulder as a warning, because P.D. was making a beeline for the stairs.

"Well, hello there, children," he cooed.

Janelle rolled her eyes at the greeting, but P.D. seemingly ignored the slight.

"Boys, you go get the paint from my truck," said P.D. as he unlocked the doors to the hall. "Girls, you follow me for the dressing up of the place." He winked, as though he were irresistible.

"Ugh," Wanda whispered in Jessica's ear, and they giggled furiously.

P.D., misinterpreting the laughter, turned and gave them all what he assumed to be a captivating smile.

The four girls laughed again, and nudged one another with the points of their elbows, releasing the tension of being in proximity to creepy old Mr. Pervis.

While the boys carried in the cans of paint and tools for the project, P.D. directed the four girls in hanging plastic across the windows, and sealing the sheets with blue painter's tape.

"Why, Mr. Pervis, how did you *ever* learn all of this?" Janelle asked in exaggerated drawl.

P.D. was hazy-eyed from the speculative accessibility of young women, and flattered by the attention, so he was clueless to her sarcasm.

"In the Navy, my dear." P.D. winked again.

"Eeeuw!" Gina wrinkled her nose.

"You must have some adventures to tell us about, Mr. Pervis," Janelle coaxed, jumping off the step stool she'd been standing on to reach the tops of the windows.

"I don't know," P.D. hedged. "Are you asking about my being shipped out with rough fellows, or what we did when we got to port?"

Wanda was on her knees, taping the baseboards. "I don't think we're old enough to hear any of your stories, Mr. Pervis," she warned, shutting him down. "It's not appropriate for you to talk about it." Done, she rose to her feet with an expression of open revulsion on her face.

"Don't mind Wanda, Mr. Pervis." Janelle smiled. "She kind of looks out for all of us, like a mother."

Wanda shot Janelle a glare from across the room.

"Like a mother," P.D. repeated, rubbing his whiskers, which he'd neglected to shave that morning.

Sundays were his day of glory in the Lord, spending two hours at the religious service at the Church of the Glen, while Saturdays were his true day of rest, when he allowed himself to go to pot. Not bathing on a Saturday was another bad habit of his—especially if he'd nailed a woman the previous evening.

Jessica and Gina completed taping plastic to the floor, and returned for another tarp. P.D., slightly distracted, handed off the folded sheet, eyes on some distant spot, roving the room, until his gaze happened to fall upon Janelle.

Janelle, who preferred the more bad-tempered horses on her father's ranch, had thighs like vises, her trademark. Rarely unseated, she could grip a horse bareback as easily as she could scissor her fellow male students, being a member of the boys' wrestling team at Susanville High. Her skills had become legendary due to her cunning ability to swiftly counter every move of the opposition.

P.D. recognized Janelle's athleticism, the bearing of the hunting cat at rest. A cold chill of deep dread went through him, followed by the hot flash of fear that overwhelms one about to be revealed. His reddening face broke out in a sweat.

"You kids're fine here, so I gotta go," he hurriedly spoke. "When you leave, just lock the doors behind you. You don't need my key."

He fled with boots in crunching haste across the plastic.

Wanda, who was crouched down filling a roller pan with paint, eyed Janelle curiously.

"Just what did you say to that Mr. Pervert to get him running, Jannie?"

"Nothing."

From the opened doors, Janelle observed P.D. leap into his truck, cut a gravel-spitting circle in the parking lot, and then bounce out into the roadway, before smoking down the road.

"What'd you tell him, Janelle?" asked Randy Sorenson, one of Janelle's wrestling teammates. Because of his awe of Janelle—and deeply buried infatuation—he'd nicknamed her "Mighty Fighty."

"Nothing!" Janelle insisted. "He just…*looked* at me, and then he got all red-faced, and took off."

"Maybe you remind him of someone," Steven Haskins teased.

Janelle punched Steven hard in the upper arm, and he stumbled away, moaning in pain.

Thoroughly annoyed, and impatient with that state of mind, Janelle shrugged it off, and went to work taping plastic to the last window, P.D. Pervis long gone from mind or view.

* * * *

P.D. met her at an Al-Anon meeting in Taylorsville, presumably distant enough from Lassen County to offer him anonymity.

The woman was frumpy and a bit apprehensive, and carried a Bible in her handbag. The Bible attracted P.D. He considered the Good Book an indicator of a wavering soul, fighting alcohol addiction, traded for repetitive religious guilt.

P.D. had taken to tracking down these collectives of small-town self-torment, where the percentage of dysfunction surpassed the demographics of the neighborhood bar. P.D. seated himself in the midst of the self-help collectives from Quincy to Loyalton, and proceeded to gauge the women for moral vulnerability.

Why he seldom loitered in his immediate county was a no-brainer. P.D. was a known player, a benighted skank self-portrayed as an upright man. Even the sluttier of Susanville's drunks wouldn't stoop to conversation with P.D.; a waste of time better spent chasing less offensive prey.

But in a distant realm like Taylorsville, he was bound to pick up on uncertainty by offering his brand of fake devoutness. He'd cajole them to a neutral site, like a motel, or their own living room if they lived alone, and then con them into sex. P.D. didn't care whether the women enjoyed sex or not. Their passive guilt made him powerful, and his God-fearing facade worked every time.

This evening, he sat at a table in the woman's cottage off the main highway, and allowed her to serve him tea first, prior to sex. Her name was Rhonda, a retired schoolteacher with a tendency to blush and giggle.

"I'm fifty-six," she gushed, and face reddening with what P.D. thought was embarrassment.

"Couldn't tell," he lied. "I'm forty-two." From the high-desert air and the harsh sun damage that dogged P.D.'s delicate hide, he appeared to be Rhonda's contemporary.

"Well. A younger man." She toyed with her tea bag.

"Rhonda." He laid a hand across hers. "I can see you're a woman of God."

"I'm a woman all right, but you being here's got nothing to do with God."

He almost choked at that point. Since Rhonda hadn't witnessed, he was clueless as to her reasons for joining up with Al-Anon.

"What do you mean? What were you doing at that meeting?"

"I lost my husband to his drinking," she explained. "It killed him, and I never really got over my loss."

He leaned forward. "You're not an alcoholic?"

"Oh, certainly not. My husband drank himself to death. It ran in his family."

"What about that Bible you carry?"

She considered his question for a moment, and then fetched her handbag. She slapped a book onto the table, Gideon's Bible, found in the nightstand of nearly every lodging rental in the United States.

P.D. felt conflicted. "That's a Bible, all right." He pulled at his collar. "Most folks carrying a Bible are looking for something that's missing from their faith."

"Oh, I'm not a religious person," she said frankly, opening the front cover, which had the appearance of frequent handling. "This here's an inscription: All my love to you, Andrew J. Pearson."

"What does *that* mean?" he asked, perplexed.

She giggled in a naughty manner, one trembling hand pressed to her lips.

"That was a note my husband left me the very first night we made love. He wrote it in the motel room Bible." She smiled. "We were only twenty back then. It's a very old book. I've been carrying it everywhere since he died, a memento of my past sex life."

"So...so you're not some lost, Bible-toting woman?" he cried, rising to his feet, feeling faint. His fear was about as profound as nearly being figured out by that teenaged girl in the hall of the Church of the Glen. P.D. seemed to be losing his God-given talent of assessing the weakness of his prey.

"Not at all." She jumped up, and grabbed his shirt with both hands, her fingers locked in the fabric.

P.D. could feel her strength as she yanked him off his feet, and dragged him toward the back room. As darkness approached he noted with trepidation a double bed.

"I'm just a horny fifty-six year-old grandma." She shoved him up against the wall, and began to expertly undress him.

P.D. was thinking he'd been had as the event progressed, much to his chagrin. Sexual aggression in a woman was revolting, and yet unable to resist, he could only watch in horror as Rhonda quickly stripped him down to goose-pimpled flesh.

* * * *

Three girls were jammed onto the bench seat in the cab of Janelle Call's pickup truck. Besides Janelle at the wheel were Wanda Ray and Jessica Espinoza. Gina Hannigan, the missing of the "Fractious Four," was absent from their high jinks due to a Masonic engagement.

"I don't think we should do this, Jannie."

Wanda voiced her misgiving, but it was too late as they were already driving up the narrow access road to PD's place. There would be no turning around until they reached the top of the road.

"At least cut the lights," Jessica suggested, her teeth chattering from the thrill of it.

"I'm not worried," Janelle assured. "I *told* you, he's gone. I saw him driving west on the Lassen Grade an hour ago."

"That's an hour closer to him coming home," Wanda reasoned.

"Hush up," Janelle growled. "We're almost there."

The singlewide and its exterior light were revealed through the parted woods. Reaching the yard, they could see the Honey Lake Valley below, sparks of illumination from ranches and towns, the orange glare of prisons, and pinpoints of light from vehicles threading the distant roads.

"That's pretty," Janelle said appreciatively. "What a view the freak has. Kind of scary, too, if you really think about it."

"Why?" Jessica spoke through clenched teeth to keep from shivering.

"It's like he's watching everyone from up here. I hope you close your curtains at night."

Janelle climbed out, and the two followed timidly. Janelle confidently approached the house. P.D. didn't own a dog, or else barking would have begun as soon as they hit the bottom of the road. For now, there was only a cat lying on the porch rail fluffed up and snoozing.

"Hi, kitty," said Janelle.

The cat opened one sinister eye, and Janelle, reading its silent hint, admonished the other two not to pet it.

"It looks like it could bite off a finger," she warned.

"Yeah, for his collection," Wanda muttered, caught up in the overtone of horror invoked by standing on P.D. Pervis's front porch.

Having assumed authority in their current situation, Janelle opened the unlocked front door and entered the house, while Wanda and Jessica hung back on the porch.

"It's breaking and entering," Jessica argued.

"Nothing doing, Jessie, the door's unlocked, so come on in." Janelle beckoned. When they failed to budge, she reached out and pulled the two girls across the threshold and into the house.

"Wow!" Wanda whistled, as they gazed around the room in stunned fascination.

"This sure explains a lot," Jessica said.

"Mr. Pervert's got delusions of self-grandeur," Janelle spoke.

Encompassing the entire front room of P.D.'s mobile home were images of Elvis Presley, a shrine to the King. Framed photographs, statuettes, sofa pillows and even the lampshades were boldly imprinted with Elvis's image. A throw blanket hanging over the back of a couch sported the likeness of young Elvis in flowered lei, captioned with, "Blue Hawaii."

"This guy's a creepo," Wanda moaned. "I tell you, he's probably got dead bodies in his basement."

"Aw, it's a trailer, Wan, he doesn't have a basement," Janelle reasoned.

"Okay, then he's got 'em stuffed into the crawl space."

Janelle wandered off, spotting the ponderous Bible, P.D.'s steadfast rock. She lifted it off the end table where it lay.

"What do you think's in this thing?" She snapped it open. Carefully trimmed handwritten papers had been taped over the text.

"Whatcha got there?" Jessica asked, looking over Janelle's shoulder.

"Look here." Janelle proceeded to read aloud from the notes. "'JoAnna Franco: size 36C breast, age 32, guilt over abortion. Got laid 3X, February 12, 2001.'"

"Sick!" Wanda stuck out her tongue, making a gagging noise.

"There's more, 'Loraine Hudson, size 40DD breast, age 38, guilt about rape by father. Laid her 2X, September 23, 2002.'"

"It's a record-keeping book, *that's* what it is!" Jessica exclaimed.

"There's a lot of these papers keeping score on women. Could be a hundred, even." Janelle flipped through the pages. "And what's worse, is I recognize some of these names, like that Loraine lady. Doesn't she go to our church?"

"Maybe." Wanda was fidgety, and kept peering out the window toward Janelle's truck and the access road.

"Listen, here's one that doesn't feel right. 'Shawnee Pryce, size 32A breast, age 17, made her feel guilty about being a slut, got her once by the communion juice glasses, October 19, 2005.'"

"Shawnee Pryce went to our church," said Wanda with some excitement, as Janelle plopped the Bible shut, and returned the unwieldy book to the table.

"She went to Susanville High, until last spring," Janelle added, "and then she moved away to go live with her aunt or something."

"Maybe she got pregnant," Wanda reasoned.

Jessica rubbed her hands together. "Maybe she had a baby."

"She was underaged, and this Mr. Pervert did something to her anyway," Janelle concluded with disgust. "I mean, look, he wrote in her age as seventeen. That's a crime, and he *knew!*" She was furious. "We're taking this freak down, though I'm not sure how."

"Wait until Gina's done with her cult initiation, she'll think of something," Wanda said. "She's a criminal mastermind. Look at that toilet-papering job after the basketball tournament."

"We've only done harmless stuff," Janelle reminded. "This is serious." She paused, and grinned maliciously. "This is provoking Mr. Pervert into doing something he could be arrested for."

"What do you mean by provoking?" Wanda asked. "Do you mean a come-on to that freaking pervert?"

"Why not find Shawnee Pryce?" Jessica posed. "I'll bet she could get Mr. Pervert arrested. It didn't happen that long ago."

Janelle shook her head. "Forget it, I won't traumatize that girl. No, this is up to us, we're taking that social deformity out ourselves."

With a snort, she stomped her way out of the trailer, the others close on her heels, terrified P.D. would return prematurely.

* * * *

The Reno Convention Center was filled with Elvis memorabilia. Countless Elvis impersonators strolled the aisles decked out in sequined jumpsuits and exaggerated hair-flips, along with the trashy sunglasses, crooning and pumping their hips in parody of The King.

P.D. was just about ready to ejaculate in his boxers. Not that Elvis sexually excited him, but the lavish implication of it all, the glow of Elvis's fame, just before he keeled over dead from his lascivious ways entranced P.D. Perhaps if Elvis had been a woman, defenseless and bloated, P.D. would have considered The King bonk-worthy. That small thought made his erection even harder, and more difficult to conceal while walking.

P.D. didn't want a man. He was on the prowl for a single female with drink in hand, possibly a little fleshy, painfully self-effacing, and meek enough for him to manipulate into guilt-ridden sex.

He thought he'd found one, his excitement heady. He approached his prey from the back, tapping her on the shoulder. As she turned, he experienced the horror of a familiar face from his past.

"My, my," said Karleen Felton. "If it ain't old Juicy Pants himself, P.D. Pervis."

Three years ago in Litchfield, she had permitted P.D. to pick her up by feigning submissive. She then pounced on him in the covered bed of her pickup truck. While she rode his skinny body amidst a stash of towels, naked ass buried in an ancient mattress, he'd noticed that she failed to hang curtains in the windows of the shell, their romp easily observed.

P.D. backed off. "Excuse me, I've made a mistake," he stammered.

She grabbed him firmly by the upper arm.

"I got a room this time." She pinched his nose. "I'll bet you couldn't forget me, P.D."

That was true, though he'd desperately tried. She was not his accustomed taste, a woman with a sexual appetite. He liked them reluctant and wounded, a slim step away from the technicality of rape. Women who lusted were worse than P.D.'s rabid desires, and could easily turn him limp.

But then, Karleen Felton and that Rhonda back in Taylorsville were women who demanded their pleasures be met, and wouldn't accept the defeat of erectile dysfunction.

Rhonda coaxed his "Wee Man" for nearly an hour. She was a patient woman, and soon had her fill. To wrap it up, he finally fantasized that Rhonda was passive, solving the problem.

After she ravaged him in the back room, P.D. seemed to lose all sensation in his lower extremities. Without so much as an orgasm for P.D.—because that would have *really* meant putting his mind to work, impossible with Rhonda grunting and groaning on top of him. He managed to put on his clothes, and leave, completely whipped. He couldn't masturbate while he drove, too damaged to get himself off in the relative privacy of his truck.

By the time he reached his singlewide, he was exhausted, and failed to note the scent of teenaged girls in the air. For once, instead of hoarding the lady goo left behind from intercourse like cheap perfume, he stood in the shower to rid himself of unwelcome physical contact.

In the morning, hauling himself out of bed, he experienced a strange sensation, which he could only define as despondency from being misled.

At the Convention Center, he recalled Rhonda's deception, while tight in Karleen's grasp. Even his now-flaccid penis had broken into a sweat.

"I couldn't," he balked. "I—I—I...haven't been...feeling very well lately."

But she kept her hold on him, moving toward the elevators that accessed the adjacent hotel.

"You can," she said firmly, her face so close to his that he could feel the wash of her hot breath across his lips. "And you will."

* * * *

Wanda stood behind Janelle in the downstairs bathroom of the Ray house in Susanville, observing her skillfully apply makeup.

"Jannie, I have to say, you look like a whore."

"Thanks, 'cause I'm going for the hooker look."

"I don't know. I would bet Mr. Pervert likes modest better."

"Do you think?" Janelle searched Wanda's eyes in the mirror for a moment. "Maybe you're right."

They had all looked up Shawnee Pryce's photo in last-year's Susanville High yearbook. Though Shawnee was close to seventeen in the photo, the unfortunate girl appeared to be around age twelve, with straw-like hair and huge opaque spectacles through which her eyes showed fear and uncertainty.

"This was taken before Mr. Pervert spoiled her," Jessica determined.

Now, in the bathroom, Janelle pondered Wanda's statement.

"I got it." Janelle slapped the countertop. "Jessica has to be bait."

"What?" Jessica gasped. "Are you freaking crazy?"

"Relax," said Janelle. "Come on, Jessie, you look the type. Not me, I made Mr. Pervert uncomfortable. Not Wanda, she's everyone's Mom, that's what I told him, and I'm sure he couldn't get it up for Mom." She paused. "Gina, you're too direct. You'd make him squirm."

Wanda held up her hand, because Mrs. Ray had entered the house from the laundry room, carrying in a basket of clean clothes.

"Let's go up to my bedroom," Wanda suggested, and they scuttled for the second floor, closing the door behind them.

"I have a plan," Gina announced, and then, with their heads together in whispers, they plotted it out.

* * * *

The Church of the Glen's "Autumn Leaves" concert was conducted in the hall, bright with fresh paint. Metal folding chairs were lined up in neat rows, and construction paper foliage in orange, red, and yellow hung from twine strung from open beams.

The Youth Group was there, along with Mrs. Tibblo, the church organist whose style was Ragtime interpretation of whatever sheet music was propped before her. Tonight would be awkward Jazz Standards, sung by the Crooning Cowpokes, the Church of the Glen's own thirty-member adult choir.

Pulling duty as chair monitor was P.D. Pervis, appearing worn at the corners. He observed the Fractious Four with red-rimmed eyes.

"Mr. Pervis," said Janelle, walking past, "have you been ill?"

P.D. cringed inwardly. She made him sweat, and in all the wrong places. She was one of those Amazons, and someday, she'd find a meek unfortunate and wear him down to nothing. High time that she-devil got what was coming to her.

He hitched up his pants and stuck his nose in the air, taking the haughty approach. "That's rude, young lady," he scolded, and stalked off.

Janelle grinned, and motioned for Jessica, who hurried over.

"As soon as they begin," she said in Jessica's ear, "you ask him for more chairs."

"But—there's *plenty* of chairs!" Jessica protested.

"Jessie, are you freaking blond or something?"

"Well, yeah." Jessica pointed at her shining locks.

Janelle patted her friend's back. "It's his cue. Act innocent. Try to get him to be alone with you, so he can say something incriminating. And don't worry, we'll be right behind you."

The crowd gathered in their seats. Many were nonmembers of the Church of the Glen, attracted every year to the nonreligious event, due to the unintentional humor that swelled the ranks of the audience.

"Go." Gina nudged Jessica, who took off toward P.D.

29

"Mr. Pervis," Jessica said nervously, "I think we need more chairs. Do you know where we can find more chairs? Are they in the storeroom? Can you help me get more chairs from the storeroom?"

He gave her a strange glance. "What in the blazes do you need me for?" he asked in a cranky tone. "Get those heathenish young men from the Youth Group to help you." He turned back to the performance.

Across the room, Jessica gave the conspirators an expression of bemused failure. Wanda waved her back, and they regrouped. As they scuffled with the little tape recorder of Jessica's in the top of her pantyhose, Janelle's bladder reminded her to visit the restroom.

"I've got to go," Janelle said, and took off for the stairs leading to the basement, where the bathroom lurked in concrete gloom.

Down here, she couldn't hear much, except the faint lilt of singing, and the foot pounding of Mrs. Tibblo as she Ragtimed herself to death on the piano.

Suddenly, Janelle was forced into the tiny dark basement bathroom by a pair of rough male hands. The door slammed shut. She could hear the click of the lock and the labored breathing of a man, as he shoved Janelle toward the wall, the sink digging into her back. There was a jangle of a belt, the hasty saw of a zipper, and the pressing of knees and hands. Though she couldn't see a damned thing, she stomped and kicked; clawed and punched as hard as she could, until the crushing deadweight of the person backed off, and the door was swiftly opened.

In the throw of fading light, she could see the backside of P.D. Pervis, making a run for the stairs.

Janelle sprinted after him, unaware that her shirt was ripped from neck to waist, showing her sports bra, which thankfully kept her modest. She chased him up the steps two at a time, nearly grabbing him just at the threshold, as they lurched through the door and into the church hall.

Together, they spilled into the light, framed by the freshly painted walls.

Mrs. Tibblo halted in horror. The singers' voices trailed away, and the crowd gave a mighty gasp, as P.D. Pervis, bloodied and torn, stood uncertainly before a sea of witnesses.

Janelle gave a dramatic shriek, and sank onto her knees. "Rape!" she cried. "He tried to rape me! He attacked me in the bathroom, and tried to rape me!"

She played it to the hilt, as she assured her friends afterward. Truthfully, she was as traumatized as she could be in an entire lifetime, imprisoned in the john with P.D.'s excitement; the monumental terror in the dark, filled with heavy breathing and what seemed like a thousand hands grasping and groping.

He's a lucky bastard that I didn't kill him, she thought, recalling Kristina Sumner having executed Tucker Parker a year ago.

The crowd surrounded P.D., restraining him for the police. Gentle hands lifted Janelle, wrapped her shirt around her, and soothed her. The pain and embarrassment were worthy, she knew, looking back over her shoulder as she was escorted to safe haven by a group of churchwomen. Some she recognized by name in P.D. Pervis's Bible count—these were the most protective and indignant.

Janelle thought about Shawnee Pryce, and the clueless eyes behind the thick, Coke-bottle glasses. Given the true face of that voiceless victim, Janelle was deeply gratified to see old P.D. Pervis go down in flames.

Chapter Three
Get a Room

Paul and Katherine Sumner had been married for close to eighteen years, and yet their physical passion was more ardent than it had been in their youth.

Sharpened by long winter nights, and affectionate familiarity, theirs was a new lease on a sex life that was already a daily occurrence. Instead of wasting time watching the satellite television, they would lock the bedroom door, and make up for the potential of lost time—not the moments they'd forfeited apart, but as a preventative for all possible future sexual deficiency.

Three of their five children still living at home recognized the sexual attraction between their parents, and mocked them. "For God's sake, get a room!" was the common phrase.

At the Rotary banquets or the Solstice Festival, Paul and Kate would hear people talk about the "Sumners' teenaged lust," carefully balanced with political ardor. The emotion was so intense they could barely keep their hands off one other, even in public.

"It's a sickness," explained one of Kate's ex-lovers, Victor White Owl, at the ranch for a pre-Christmas visit. "You're deluding yourself."

"How's that?" Paul asked good-naturedly. Though Victor was the biological father of Kate's eldest daughter, Sara, no rivalry existed between the two men, who had been good friends for decades.

"Your libido," Victor clarified. "It'll take you for a spin, and then let you down."

"Is that where you are now?" Kate asked innocently. "Have you gassed out?"

"Yes," Victor admitted without ego. "I had my first episode of erectile dysfunction a week ago."

"La-la-la-la-la!" Kristina Sumner sang, covering her ears. She had entered the room with a bowl of popcorn, and then scooted out at Victor's statement, in her haste leaving behind the popcorn.

"Works every time," said Victor smugly, eating from the bowl. "Creep out the kids, and they abandon their favorite food."

"I'll go find that vintage I was telling you about, so you can wash it down," said Paul. "Meet me in the wine cellar."

Paul had once been a vintner, and still owned a share in a Lodi-area winery. Ten years ago, Paul had hired a contractor to finish the basement beneath the ranch house, and install a wine cellar. They couldn't drink all that wine in a hundred years, and had taken to donating cases to auctions for various Lassen County philanthropic organizations, or supplying the bar at dinner dances for Our Lady of Mercy Church.

Victor grinned. "Good, hopefully it'll go well with popcorn."

"I guarantee it," said Paul, and left to ferret out the wine.

Seated by the wood stove, Kate was darning a gaping hole in her eldest son's sweater. Daniel, who attended UC Santa Cruz, a ten-hour drive, occasionally visited home with boxes of laundry and sewing projects for his mother.

"You were saying? About dysfunction?" Kate prompted.

"Erectile Dysfunction," Victor corrected.

"Gee, I never thought it would happen to you. I would venture to guess that's almost life-ending for a man."

"Well, face it, it *has*." He ate more popcorn, as though to compensate.

"What was the, ah, situation, if I may ask?"

"I picked up this college-aged girl at a bar. It got very hot and heavy." He leaned forward in his chair. "She was hot, hot, *hot!*" And he laughed. "But I couldn't get it up."

She closed the hole in the sweater with a knot of the thread. "Is it...physical?"

"Nah, most likely it's all in my head." He sighed. "Still get the morning knocker as proof."

"But...what happened to Lora?" referring to Victor's estranged wife. "I thought you two were working it out."

"Yeah, well." He rose to his feet, uncomfortable at the conversation's direction, because Kate had mentioned his wife, from whom he'd been completely estranged for four months. "I'm going to find that well-endowed husband of yours," he promised, and he wandered out to find the wine cellar stairs.

Turning back to the sweater, Kate stared at it without seeing it, threaded needle in one hand, and the sweater in the other. She was pondering the problem of Victor, and his wife, Lora, the only woman Victor had ever stooped to marry.

Kate's pride wasn't bothered. Certainly Victor, during their brief and passionate interim, hadn't posed the question to Kate. What vexed her was the rift between Victor and Lora, and all because of a stubborn misunderstanding.

Sighing, she cleared her throat, and returned to the task at hand.

* * * *

Victor made his way down the stairs to the wine cellar. Though the temperature of the upper level was toasty from the Sumners' wood stove, a billowing cold rose up from the depths of the basement. The closer he came to the bottom of the steps, the colder it felt. After passing down a short hallway, he emerged in the Sumners' expansive wine cellar.

Paul was crouched down, examining a rack of wines, and scrambled to his feet when Victor appeared. A bottle of 1989 Clay Creek cabernet sauvignon stood on an oak table, one of the prizes in his considerable collection, along with a mechanical decanter, and a half-dozen long-stemmed glasses.

"It feels like the reach of Hell down here," said Victor. He shivered as he picked up the bottle, and studied the label, a printed copy of one of Kate's paintings of the Clay Creek Winery vineyards.

"I hear Hell's pretty hot."

"No way. It's the fun afterlife that's hot, and I for one intend to hang out with half-naked girls in bikinis after I die." Victor shook the bottle gently. "I remember when you hired Kate for that wine label art commission. She was really pissed off at you back then."

Paul grimaced in recalling the rocky early days of courting his wife, and their brief contention.

"Yeah, I guess that's one way to win a woman's heart. Speaking of relationship impasses, how is Lora?" he asked, about Victor's estranged wife.

"Hell, I don't know." Victor set the bottle on the tabletop. "Some women don't like being pissed off, *kola*. It ruins romance for them."

Paul uncorked the bottle, turned two glasses upright, and poured about a half-inch. He handed one to Victor, who swirled the wine in the glass.

"Victor, if you don't mind me asking, what exactly happened between you and Lora?"

Victor shrugged, and gazed up at the ceiling.

"I don't know. We argued. I guess she got tired, Paul. We were happy-go-lucky for a few years, but I lived too far away. I refused to leave Truckee, and she wouldn't leave that fucking stockade her father bought for her in Susanville." He swilled the wine in one blasphemous gulp. "Sorry." He grunted, standing the wine glass delicately on the oak tabletop. "I know that's not the custom."

"A man creates his own custom," Paul concluded. "So, whatever works." He regarded Victor steadily. "Or in your case, what *doesn't* work." He finished his wine. "What happened, exactly?"

"I hadn't been with Lora for about four months." Victor rubbed his face. "I got restless."

"Horny?"

Victor laughed. "Yeah, so, I picked up a woman at a club in Tahoe last week, and one thing led to another. But when I got down to business, I just couldn't get it up. Never had that trouble before." He looked up, and flashed a grin at Paul. "I don't suppose you and Kate have ever had an issue?"

Paul simply shook his head. "Never have, happy to say."

"Yeah, Kate and I never did, either." Victor clapped Paul on the shoulder companionably. "What do you say we go back up, and bring your old lady a glass of that wine?"

* * * *

Kate and Paul's bedroom occupied the first floor of the Sumner ranch house. The large room had formerly been a library/den, and the built-in shelves housed an extensive collection of books.

Kate had arranged the room with two armoires, a king-sized bed, a love seat and recliner, for the evenings when she and her husband, winding down from ranch activities, sat before the fire and read together. There was a desk with a computer, and when not in use was hidden behind hutch doors.

Along the windows were padded seats, and here Kate sat, removing her socks while she watched her husband undress.

"Eighteen years of marriage," she said, grabbing up soiled clothing, and tossing it into the bathroom hamper, just a step around the far corner.

"Hmm." By now, Paul was naked, and was rummaging in his armoire for a clean towel.

"Here, have one of mine," she offered, and tossed him an extra towel from her wardrobe.

They entered the shower together. Kate refused to tuck between the sheets until she bathed, and Paul always claimed he needed someone to scrub his back. This dual excuse was a mutually tasteful manner of initiating shower sex, or a sensual wash-down before making love in a way that erotically fulfilled their most primal desires.

"Eighteen years of showers," he said, soaping her, though feeling her muscular curves and sexy roundness was more of a focal point than getting her clean.

"Eighteen years of...oatmeal." She mentioned the mundane breakfast fare, her eyes half-closed to the pleasure of his touch.

"Okay, well, eighteen years of manure."

She laughed, breaking the spell of seduction by shower.

He hushed her with a finger to her lips.

35

"You know, the kids can probably hear us from upstairs," he reminded her.

"No kidding." She snorted. "You know, one of these days, we'll do it, then open the door, and they'll fall inward."

"Victor's here, too." He referred to their houseguest, asleep in Charlie Kat's room, while Charlie Kat bunked with Dakota.

She rinsed her hair, long enough to reach the up-curve of her buttocks. "He probably listens in more than the kids."

"The kids don't listen, Kate. They get grossed out by us, face it."

"But we're not gross," she protested, putting her arms around his neck.

"You're doubly not gross," he agreed, teasingly, and licked her breasts.

She rubbed the water from her eyes. "Speaking of Victor, he has a problem. Besides being quite a pain in the ass himself."

"I know. He was kind of graphic about it."

"You too?" She sighed, and shut off the water, and they were contemplative while they dried off.

"I'm lucky, Kate," he finally said. "An extremely lucky man." He looked down at his erect penis, and presented his lack of an issue with steady fingers.

She kissed his lips, sinking into him, their skin damp, and her hand on his cock.

"No dysfunction," she agreed leading him to bed for some very hot and quiet lovemaking.

* * * *

She noted the paleness of dawn through the curtains as the phone rang on her nightstand.

For a call to come at such an ungodly hour meant disaster in Kate's mind. Her first thought was something had happened to one of her older children, either Sara, working toward her veterinary certification at UC Davis, or Daniel, far away at UC Santa Cruz, studying political science.

She grabbed up the receiver, before Paul could stumble out of bed.

"Hello?" she spoke, hating how her voice sounded in the morning, like an old woman with gravel in her speech.

"I'm looking for Katherine McLain," a man's voice on the other end stated. The background chatter included low voices, and the cacophony of electronic tones.

"So am I," she agreed. "Frankly, I think she's still asleep, and you're part of a very bad dream."

"Are you Katherine McLain?"

She sighed, and leaned her head in her hand. "I don't know. Tell me who you are, and then I'll decide."

36

"Who is that?" Paul was awake, propped on one elbow.

"That's an excellent question," said Kate. "Who are you?"

"Ms. McLain, my name is Mort Schulz; I'm an attorney in Orlando, Florida."

"I'm listening."

"Nothing serious." He must have discerned the defensive note in her voice. "Just something you've inherited."

"I can't imagine what would live in Florida for me to inherit, Mr. Schulz."

"Does the name Mariellen Houghlen ring any bells?"

She felt her hackles rise at the name. Kate was sixteen when she lived with the Houghlen family after her foster parents were murdered. Mariellen, the Mrs. Houghlen, had been the type too personally wretched to feel joy, constantly exuding an aura of misery.

"It rings bells enough to really irritate me, Mr. Schulz," she said quickly.

"Mariellen Houghlen died two months ago," he informed.

There was a pause, as though she was expected to express condolence for Mariellen Houghlen's death, but the interruption was heavy with Kate's intentional silence.

He inhaled. "There was a box. With your name on it, instructions taped to the cover. Your address in Susanville, is it?"

"I actually don't live in Susanville at the present time."

"Your telephone number's listed in Susanville."

"Mr. Schulz, this is an unlisted telephone number." She sat fully upright, and tugged the blankets over Paul. "Come to think of it, how did you obtain this number?"

"I'll admit, I got it from an investigative service. But Mrs. Houghlen has your Susanville address written here, a rural route number off of Highway 139."

"I own the land, but I don't receive shipments at that address. And anyway, what does this box of Mrs. Houghlen's have to do with me?"

"As I stated, it contained instructions on the cover, to contact you in the event of Mrs. Houghlen's death. It's part of her will, too, a small mention in a footnote, an addendum to the original document, which was filed in nineteen sixty-eight."

"What's the date of this 'addendum'?"

"May thirtieth, nineteen eighty."

"Interesting. I left Lodi in May of nineteen eighty, and that's the last I saw of her, though she wrote me a nasty note some time later. But that's not part of our business. What's inside the box, Mr. Schulz?"

"Photo albums. Photo negatives. Some low-end jewelry, and other odds and ends."

"Tell me about the photos," she urged.

"My guess they're of family, Ms. McLain. Ranch people, old buildings. The photos seem to be circa nineteen-sixties or seventies by the looks of dress and automobiles." There was the sound of rigid pages flopping against one another. "A girl on a horse, and the same girl with blue ribbons, standing beside a different horse. Two boys and the same girl, only two of them with deer." He laughed. "You wouldn't believe it, but the girl's deer is much bigger than the boy's."

"Of course I'd believe it, Mr. Schulz. That was me at age eight. Those boys were my foster brothers. René shot a four-pointer, and Jacques lost his buck in the woods."

"I suppose that's why one of these boys looks like someone kicked him in the ass." He chuckled.

"Those photos must have survived the fire," she mused.

"What fire?"

Kate described the arson of the LeBlancs' ranch house in 1979, when her foster parents were murdered.

"Nothing would survive a fire of that magnitude," Schulz surmised. "Amazing that you did."

"My foster father threw me out of a second floor window. That's the only reason I survived, and the only reason the arsonist was caught." She pursed her lips, because the sourness of the past was threatening to rise up and choke her. "But if you used an investigative service to get my unlisted telephone number, I have to assume you already know something about me."

"Ms. McLain, I can only say that you should have enlisted. The military could've used someone like you. But anyway, there's no scorch marks or smoke damage on any of this to indicate it's been through fire."

"Maybe the photos were stored at another location," she suggested. "I remember Lance Houghlen and Pierre LeBlanc grew up together in Ripon, and then went to the Korean War together. They joined the San Joaquin County Sheriff's department after the war. They tried to keep their families together socially, but Mariellen Houghlen didn't like colored people, and she hated farming and ranching."

She bit her lip, because the historical bitterness was backing up, and she was afraid to spill the gall in her voice.

"I don't see any minority people...oh, *you?*"

"I'm Indigenous, a citizen of the Quinault Nation. Mariellen equated that with evil."

"Well, it's not of any relevance to me, Ms. McLain. I'm just the messenger."

"Sumner," she corrected. "I'm *Mrs.* Sumner." She saw Paul nod sleepily on his pillow, and she added, "It's been almost eighteen years of being Mrs. Sumner."

The close of their conversation was sealed with a promise from the lawyer to ship the box straight to the Spotted Horse Ranch.

Afterward, she settled into the body-heated bedding, her chilled breasts against Paul's warm back.

"What's the prognosis?" he asked, eyes still closed.

"I get a dead woman's leftovers," she murmured, and managed to fall back to sleep for another hour.

* * * *

Since it was winter break, and the start of the Christmas celebration, both Daniel and Sara returned to the ranch during their month-long holiday. The Sumner nest was filled again, along with the nagging presence of Victor White Owl.

Kate was making apple pies and found his hulking silence at her kitchen table particularly aggravating.

"You're like a raven at a garbage heap," she remarked.

"Thank you. I like ravens, so I'll take that as a compliment."

Nothing could sway his calm, except, of course, his marital predicament.

"I telephoned Lora," she said casually, knowing this would irk him. "I've asked her to come to supper on Christmas Day."

"No!" He predictably slapped the tabletop with the flat of his hand. "Why the hell did you do that, Kate?"

"Let's talk about possession, Victor." Her notorious indignation was revealing itself.

"Being nine-tenths of the law?"

"What an asinine proverb," she scoffed. "No, about *this* ranch, *my* privacy, and *your* wife!"

He folded his hands. "I'm listening. Say, Kate, get me a glass of Scotch, will you? That's if you expect me to keep listening."

Though it was ten o'clock in the morning, she obliged by grabbing up a tumbler, sloshing in a generous measure of whisky, and slamming it onto the table before him, like a cinematic barkeep.

"By all means, drink up," she said with exaggerated hospitality.

"By all means, keep barking."

Nevertheless, he took a large swallow, and then gave her his full attention from across the table.

"You know, Victor, I can tolerate you, I really can. It's nothing personal. We had our…time, so to speak, and we're still standing. I like you, and we'll always be friends. It's just that you wear like a smelly sock, or bad hygiene, when you stay here at the ranch for more than three days. And it's going on three weeks, so maybe you can see where this is heading."

"Humph."

"You have to get a grip on your life. That's what I'm saying. Your personal life, you have to conclude your business with Lora, one way or the other."

He raised his brows, and then finished the liquor. "How so?"

"Look, you haven't been to Truckee in how long?" She was referencing his veterinary practice of over thirty years.

"Three weeks." Which was exactly the length of time he'd stubbornly remained at the Spotted Horse Ranch.

"And who handles the practice when you're away?"

"Tom Thorn and Ben Parks." He named his partners, two Washoe veterinarians, who had been with Victor collectively for close to twenty years.

"Are you even part of the practice anymore?"

He shrugged. His fifty-ninth birthday had recently come and gone, and would become a dwindling memory. "I was thinking about retirement."

"Not that you have to retire, but you certainly can't focus on your work without resolving this thing with Lora."

"No shit!"

"I have a solution for you, *Hinhanska*." She affectionately mentioned his Lakota name, out of deference. "But you'd have to give up something."

"Hell, I'm not giving up anything the woman won't give up too!" he snarled.

"Victor, I think Lora would give something up, if it were a mutual thing." She sat back in her chair. "I would just bet that she'd leave behind that house her father bought her, if the two of you had your own place to live." She nodded sagely. "I just *bet* she would."

Now Victor was staring at the empty glass. She knew he wanted another tot, so she got up and retrieved the bottle, and splashed a few gulps into the tumbler.

But he only stared at the contents. He wasn't glowering, so she deduced he must have been working it out inside his head. She was about to rise to her feet again, and return to the pies, when he reached out and grasped her hand.

"Kate." His voice was hopeful at the edges, but plaintive, too. "Do you *really* think so, Kate?"

She gazed down at this man who for so long had been both a gigantic nuisance, and good friend. She owned memories—locked away—of their lovemaking, and was grateful that they had managed to salvage and nourish the platonic force of their relationship after so much water under the bridge.

"Yes, Victor, I *know* it. Lora said this to me."

"Good, because you really don't know how much I miss that ungrateful, bitchy wife of mine." He downed the second glass, and wiped his lips.

"I know. She misses you, too." She patted his hand kindly, and returned to her pies.

* * * *

On Christmas Eve, they shuttled to Our Lady of Mercy church in Susanville, loading into the Sumners' eight-passenger white Suburban. This included Victor, no Catholic at all, but accompanying the family if it meant avoiding being left alone at the Spotted Horse Ranch.

As Kate drove, she could see Victor eyeing her in the rearview mirror from the second bench seat, and pondered on the working of his mind. The long drive was filled with family conversation, while Victor sat mutely, his eyes probing Kate's as she took the long turns of the highway. His behavior was so uncharacteristic of Native culture that she knew he was up to some mischief.

At the church, he paused beside the Suburban, while Kate's five children tumbled out, eager to meet up with old friends inside the church.

Paul had apparently noted the intensity between Victor and Kate. She had informed him about the odd conversation at the kitchen table, and though not particularly worried about his wife's actions, he expressed concern about Victor's state of mind.

"Do you mind if I borrow your truck?" Victor was asking.

"Yes, I mind if you borrow my truck," she huffed. "Just where were you thinking of going?"

Victor rubbed his cheek. The cold was irritating, but then, it seemed Kate's attitude was getting to him.

"I was thinking of going out to see Lora," he admitted.

She shoved the wad of keys into Victor's hands. "You have at least an hour. If you so much as scratch my truck, you're going to have to answer to me. And if you forget to come back for us, I'm going to kick your ass when I finally catch up to you, is that understood?"

Victor's mouth spread in a smile that lit up his eyes. "Such words, woman, right outside of your church."

"I'm not worried. I get absolution."

With that said, she put her arm through Paul's, and they hurried after their brood.

* * * *

All along Main Street, Victor thought about Lora with a pain that ran from his head, through his heart and into his groin. Apparently, just the thought of her made him hard. By the time he reached her log battlements out on Old Johnstonville Road, he was throbbing in pain, and decided that extended foreplay wasn't going to be part of this thing at all, if he had his say. A man can resist a woman he desires for only so long.

He knocked on her door. Lora opened it. There was about a ten second silence, as they regarded each other, and then, she grasped his jacket, hauling him into the house. With an expression of total bliss on his face, Victor followed her hand, entering her "fucking stockade," as he'd termed it, without reserve.

But at least he wasn't late picking up the Sumner family outside of Our Lady of Mercy.

* * * *

They had been standing at the curb for less than two minutes, when Victor swept up in the white Suburban, and set the brake. He opened the doors with the flourish of a chauffeur, relinquishing the wheel to Kate, and loaded himself onto that rear bench seat between Charlie Kat and Dakota.

All the way to the ranch, she might have been wondering, except for the first clue, Victor's wet hair in spite of the cold. Soon after they headed up the Lassen Grade, he fell asleep, snoring forcefully, and that could only mean one thing—that Victor and Lora had broken their stalemate with vigorous sex.

She turned her head to look at her husband. Paul was smiling at her, and she grinned back.

* * * *

The box from the Florida lawyer, Mort Schulz, arrived two days past Christmas. Since all of her children were home until after the New Year, Kate was fortunate to have the opportunity to share her former life with them. The box had flung a window wide open, and a bygone era spilled out.

Seated at the kitchen table, she set out the photographs of her childhood, seven albums in all, most containing black and white stills of deer hunts and ranch work. The photos portrayed her as a tough slip of a girl driving tractors, and posing unsmilingly with her arms cradling a hunting rifle. From this uncommon childhood, she'd grown into an unyielding and calculating young woman.

One photo undermined the austerity of the entire collection.

Kate pulled the framed portrait from its paper wrapper—a photo of herself in an elaborate, lace-edged white gown, complete with a garland of white roses that defined the frame of her long, silken dark hair.

"What is that?" Paul asked, when he received the photo into eager hands.

"That's when Mommy married you, Daddy," said Dakota.

"I don't think so," Kristina disputed. "Mom's a lot younger than in that big picture in their bedroom." She mentioned the framed color portrait of Kate and Paul on their wedding day, hung above the master bedroom hearth.

"I know what this is." Sara took hold of the photo, and studied it. "It's Mom on her Confirmation day."

"You're right," said Kate, "and the only time in my life when I ever really enjoyed wearing a dress, except for my First Holy Communion. And our wedding, of course."

Daniel, whose attention had been buried in the photo albums, placed the last book aside.

"You're a paradox, Mom," he claimed.

"Mom's not even one doctor, so how could she be a pair of docs?" asked Charlie Kat seriously. Charlie Kat was a tireless jokester, and always prepared to take advantage with a pun.

"No, big guy, I meant that Mom's a real woman, even though she grew up like a boy," Daniel explained, ruffling Charlie Kat's hair, until the younger boy scooted away, giggling.

"You're right," Paul agreed, putting one arm around his wife, and feeling the tautness of the muscles she possessed even now at age forty-four. "Your mom *is* a real woman."

It might have been a tender moment, but then Kristina groaned, Charlie Kat made a gagging motion, while Dakota sat with his hands around his own throat.

"For God's sake," they chorused, "get a room!"

Chapter Four
Take it Like a Man

Sidestepping up the unstable hill in his worn institutional shoes, the gravel gave away, and he nearly slid toward the creek bed one hundred feet below.

He was sweating, and the bitch of it was carrying all those implements—the shovel and pick; a heavy black Maglite, and roll of black plastic, doomed to line a hole in the woods to repel maggots and coyotes.

He had too much to haul up to the site in one trip. In the cruiser, a white blob on the dirt road behind, he'd left the bag of lime. The sack weighed a hundred pounds, but then, that was a hell of a lot lighter than carrying a hostage. He wasn't getting any younger. The problem with turning fifty was a guaranteed decline in physical abilities. Too bad he hadn't remembered *that* before his dick got him into trouble.

Reaching a grove of trees just out of sight of the dirt road, age and exhaustion caught up with him. He decided to march her up here at gunpoint, and keep the weight off his legs.

At the site, he slipped into the pines, letting the tools fall with a *clank* upon the crinkly roll of plastic. He was panting, sweat rolling down his body beneath his clothes, adding to the stress that produced a slight fluttering beat to his heart. The heavy lined jacket with official police insignia magnified his physical discomfort.

Sitting down heavily on the edge of the slope, he listened to the creek, hopelessness like a rock in his chest. The core of his problems lay in his inability to rationalize his choices in recent weeks. Add some desperation to the mix, and a man might do anything, even if he were the police chief of Susanville.

He caught his breath, and groaning, hauled himself to his feet. Adjusting his glasses, he set the flashlight on the roll of plastic, and hefted the pick. With a grunt, he bit deep into the soil with the deadly point.

* * * *

His troubles began when his wife of twenty-five years passed away. Hers was a simple case of mistaken identity: a driver of a semi truck on Main, heading toward the Lassen Grade, had confused Diane for thin air, and plowed her down. The blood splatter still stained the asphalt, and every time Sam Pilger drove through town, he was reminded of his wife's violent death.

The Lassen County Sheriff's department handled the investigation third-party, because Diane was the wife of the Susanville police chief, and there was fear of bias.

After lengthy review, the department determined that the truck driver had heading west with the sun in his eyes, while Diane was crossing against the signal light. Between the lines, the report implied, *let's get real, and settle blame where responsibility belongs, directly on the innocent victim.*

Reading the report, Sam understood the truck driver had become, in that bloody instant, his enemy. Sam was getting up in years, despite his immaculate uniform, close-shorn black hair, and biker's goatee, designed to intimidate and impress. Losing his wife was far grimmer than losing an arm or leg.

Sam was post-military, and what a military man did to the enemy was to tear him apart, by hand if necessary. He therefore decreed in his private thoughts that the trucker should die. For a while he elaborately planned the man's death. Diane's demise was swift, but this trucker, this faceless pariah, would suffer, and only because Sam agonized behind a facade of stoic forbearance.

Externally, all seemed well, the townspeople nodding encouragement to his pain. The internal rage was twisting him into a foul wreck. Behind his eyes the real man was a savage, primed to kill, stinking with hidden, inner decay.

Hiding his rage was only the start of Sam's misery.

There were the traditional practices, the funeral, burial, and the condolences of friends and acquaintances. The tragedy had been published in the *Great Basin Register*, and people as far away as Minnesota and Florida sent sympathy cards.

Unvented rage and grief consumed him, and he was incapable of responding. The cards, stack upon stack, were shoved into a box, the lid taped shut. He fantasized about taking the box out to the desert and setting the contents ablaze, maybe pouring some kerosene over his head too, and lighting a match.

But there was a meager pinhole of light in Sam's otherwise hopeless lot. His daughter, Leslie, often too busy to take time off from her job, returned to Susanville for the funeral.

Leslie was heartbroken, as she and Diane had been so close. At twenty-four, and an only child, Leslie had built a separate life, though the umbilicus was still firmly attached.

Diane had embraced motherhood, a secret cache built around herself and Leslie, and apart from Sam. He never held it against his wife, not until she died, and he witnessed the deep pain inflicted upon their daughter.

The stark difference was that Leslie freely grieved, while Sam privatized his sorrow to the point of denial.

After the funeral, Sam and Leslie returned to his ranchette off Johnstonville Road, and pored over the photo albums. The books were final proof of their intertwined lives, and Sam had made a point to laugh, whether or not he felt like it. There were plenty of tears to come, but not in Leslie's stead. Sam would visit no grief upon his child. He was only grateful for twenty-five years with Diane. There was no need to sweep Leslie out with the uncontrollable nature of mourning.

Before Leslie returned to her career in Los Angeles—editor for the West Coast division of a textbook publisher—she secured the services of a woman to regularly clean Sam's empty house and cook a few meals. She would never hire a stranger for Sam, and chose a former schoolmate, a young woman Leslie's age, by the name of Aurora Campbell.

* * * *

Sam recalled Aurora from the distant past, a gangly, large-eyed girl with a slight overbite. She had been painfully shy and self-conscious, which had developed into clumsy puberty.

The Campbells had been a typical all-American family. The parents, Mitch and Janice, were friends of Sam and Diane when the two families lived in Salinas. Mitch and Sam had been cops on the police force in Carmel-by-the-Sea, and forged a close bond. In that sense their daughters, Leslie and Aurora, become inseparable playmates.

Just before Aurora entered junior high school, the Campbell family abruptly moved to San Diego, where Mitch continued his career in law enforcement. Sam and Diane eventually settled in Lassen County, at odds in distance from their former friends. Due to mileage, and the passing of time, the girls didn't reconnect until they crossed paths while attending Chico State University.

When advised of his caretaker, Sam was reluctant, recalling a leggy, painfully self-effacing girl. He did not expect protracted conversation with a person who'd been so introverted that she couldn't even speak in Sam's presence. He did not anticipate a shift of the girl into a woman, or the stunner she'd become.

Aurora lived in Janesville, and owned a log house on ten wooded acres of mountain slope near the base of Thompson Peak. Employed by

46

Lassen County as a building inspector, she had developed a keen manner of observation, and no compunction to hold her tongue.

She exhibited confidence and a fine intelligence, besides her obvious favorable physical attributes. The awkward teeth had been purged by orthodontia, the skinny form replaced with curves of muscle. Aurora seemed fearless, and rode a motorcycle, showing up for work at Sam's that first day on a Concours, a man's urban touring bike.

She was strictly clinical, and all business, until Sam personalized their relationship by asking her questions about her private life.

"I don't have your problem," Sam commented, about her motorcycle hobby. "I have a bike, but unlike you, I don't have a desire to ride."

His Harley-Davidson Softail languished in the garage. Diane had hated the thing, condescending to ride infrequently behind him as passenger. He had fading memories of Diane's arms latched around his waist, shivering in terror of the road.

A few days later, Aurora returned on the Concours while Sam was dithering in the front yard, pretending to give a damn about Diane's withered flowerbed.

"Who does that belong to, your boyfriend?" he asked innocently, a way to figure out her connections. In the depths of his brain, he entertained carnal aspirations with this gorgeous woman, and knew he'd never have a chance if she were already involved with another younger cock.

She shifted slightly, the swell of her breasts peeking over the top of her shirt, and stirring Sam's lonely appetite.

"This is my bike, Sam. And I don't have a boyfriend. So, you don't have any competition."

"Nice bike," Sam answered, ignoring the ringing in his ears. "Put it in the garage. You'll get it dirty."

"No, Sam," she spoke in that firm voice, one hand on his shoulder. "We're going riding."

They took a day trip, with Aurora mounted on the Concours, guiding Sam on his Harley. At first, he was a bit wobbly from lack of practice. The ride was lengthy, the sweeping miles up the Interstate and across the Madeline Plains to Alturas. They rode in staggered formation, his energy guided by her eloquent, graceful body as it lay invitingly across her bike.

They stopped to eat at a diner, not exactly jetted to romance, but comfortable together. Sam could sense his appetite was returning in all definitions of the word. The air between them seemed to crackle with electricity fueled by the misdirected power of his bottled-up grief.

Back home, he collapsed into bed with Aurora, on a mattress where he once slept with Diane, dented by the shapes of familiar bodies.

That night, he didn't approach sleep, too occupied by frisking around naked with Aurora. He considered the strangeness of being fifty, and yet conjuring youth while making love to a young woman his daughter's age. He knew with some guilt that sex with Aurora was far better than it had ever been with Diane.

"What would Leslie think?" he asked her, an inept kickoff of post-coital conversation.

"She might think that her father's happy, and deserves to be," Aurora had gauged.

Without his glasses, his blue eyes filled with a fuzzy notion of Aurora's shapely body.

"I can see happy around the bend," he agreed, "but I also see a lot of sadness."

"I'll stay with you, Sam, and then maybe you won't be sad."

"I'll always be sad."

Which meant, in translation, that he owned no intention of a commitment, marital or otherwise.

"Sadness can be an infinite pit," she explained, while sitting up on one elbow, so she could look into his unfocused eyes. "But there's always hope enough to pull a person up out of it no matter how deep they've fallen."

He reasoned that for her he would pass, like the weather, and she would find herself young male comfort. She had no need to be chained to an old man. He told her this, as though he were a repository of wisdom.

But the truth was Sam would never be able to face his community, nor his own daughter, if he admitted to a sexual relationship with a woman who was young enough to be his child.

"We're both adults," she reminded. "It's nobody's business what we do behind closed doors."

"I remember," Sam told Aurora, seeking another tack, "a time when you were naked."

She stretched like a cat, her body dumbfounding. "Like this?"

"No, in a tub, splashing. You were a baby. Diane was baby-sitting you, and you took a bath with my daughter, Leslie. As a baby."

Aurora wasn't an idiot. She understood the significance of his statement, and stopped coming over to cook and clean for Sam. She seemed to know the inevitability of their relationship had no resolution except a brick wall.

He learned to cook, awkwardly, but at least without burning the food. He cleaned the house, and washed his dirty laundry. The saving grace was reticence of the grocers' and his public position that prevented him from turning to alcohol.

* * * *

He received a telephone call from Leslie in a lull between her work projects. She wondered about her father's comfort, and his emotional health.

"How's Aurora working out for you, Dad?" she asked, an expectant tone in her voice.

"Fine," Sam answered quickly, hoping the lie would placate his daughter. "I'm fine."

"Are you sure, Dad?" Her loving concern ate through to the tainted core of him.

"Just fine," he repeated, which clearly demonstrated he wasn't.

"Look, I have a plane ticket, Dad. I'll be in Reno Friday night. And then I'll get a rental, and meet you at the house."

"Fine."

"That's five days. Will you be okay until then? Please tell me you'll be okay."

"I'll be okay," he promised, words spoken through wooden lips.

When he hung up, Sam again entertained the concept of self-immolation—after a thorough dousing with kerosene—but the prospect of inconceivable physical pain stopped him. Pondering, he reached into the drawer of the table beside him, and brought out his antiquated service revolver, a thirty-eight, which he'd replaced with a forty-caliber semi-automatic.

He opened the empty action, and shut it. Holding the muzzle to his head, he pulled the trigger over and over, listening to the sound of the chamber turning, growing accustomed to its metallic voice.

* * * *

In the blank hours before sunrise, he awoke, feeling with desperate fingers along the opposite side of the bed, telling himself that he was relieved at its emptiness. That mighty weight fled, while the fact of his need to urinate reminded him that he should visit the bathroom.

He swung his legs to the side of the bed, and scuffed across the carpet, and into the bathroom, where carpet ended at linoleum. The shuffle-walk had nothing to do with infirmity, but a blind-man's quest in the dark. Not that Sam was sightless—far from it—but far easier to negotiate the unlit rooms with his eyes closed, than to pick through murky shadow, especially with his glasses tucked into their case on the nightstand.

In the bathroom, he resorted to the light, and blinking at the impact, shakily opened the toilet and filled the bowl with his stream. Relief bordered on fleeting pleasure, those sporadic occurrences hinging on his physical body, not his emotions. He was far from possessing an elderly man's urinary-tract issues, but close to a limp-dicked riddle of a sexless future. He had a serious problem with timing, from pissing, to the ills of sorrow, and he began to cry.

Finished, he shook off his penis, flushed, washed his hands absent-mindedly, and then after shutting off the light, he felt his way back to bed with the points of his toes.

I'm lonely to my bones. If he kept talking to himself in the silence of his own head, he'd lose it for sure.

Wide-awake, staring at the ceiling, lights swelled up from the darkness, and through the lace curtains, patterning the walls. He shot upright, listening to a truck roll up the driveway, circling in the crisp gravel. A door slammed, and someone light-footed ran up to the porch. Even as a fist pounded the front door, he was fumbling with his glasses as he hurried to the foyer, not caring whether he wore just a set of briefs, but otherwise naked.

Aurora stood, cheeks shiny with tears.

"Aurora," he managed to speak, and then his voice caught in his throat.

"Listen, Sam." She wiped the tears with her fingers. "I don't care if you never marry me. I just don't want you to be alone. I know what that's like, and I can tell you from personal experience it ain't pretty. Loneliness makes a person depressed. So, if I can't change your sadness, at least you shouldn't be sad alone."

He drew her into the house, hands around her wrists. She pressed up against him, her face on his naked chest.

"I missed you," he admitted. He let go of her wrists, and while holding her in a clumsy embrace, felt his cock rise up with a vengeance.

Her arms went around his neck. "I love you, Sam. I've loved you since I was twelve."

"What?"

"It was my secret, one that I figured nobody ever knew. Well, and then my mother found out."

"How in the hell did that happen?"

"She read my diary. That's why we had to move to San Diego. Dad didn't want you to be tempted by willing jailbait."

"Oh, God! I never would've touched you back then. I hope you know that."

"As long as you want to touch me now, Sam. I'm more than ready for you now."

With her soft face pressed into his neck, he began to sob.

She grasped his hand firmly, and led him to the bedroom. On the creaky, sagging mattress, they made love. He held her close when he fucked her, loving the silkiness of her taut flesh. Her orgasm arrived with a surge so violent that she cried out painfully when she came.

Afterward, when she was asleep with her face snugged up to his shoulder, he envisioned the scenario of Leslie's return and cringed at the thought of disclosure. He imagined the people of Susanville, knowing their aging, fifty-year-old police chief, Sam Pilger, was fornicating with a woman half his age. In the small-town atmosphere, he'd be crucified.

That was when he grew the plan. He thought about crime scenes and the buried dead, the missing never found, the thousands of acres of hiding places, and how to conceal the smell of a corpse.

As he turned to Aurora, his hands on her body—and her trust—he knew that he loved her. He wept, because of what he had to do.

* * * *

Thursday night, Sam carried the tools and the plastic to the secluded clearing on the overlook of Goodrich Creek. Out of sight of dirt roads, of air search and rescue, and no ranches or trail access, despite the logging road.

After he dug and lined the hole, he slipped and slid back to the cruiser, and hauled up the sack of lime, struggling over gravel and through fire flowers, and hanks of bunch grass.

He drove back through town, and continued home, where he telephoned Aurora. She was bright and eager to make love to him, and came straight into his arms.

He produced the gun. She shook her head, trying to understand, as he secured her with plastic cuffs and placed tape over her mouth.

"I love you, Aurora, you're precious to me," he kept saying, his face wet with tears. "I love you, and I'm so sorry about what I have to do."

On the back seat of the cruiser, she lay still in disbelief, gazing up at the trunks of trees illuminated by the wash of the cruiser's headlights. All the years she had been waiting for him, and must now presume life and love would be annihilated in the flash of a bullet.

He parked near the creek, and together beneath the stars, by the glare of the Maglite, they climbed the hill. He could see her determination, even with her hands behind her in cuffs. She climbed for him, submitting to the gun, doing it for her love of Sam, or else numbed by his deceit.

At the clearing, he pushed her through the trees. She went to the edge of the pit without force, leaning over the hole, ready for the final leap.

He took a deep breath, and stood back, holstering the gun.

"No, not this way, it was *never* you," he insisted.

He removed her from the pit's rim. With a pocketknife, he sawed through the plastic cuffs, until he'd cut the ties, and then pulled the tape from her mouth. She was free, rubbing her wrists, and gazing at him in love and confusion.

He perched on the edge of the pit, gun in hand, and shoes squeaking on the plastic.

"I'm going to shoot myself," he explained. "Let me fall into the hole, cover me with lime and earth and plastic, so I can sleep."

"Sam!" She was sobbing, though fighting hysteria. "I can't do this! You don't have to do this!"

He maneuvered the gun, pressed against his temple.

"Watch me, I'll do it, and you can cover me up, and then I can sleep."

She cried out, and curling her fingers around the grip, yanked the gun from his fist.

He dropped his face into his hands. "I'm so tired. I just want to sleep. I'm...*so* ashamed," he wailed softly.

His heart was jiggling off-kilter, and he pressed his hand to his chest, as though to ease the rhythm, feeling light-headed.

"But Sam!"

She snapped her hand back, tossing the gun toward the creek. It sailed through the air, hit somewhere down the slope, and clattered away in the rocks.

"There *is* a purpose, Sam."

Pressure began to gather in his chest, and spread into his lungs, clenching him.

"Leslie is coming tomorrow," he pleaded, struggling to speak. "I don't want her to know. It would kill her if she knew about us. How will I ever be able to face her?"

"But, Sam."

Aurora smiled tenderly. She'd let him bring her here with the gun and cuffs, to a remote location that had been for his death, not hers.

"It was Leslie who put us together, Sam. She asked me to be with you."

"What?" He sat down, hard. His chest was burning, and he was dizzy. "What?" he repeated, unable to believe that his daughter had pimped Aurora from the beginning.

"She knows about us, Sam, she put us together, she knows I love you. That I've always loved you."

Now the pain flowed up from his chest, stabbed up his left arm, traced up his neck to his jaw. He shuddered, as pain clamped tight in his throat. Besides the pain, he felt the unbalanced fluttering of his heart.

She sat down beside him, cradling him with one arm. He was crying, because he'd lost in love all over again.

"No one will die tonight, Sam. It's over. We can go home. Leslie's given us her blessing."

Sam wanted to tell Aurora how he felt—but he couldn't speak. His heart seemed to have given out from the strain. Suffering against the pressure, eyes glazed at the night, his feet in the bottom of the plastic-lined pit, with Aurora's arm around his shoulder. The creek called from deep in its rocky bed.

"Goddamn you, Sam!"

As though from afar, he watched as Aurora hauled him out of the pit. She seemed to have gone berserk, pounding his chest with one fist beneath a serene, star-filled sky.

Chapter Five
In the Bag

Newcomers were fair game in Lassen County. Locals often wavered between the need to extend small-town hospitality, or to swiftly withdraw. Suspicion toward outsiders was predictable in a community that survived California tax collectors, hostile bandits and butchered Indians.

These Johnny-come-latelies were referred to as "Carpetbaggers," a reference to the idiom of contempt and animosity used by white Southerners to depict Northerners active in the Republican Party who invaded the South during the era of Reconstruction. Post-Civil War was harrowing times when Carpetbaggers enacted the insanity of granting blacks the right to vote, established public schools, and allowed social opportunities for common whites not born into the Southern Plantation culture.

In essence, the terminology was a modern-day jab at anyone who relocated to Lassen County, and tried to exert influence where authority was not wanted.

Take the slogan of Lassen County: "Land of the Never Sweats." The *Great Basin Register* argued the platitude had earned citizens a reputation for being shiftless and lackadaisical—*The people of Lassen County must rid themselves of a catchphrase that belittles us all*. The glaring irony was a one hundred-thirty year-old newspaper owned by Carpetbaggers telling the white natives how to handle their business. The only redeeming qualities to the *Register* were the editorials provided by its editor, Velma Harris, who was narrow-minded and religiously right-winged, and often mistaken for a native-born Never Sweat.

Liberal ideas were strictly avoided, while religious jubilation was deeply embraced. One would be foolhardy to reveal an association with Lassen Progressives, or to publicly oppose the conservative majority. An NRA membership served dual purpose as conversation prompt and safe house.

Lassen County owned a disproportionate number of churches, exclusive to Christianity. For any Jewish citizens living among these

Jesus-loving brethren, there was a Temple in Reno, and then none until you hit Lake Tahoe or the Central Valley. "Foreign" ideals espoused by Buddhists, Muslims, Sikhs, or Hindus were woefully absent in this neck of the woods.

The inclination to gather like docile sheep tended to magnify sensitivities. Religion was firmly carved into the cornerstone of America, displayed in the Masonic Square & Compasses imprinting the buildings in Uptown. Northeastern California was rich with Christian history, and drunken to the gills with Protestants, Catholics, Mormons, and a generous helping of the Masonic creed. "Praise the Lord!" seemed to thunderously echo off the vaulting sky.

But apparently a few locals determined that Carpetbaggers and their new-fangled ideas threatened to put to death the fragile social order of Lassen County.

* * * *

It seems like nobody these days really cares about what first went on in Lassen County. Nobody remembers because all of history is coming unglued by the Carpetbaggers. They move in here thinking they like the way we live in small town, and then they want to jump up and change everything! They start with the town slogan, and next they'll go on to stop the town meetings, and pretty soon they'll finish off the Susan River with some big dam the Corps. or the Bureau of Reclamation wants to build, and flood us all out. I think if the Carpetbaggers want to change, they should change to our way, and if they don't like it, they can just go back to the city they came from. Forget about us, we don't want you.

Palmer H. Forrest, Ravendale.

"Good God," said Paul Sumner, opening the *Great Basin Register*, and coming face to face with blunt scrawl from Mr. Forrest. "Listen to this," he addressed his wife, Kate.

"Okay."

Kate sat across the table, working on a reconditioned laptop computer her eldest son, Daniel, had shipped from Santa Cruz. Kate had no difficulty familiarizing to technology's idiosyncratic nature, but she required focus when doing so. Something in Paul's tone promised a good laugh, and she tore her attention away from the laptop.

Paul read her the brief letter from Mr. Forrest.

"Ugh," she said.

"I wonder how far *his* kin go back, in Carpetbaggerism," Paul mused.

"Probably not as far back as the people living at the Indian Rancheria."

"Unless, of course, Mr. Forrest has relatives of your ilk."

She came around the table, and sat on Paul's lap. "What do you mean, my ilk?"

"Indians, baby, the First People, the Carpetbaggers to defy all Carpetbaggers who had the impertinence to come along afterward."

"Not a chance." She nudged her husband's chest gently with one hand. "I know you've had some experience with Mr. Forrest yourself."

"Ah, so true! Forrest's that horrible, crabby little man who tries to get to the podium mic at city council meetings, always suggesting separate laws for locals and transplants. Yuck! He's unpleasant." He buried his nose in her long hair, as though trying to purge the memory of nasty Mr. Forrest.

Kate started speaking, using an urbane radio voice, which meant that Paul would be served a history lesson.

"About ten years ago, the Sheriff's department arrested a man up in Madeline by the name of Jamison Furly. He was burying weapons in a cache."

"What does that have to do with Mr. Forrest?"

"It's my point. Jamison Furly was a Nazi, he owned land in Madeline he called Furly's Fort, and there were approximately fifty people, all men, living on the place, and training as a militia. A deputy infiltrated the group, found out they were stashing a weapons arsenal, and that's how Furly came to be arrested."

"Not because he was a Nazi?"

"Paul, even Nazis have a constitutional right to freedom of assembly," she reminded. "And I happen to think that Nazis make the American Indian Movement look pretty tame."

"Can we go back to your explanation, so I can understand how any of this ties into Mr. Forrest?"

"Palmer Forrest was their supply man. He brought them food and drink. I think he might have been a member, though after the arrest of Furly and a few others, the group disbanded, and Mr. Forrest went back to Ravendale. Furly was convicted of the weapons charge, the man's ranch was sold by the ATF, with the Lassen County Sheriff's department taking a cut."

"How do you know all of this, woman?" he demanded, arms around her shoulders.

On a school day, the house was empty save for the two of them, and Kate had an idea of what was to follow. Paul had absolutely no interest in history at the moment, just a riveted male fixation upon his wife's body. He proved his carnal interest by shoving his lips into the warm cleft between her breasts.

"Because of our old friend, Dennis Caldwell," she went on, while Paul hummed blissfully between her breasts. "He was the deputy who infiltrated the group. He told me about it a few years ago during that barbecue at Green Earth, remember?"

"You just get better and better with age," Paul said, redirecting, and eyes closed.

"Hmm," came that thoughtful sound, which indicated that Kate Sumner would soon unleash a brilliant Op/Ed piece upon the *Register*.

In the meantime, the two climbed the stairs giggling and dropping their clothes the way trees shed leaves in autumn—messily, and without any concern where they might fall.

* * * *

I fully agree with Mr. Forrest. He paints a valid point, that all Carpetbaggers should be expelled.

Mr. Forrest is a descendant of Cooper Forrest, one of the original settlers of the Honey Lake Valley, and a proud former member of the Susanville Armed Militia, who assisted the U.S. Army in three major military campaigns against Indigenous people—the 1866 massacre of extended Paiute families at Papoose Meadows, the 1868 massacre of a Maidu Indian encampment in Antelope Valley, and the 1872 routing out of the Modoc tribe up in the Tulé Lake area. Cooper Forrest was willing to do anything—including outright murder—to establish a whites-only America. Our contemporary, Palmer Forrest, seems just as intent on establishing his own "Amerika" in Lassen County.

Using both cases and both Mr. Forrests, I will advise readers to the fact that the Maidu, Washoe, Paiute, Shoshone, Miwok, Wintun, Yurok— and the unfortunate Modoc—are the "Aboriginals," and therefore, Palmer Forrest, and every non-Indian who allegedly "settled" the Honey Lake Valley, are afoul of the system of restitution and natural progress. This would define all peoples who arrived after the Native Americans, as Carpetbaggers.

This includes 50% of me, as my other 50% is derived of aboriginal genes from the Quinault Indians of Washington State. We all know that Washington State is really a continuation of Oregon, which includes California. So in conclusion, I am a Carpetbagger and also a member of the Original People.

With this ridiculous, irreverent point, I urge the "locals" who have nothing better to do but complain, to grow up and smell the coffee.

Katherine Sumner, Spotted Horse Ranch.

* * * *

"You're a great wit!" said Gladiola Parker, to Kate.

They stood in the Parker Gallery along Main Street, a copy of the latest editorial section of the *Great Basin Register* spread on the glass-topped counter. The newspaper was awash in a large brown stain, as

Gladiola had been drinking coffee, and upset the cup when Kate arrived with a very large wrapped canvas.

"If you weren't already married, I'd ask you to marry me," Gladiola added, as though in praise.

Kate rolled her eyes. "Really, Gladiola."

"All I have to say is you add magic to plain speak."

"I couldn't stay silent forever." Kate removed the paper covering from the canvas.

"You say so much with so few words. Remember, my ancestor is *Nama'dzadzibua*."

"Who?"

"Uh, *Nama'dzadzibua*. You know, Selma Richards—"

"Yes, the unwilling Paiute concubine." Kate sighed in obvious irritation. "What's the point you're trying to make?"

"So…I get credit for being part Paiute."

"And yet you earn a special demerit for being related to Anton Parker." Kate clucked her tongue. "That wipes your Indian heritage right off the board."

"At least Parker wasn't an Indian killer," Gladiola said in defense of her lunatic white ancestor.

Kate lifted the canvas onto an easel placed beneath a rack of lights.

"That's because Anton Parker was too busy nailing every Indian woman in sight with his stupid dick."

The conversation faltered as they leaned close to inspect Kate's newest work.

The odd painting revealed of a collection of pitifully tiny buildings, surrounded by the enormity of sagebrush flatlands. On the horizon lurked the familiar shapes of mountains bounding the Madeline Plains, and immense sky traced with clouds. The silhouettes of vultures wheeling on an updraft, just over the boxy, miniature compound, suggested carrion. Displayed upon one of the buildings, was a red banner with the distinctive emblem of a swastika.

"I've called it, 'Amerika,'" said Kate, with satisfaction. "With a 'K.'"

"This is that…that *place*, isn't it?" Gladiola seemed disturbed. "That former white supremacist ranch up north."

"I suppose. I've never actually seen it, but doesn't it look right?"

"Oh, boy, I'd have to really distance myself from this." As though to prove her statement, Gladiola deliberately stepped away from the painting.

"Why? It's art." Having never had a painting rejected by Gladiola before, she was at a loss as to how to handle this turn of events.

"But it's contentious, and not exactly uplifting. And I'd rather sell uplifting to stupid people. This is far too intellectual."

"I just thought that it's history, and it has relevancy in Lassen County."

"So does a massacre."

"No one alive recalls the massacres, but there are people who remember Furly's Fort."

"I can appreciate the piece, Kate, don't get me wrong. It's just not for this gallery. People would think I'm condoning the KKK or Nazis, and I just don't, I do *not*."

"Well, that's okay. I'll take it home. Paul warned me that it might be too controversial." She picked it up, and was about to wrap it, when Gladiola stopped her with a hand on her forearm.

"Wait, I think I know a museum that might take it. I may be able to get you a sale after all."

Gladiola went to a drawer behind the counter, where she kept all of her business cards in grand disorder, shuffling through the mess, until she found what she was looking for. Closing the drawer, she placed a dog-eared card onto the countertop.

"It's an historical center in Houston," Gladiola explained, picking up the telephone and pressing out the numbers. "They keep all sorts of art, from sculptures about the Holocaust, to vintage gallows from the real Old West." She paused, and held up one hand. "Hello, may I speak to Lawrence Haynes? Yes, please tell him this is Gladiola Parker, from California." She covered the mouthpiece. "I think I could sell this to them, Kate. Would you mind if I photograph it, and e-mail them a copy?"

Kate set the canvas back onto the easel. "Whatever you must do, go right ahead. I'll just go about my business."

Gladiola smiled. "I'll talk to you soon," she promised.

As Kate ducked out, into the half-light of a cloud shadow, she felt suddenly different, as though the world had changed in a subtle, yet obvious manner.

* * * *

"Amerika" Turns Heads
By Jake Weatherby, Staff Writer, Great Basin Register

Once again, our unique little town of Susanville, which plays host to a wide variety of artists and intellectuals, has the chance to study many differing points of view. In the last two issues of the Great Basin Register there have been opinions submitted by readers who stand at opposite points of the compass in regard to whom is considered a "Local," and whom might be termed "Carpetbagger."

To drive home her opinion piece, artist and rancher Katherine Sumner, who lives in unincorporated Lassen County, has produced a portrait for viewing, entitled "Amerika," which not only portrays the great wide-open country we enjoy here in Lassen County, but also the diverse views on race and politics.

In 1997, the Lassen County Sheriff's department, in conjunction with Alcohol Tobacco & Firearms (ATF), infiltrated a substantial gathering of white supremacist members of an unofficial militia established in a rural compound in the Madeline area, on ranch land owned by Mr. Jamison Furly. Law enforcement agencies involved determined this particular group was preparing for a race war by hoarding an illegal weapons arsenal beneath the floor of a building within the compound. The ring was broken, the conspiracy uncovered, and within ten months, the seized property was sold to satisfy terms handed down by the Federal Court in San Francisco, in accordance with plea deals by many former members of Mr. Furly's group.

There has not been any sign of a resurgence of Nazis, the KKK or related white supremacist groups in Lassen County in the past decade, except among certain isolated individuals, and within the inmate populations of the local prisons. However, due to recent revelations of Mr. Palmer H. Forrest of Ravendale, who submitted an opinion letter to our esteemed editorial staff, it would seem that white supremacy is alive and rising in our county.

In response to Mr. Forrest, Mrs. Sumner—who signs her art as Kate McLain—created an interpretation of that 1997 compound in her piece, "Amerika," now on display in the Susanville City Library on Main Street. The painting will be available for viewing through the end of this month, during regular library business hours.

Mrs. Sumner has lived in Lassen County since 1984, and is a member of the Quinault Indian Nation of Washington State. When asked about her purpose for creating the painting, "Amerika," Mrs. Sumner simply stated, "My husband warned me that it might be too controversial."

* * * *

Gladiola Parker observed as Kate Sumner, mindful of the slippery ice on the sidewalk, made her way into the Parker Galley with a swish of her long, loose hair.

"My goodness!" was Gladiola's comment, as Kate closed the door firmly behind her. "I didn't realize how long your hair really is."

"I'm on my way to get it trimmed." Kate shook a finger at the stout, smiling woman. "Gladiola, if I didn't know you better, I'd wonder about your motives. You told me you were getting rid of that piece to some outfit in Houston."

Gladiola shrugged. "Sorry, the City of Susanville purchased it from my gallery."

"How could you pimp that thing to the City like an ugly hooker, when you swore to me you were going to have to distance yourself from it? Isn't having it in Susanville still a little too close for your comfort?"

"Have a moment?"

"You bet I do."

Gladiola motioned to a bar table and tall stools positioned near a front window, where she often took her breaks, and stared at passing foot traffic. On those days Kate was inclined to take a breather with the hearty Gladiola, she would be subjected to the gallery owner's sly comment about every person, as she termed it, "slinking past."

Kate had no doubt whatsoever that she was included in these monologues of titillating scrutiny once out of earshot.

She pulled out a stool, and perched across from Gladiola, nearly sitting upon her fall of hair, which she threw across her back, so it dangled down the stool.

Gladiola, a heavyset woman, teetered on her own chair, looking a bit top-heavy on the fragile oak legs.

"Now all we need is beer," said Gladiola.

"Yes, clink our bottles together and laugh it up," Kate agreed without smiling.

"Ah, lighten up," said Gladiola. "Listen, I was going to get rid of that...*thing*, if you don't mind me calling it, but then, you'll never guess who paid me a visit."

* * * *

In the minutes following Kate's departure—and while Gladiola was still on hold for Lawrence Haynes of Houston—off-duty Sheriff's deputy, Dennis Caldwell, strolled into the Gallery.

"I didn't know you liked art," Gladiola commented, but Dennis merely smirked, catching her sarcasm and throwing it back in her face.

"If you ask me, art's a waste of time, but my girlfriend sure appreciates it."

"Your girlfriend?"

"I'm dating Cherry Parker."

"Well, good for you!" Though Gladiola didn't particularly consider rough and gray-haired Dennis Caldwell a good match for the refined Cherry Parker.

"Yeah, here's what I figured. I get her a painting, and she'll give me a return on my investment." And he started to laugh, until Gladiola's glare cut him off in mid-cackle.

"Look around while I take this call," she spoke through her teeth.

While she held for Mr. Haynes, Dennis walked back and forth, squinting at art hanging on the walls and propped on easels, his face screwed up with loathing.

When he spied "Amerika," he just stood dumb in his tracks before the piece, mouth unconsciously slack.

The Houston people, having been unable to locate Mr. Haynes on their premises, took Gladiola's name and telephone number, accepting the offer of a photographic e-mail attachment of Kate's painting in the interim, until Mr. Haynes could return the call.

Gladiola was fiddling with a digital camera, and finally realized that Dennis was simply standing like a geriatric inmate in front of the painting.

"Hey, Dennis, excuse me a moment, I need to take a picture of that piece of work."

"What the hell is this?" he spoke, the intensity of his voice shaking out of each word.

"Something Kate Sumner brought in. You just missed her." Gladiola sniffed. "Personally, I hate it. I'm going to purge my gallery of its reek."

He ignored her, and picked up the painting, turning it into the light that came through the plate glass windows.

"This is what it looked like from the air."

"*What* did?"

"Furly's Fort. It looked *just* like this. She remembered what I told her." He set the painting on the easel with an abrupt clatter, and headed for the door.

"Where are you going?" Gladiola called after him.

He put a finger in the air, as though holding a sword. "I'll be back, I promise." And he trotted away.

In the meantime, Gladiola photographed the painting, and managed to e-mail it to Mr. Haynes in Houston.

Less than an hour later, Dennis returned with the mayor, Skipper James, and Jake Weatherby, a *Register* correspondent. The trio fussed and conferred before the painting in hushed, tight tones for approximately ten minutes, and all the while Gladiola eyed them cautiously from behind her glass-topped counter, pretending to organize the drawer where her collection of business cards lay in a pile of disarray.

After some wrangling, Mayor James stepped up to Gladiola, and inquired about a price.

Gladiola shook her head strenuously. "No, it's not for sale. It's pretty much in the bag already."

"Maybe you'd reconsider," said the Mayor. "Do you have a firm offer from another party?"

"She doesn't have a damn thing," said Dennis, his beefy arms crossed. "She was on the phone, on hold, when I came in. She's still in the process of trying to sell it, because she was going to take a picture of it before I left."

"Is that true?" the Mayor asked, brows furrowed.

"Yes," admitted Gladiola, refusing to be involved in a blatant lie. "But I have the impression this museum in Houston will be interested, because it's right down their alley. I've already e-mailed a photo, so, like I said, it's in the bag."

Dennis whispered something into Jake Weatherby's ear, and the reporter nodded.

"I think you might be talking about the Forbes Museum, correct?" Jake ventured.

"Of course, that's who I'm talking about!" Gladiola snapped, growing restive from this useless conversation.

"It's a collection of art and relics related to genocide, capital punishment, and social mayhem," Jake explained, for the Mayor's benefit. "Very worldly and renowned."

Gladiola intended to expel the feeling of doom. "Gentlemen, I'm going to be frank. I don't really care who gets the piece. I just don't want it in this gallery."

"Done!" Dennis clapped his hands once. "The City will happily buy it from you, Gladiola."

"Now, just wait a minute," Mayor James parried. "The City's going to buy it?"

"Don't you have to submit a proposal to the City Council?" asked Jake.

"The City's buying it, all right," said Dennis, nodding. "It's a human interest piece, Mayor."

"And why are you trying to get rid of it?" Jake asked Gladiola.

"I told Kate Sumner that it wasn't my kind of subject matter, that I didn't want people thinking I'm a party to this white supremacist thing. How could I be? I'm part Indian."

"And what did Mrs. Sumner say to you?" Jake persisted.

"She told me that her husband warned her it might be too controversial."

"It looked just like that, when we came in the helicopters," said Dennis, rather dreamily, as though his reminiscence involved droll summer activities, or Christmas fanfare. "Their banner was face up, toward the sky. Scattering like ants, all of them."

He stuck a fingertip toward tiny men painted in positions that suggested running hell-bent for cover.

"Good God, I never saw that before," Gladiola spoke, and they leaned close to study the details.

"There's more, how about a coyote?" The Mayor motioned with a pinky finger.

"She painted a fucking antelope, too," Dennis said.

"And there's a skunk," said Jake, not wanting to be left out of their brief amusement.

"That's Kate, she hides stuff everywhere," Gladiola claimed, with pride.

"Look, how much?" Dennis asked bluntly.

"I really hadn't given it much thought," Gladiola confessed.

"Well, what do you sell Mrs. Sumner's other work for?" Skipper James asked, with a tone of exasperation in his voice.

Gladiola privately wondered how the hell the man could endure the daily stresses of his elected position, and then, she remembered Mayor James's love of drink.

"Twelve-hundred dollars," said Gladiola quickly, without blinking an eye.

* * * *

"One-thousand two-hundred dollars," said Kate, in paraphrase. "You asked the City to pay that much for the painting?" She shook her head. "Don't they require a referendum? An approval at a City Council meeting?"

"Kate, it's supply and demand—" Gladiola began, but Kate cut her off.

"I've heard this spiel before, years ago, when you sold old Joseph Muir those first works. I was astonished then, and I'm flabbergasted now, because *you*, Gladiola Parker, never cease to amaze me." She pulled a folded newspaper section from her pocket, and slapped it onto the table. "Somehow, that *Register* reporter, Weatherby, thinks that Mr. Forrest was talking race wars in Lassen County, when all he was doing was his usual whining about outsiders."

Gladiola smirked. "Forrest's not the only kook out in the sticks."

"I live out in the sticks," said Kate warily. "Now, Gladiola—just when did Jake Weatherby interview me? Was I asleep at the time? Or perhaps *you* were drunk."

"Of course, you know he never did, I just told him what to say."

"I said that to you, 'my husband warned me that it might be too controversial.' Is that what I said to you, Gladiola?"

"Well, no, your exact words were, 'Paul warned me that it might be too controversial.' I know. I have a photographic memory."

"Over a thousand dollars." Kate shook her head in disgust. "And so when is the City of Susanville expected to pay you?"

"In ten days, they'll have the check cut through the proper channels."

"And Jake Weatherby." Kate snapped the paper violently. "I received a phone message from him. He wants to interview me. Gladiola, I am *not* interested in notoriety."

"But why?"

"I like being a mother, and painting my inspirations from time to time, and I certainly don't need media attention to get my work into the gallery market. Do you know that some journalist from *Newsweek* left a message on my machine? And a man from the *Sacramento Bee* called. It's my good fortune that he spoke with Paul, and got the husband's brick wall."

Gladiola rubbed her hands. "It's only up from here, Kate."

"*What's* only up?" Kate asked suspiciously.

Gladiola held both hands upward, and spread, as though tilted at a marquee.

"Fame!"

There came a flash of irritation, as Kate fairly leaped off the stool, and hit the floor.

"*Screw* fame!" she growled, and left the Gallery in a swish of long, silky hair.

* * * *

They were driving home from Richard and Sue Jenks's Milford ranch on a Saturday afternoon, heading northbound, toward Susanville, and into the wind. Sleet was bashing against the windshield, and whatever sparse traffic cruised the Interstate seemed as hurried as the Sumner family to find a warm, dry space.

Kate was at the wheel, the designated driver following one of Sue's famous casserole dinners, after which Paul Sumner and Richard Jenks involved themselves in pool and whiskey.

While Kate and Sue cleared the dishes, the two Sumner children still young enough for parental supervision, Dakota and Charlie Kat, ages twelve and fifteen, watched the Jenks's satellite television in peaceful fellowship. The sound of clinking glasses and laughter leaked out from the closed Game Room door, indicating, as Sue liked to describe, "a state of simpleminded infancy."

For being a logical man, Paul gets to act like a fool every now and then, was Kate's generous thought, pushing forward through the storm with two adolescent boys giggling on their bench seat, and her husband snoring gently beside her.

Somewhere close to Janesville, the sleet thickened into true falling snow. A truck entered the roadway behind their Suburban, and churned through the wind, gliding onto Kate's tail. In vain, she searched for a place to pull over, but the roadside shoulders were notoriously soft with the tendency to give 'way. With the following vehicle aggressively flashing its headlights, she chose the mouth of a ranch access road, and turned to allow that bastard behind her to pass.

Instead of safely passing, the truck followed their Suburban, crashing into the vehicle, causing the SUV to shudder, and slide into a barbed wire fence. The truck then slammed into the Suburban's rear bumper a second time, pinning it.

Dakota and Charlie Kat were yelling from their seat, and the lurch and sudden stop, along with the vocal commotion, awoke slumbering Paul, who came to with a start.

"We've been run off the road," said Kate, who was legendary for her ability to think swiftly in emergency situations. "Charlie Kat, call for a deputy," she instructed, and she tossed her son a cellular phone. "Paul, take this." She pulled a crowbar from beneath the driver's seat.

"What about your Big Boy, Mommy?" Dakota asked, while Charlie Kat worked on the phone call.

Having temporarily trapped the Sumners' Suburban, the other driver pounded on the driver side window, eliciting a cry from the two children in the back.

Kate was curiously calm. "The doors are locked," she assured her family.

Her window exploded into glass crumbles beneath a tire iron. She could feel the fragments fly past her face, backed by the storm wind. With the window's destruction, a pair of hands yanked her through her seat belt, and hauled her bodily from the truck, dragging her across the snowy ground.

He was a large man. She couldn't see his face, but she could read his posture through the whirling snow, as she felt the slickness of the ground beneath her. She struggled, trying to brace her feet against the ground. The man sensed her resistance, and halted, locking his legs as he lifted her into the air.

His grip shifted, hands now around her throat with an unbelievable pressure, heightened by the weight of her own body. Black circles began to whirl in her vision, but she fought it with the rationale that a large man is just as breakable as any other. Curving her body in sudden motion, she brought her feet forward, and snapped both of his legs at the knees.

Down they went, the man hollering in agony, and Kate gasping for air. Another dark figure emerged from the falling snow, grasped her by the rope of her braid, and thrust her face into the ground. She could feel small stones beneath the snow graze her flesh, as she held her breath, counting the seconds, all the while scrabbling fruitlessly with her hands to find the man's ankles.

The hands picked her up, the fallen man still screaming, anchored to immobility and howling in pain. The second attacker tossed her through the air. She heard the sound of wind rushing past her ears, and then felt the impact as her body slammed into a boulder. A grunt was pulled from deep in her chest, as three ribs on the right side of her body fractured.

Kate was enraged, yet perfectly focused, the screams of the fallen man dulled by her absolute purpose. She was more afraid for her children, and for her semi-intoxicated husband. She floundered through the slippery snow, hurrying toward the pale bulk of the white Suburban. She could only walk so fast, as the cracked ribs slowed her progress.

At the two linked vehicles, the second man, the one who had thrown Kate like a bale of hay, was attempting to pull Paul Sumner from the vehicle.

"Fuck this!" she gasped, an animalistic cry pouring from her mouth. She leaped upon the man, one arm meant to lock around his bull neck, but the fractured ribs caught her up short. The bruiser of a man was dodging Paul's crowbar sweeps, and yanked her off his shoulder, throwing her to the ground like a rag doll.

Rising to her knees, the cracked ribs stabbed. She tottered to her feet, prepared to launch again, when out of the curtain of wind-driven snow came Dakota, carrying a large, indeterminate item in his hands.

"I have your Big Boy, Mommy!" He thrust it upon her, a Smith & Wesson forty-four Magnum revolver.

* * * *

"Why do you carry that thing?" Paul had asked, back in the early days of their marriage, after she killed a man who threatened the life of herself and her eldest daughter, Sara, then a toddler.

"I carry it for the sake of my safety and emotional comfort," she'd answered.

Former Sheriff Butch Adams had been only too happy to issue Kate a concealed carry weapon permit. She'd retained the revolver since the fearful home invasion, hidden beneath the passenger seat of whatever vehicle she drove. The gun was never armed, but two speed loaders, containing a total of twelve cartridges, lay in the case with the revolver.

She warned her children, who were well versed with small caliber firearms, "This is for big boys, and you must never touch it."

Somehow, with Dakota, the phrase had christened the gun itself as "Big Boy."

* * * *

Kate panted, and grasping the revolver, opened the action. Each chamber was neatly filled with a fat, hollow-point cartridge.

Dakota was beaming proudly, a strange contrast to their life-or-death situation.

"I loaded it for you, Mommy."

The man had his hands around Paul's throat, throttling Kate's husband so thoroughly that Paul's eyes were beginning to bulge. The crowbar had tumbled to the ground during the struggle, and was now clamped beneath the stranger's heavy left boot.

Despite being strangled, Paul was kicking out with his feet, but the larger man was immovable. The uneven sound of spasmodic laughter whirled from the assailant's mouth with a plume of freezing exhalation.

Staggering, with her fractured ribs so painful that she was streaming sweat in the freezing air, Kate came forth and stuck the gun upward, mindful to aim it away from Paul. Their attacker was well beyond the threshold of the rules of civilized behavior, and there would be no begging for mercy. Pressed against the base of the man's skull, she quickly pulled the trigger.

Simultaneous to the loud report, the man's head exploded, fountaining blood and brains through beautiful flakes of snow, illuminated by the revolving blue and red lights of an advancing Sheriff's cruiser, and the haunting screams of the crippled man beyond.

* * * *

Jake Weatherby was a man in a hurry. He jogged as fast as his feet could carry him across the icy parking lot behind the County Jail. Out in the protected valley between Susanville and Johnstonville, the jail was nearly in the shadow of High Desert State Prison, which appeared like a battlement of science-fiction warfare through intermittently falling snow.

Over the Sheriff's band, he heard the call of a roadside attack on a family near Janesville. The chatter on the radio was rapid as information was relayed back and forth from a possible accident, then vehicular assault, to a shooting death. He wrote down details, and recorded plate numbers, determining the victims of the initial assault were in a vehicle owned by Paul and Katherine Sumner.

But the shooting was the kicker. As Jake untangled the facts, he concluded that two men had initially run the Sumners off the highway, attacked the family, and the tables were turned, as one of the two attackers was disabled, and the other killed.

Showing his press badge at the jail, Jake passed through the metal detectors, and hustled to the desk to sign in as a visitor.

The C.O. on desk repeated three times, there was no Katherine McLain Sumner brought in custody to the County Jail. Maybe Jake was too late, or perhaps Mrs. Sumner had already been moved to holding for arraignment at the County courthouse in Susanville.

Jake rubbed his chin, frustrated. He was certain he'd heard it correctly on the band frequency he routinely monitored for just such a story. As he turned, he glimpsed the half-shielded windows of a conference room, and there, at a long table, sat Mr. and Mrs. Sumner, two young boys, and a plainclothes investigator. Two C.O.s in uniform stood against the wall, and a female deputy sat along the table, straight-faced and collected.

Not a lawyer in sight, he thought. Taking a seat in the foyer, he settled in for a long wait.

* * * *

Through the snowfall, the cruiser turned a half-circle, halted sharply, and Deputy Cherry Parker hustled out, sidearm at the ready. She ran toward the Suburban, her weapon drawn and trained forward. As she approached the Sumners, the wind was blowing snow directly into Deputy Parker's eyes, so she was forced to squint at the scene of the family, gathered around a steaming corpse.

Kate had already dropped the Big Boy to the ice-crusted earth, and was staring down at the man she'd shot through the head. Death had slumped his heavy body forward to lie at the feet of a stunned Paul Sumner, who wore blood splatters across his face. There was more blood pumping from the dead man's shattered skull, running in a rivulet of deep red as it melted the coating of snow. Their young sons, stood behind their mother, clinging together in shivering silence, as the snow hissed past.

Deputy Parker, having quickly decided the Sumner family was reasonably safe, ran to the man with the broken legs. He had been dragging himself, inch by excruciating inch, toward the pickup truck still attached to the Suburban's rear bumper. How he figured he'd ever climb in, much less drive away, was anyone's guess, but the Deputy cuffed him as a formality.

* * * *

There were many more sirens upon approach, adding up to three more Sheriff's cruisers, two CHP, and two ambulances, one from Janesville, the other from Susanville. The coroner's van came from Lassen-Flagg Hospital, and two tow trucks arrived to unlink and remove the crashed vehicles.

Law enforcement clamor marked the ground as swiftly as the falling snow obliterated the damage. Kate, spotted in blood and sporting abrasions on her face, gathered her family in the lee of Cherry's cruiser, out of the wind-driven snow.

Kate was not exactly arrested—though, after being examined briefly by paramedics, she, Paul, and the boys were bundled into one of the ambulances, and shuttled to the County Jail in Johnstonville.

The deputy followed in a cruiser, and Kate fixated on the turning lights. The boys sat between their parents, arms linked for comfort. She listened to the sound of the ambulance wipers whisking back and forth, while her nerves slowly tightened.

At the jail, they were placed in a conference room, guarded by two hulking Correctional Officers, while they waited for…what? She could only guess.

A female C.O. brought in a box of donuts, and cups of hot chocolate, but the Sumners only stared at the food blankly.

After some time, Deputy Cherry Parker came through the door with a notebook, accompanied by Deputy Freddie Snake, who held a file folder in one hand.

Still, Kate retained a wary pose of the hunted.

"Kate." Freddie touched her shoulder. "Tell me what happened out there."

"Am I being placed under arrest?" At least she still had her wits.

"At this time, no crime has been determined to have been committed."

"Will the D.A.'s office be contacting me?"

"I don't know. We have to get past this first."

"Will you be reading me my rights?" she pressed. "Should I call a lawyer?"

"Not unless this shooting turns out to be something you planned to do."

"Not in a million years."

He sat in a chair, and referred to pencil scribbling on the face of the folder.

"I see you have a license to carry."

"I've had CCW permit for twenty years. But you already know all about that."

"I do, yes." Freddie studied her face for a moment, the dark circles of exhaustion beneath her eyes, and the sheen of perspiration on her forehead. Abruptly he smiled. "I'm not inclined to arrest you, Kate."

She inhaled, interrupted by a small grunt of pain. "In that case, you'd better record this."

He pulled out a small cassette recorder from a jacket pocket, and set it on the table.

"I'll tell you, one time, and that's it." In her capable voice, she proceeded to describe everything that happened that day, including their meal at the Jenks's home, to when she shot the man in the head. As she spoke, Freddie took notes in pencil on the outside of the closed folder.

"Remarkable," Freddie marveled, "that you should be able to recall it all with such clarity and detail."

"I was raised by a man who was a San Joaquin County Sheriff's deputy." She paused, distracted by physical pain. "A rapist attacked me unsuccessfully when I was thirteen, and my foster parents were murdered when I was sixteen. Another man tried to kill me—and my daughter Sara—twenty years ago. Some events, you remember. Others are like dust, worthy to forget. How do you suggest I should conduct myself when my family is attacked?"

Charlie Kat and Dakota, normally long-suffering, had begun to cry—not during Kate's narrative of the attack, but when she described the violence of her early years, and the fact that their eldest sister had been nearly killed as a baby. They had been aware of this event in a vague sense, though after today, they could relate deeply to their mother's need for family preservation.

"You shot a forty-four at pointblank range," Freddie commented. "It's like a small cannon. Weren't you worried you'd kill your husband, too?"

"I've been using firearms since I was eight years old," she contended. "I aimed upward. And anyway, I use hollow-points. They're designed to do a lot of internal damage, without collateral."

"Okay, so either way you knew enough to shoot upward. Enough time to think, to evaluate. Hell, any cop would be lucky to have that kind of time when they have to shoot a perp."

"I've always been able to think logically with my back to the wall. I've been trained to hunt game for more than thirty years. You learn to react predictably in unpredictable situations."

"Therefore, shooting a man is like shooting a deer," Freddie summed.

"No, I'd kill a deer in order to eat, but I'd shoot a man so my family won't be murdered. Once I put that gun to his head, there was no turning back, Freddie."

"Still, there's a fine line between reaction and premeditation."

"Look at Paul's neck!" Kate snarled.

She tenderly pulled open her husband's sweater to reveal the bruises from being strangled by a pair of giant hands.

"Tell me how long I have to stand there watching my husband almost die, before reaction turns into premeditation."

She rolled down the top of her own turtleneck, unable to see the bruising she felt, but Freddie's expression was enough.

"I want to know who would do this to us," said Paul.

Freddie opened the folder, which had been lying closed on the tabletop, but for his penciled scrawl.

"The truck is registered to Charles James Simms, deceased. He was a rancher outside of Susanville."

"We knew him," Paul said, grasping his wife's hand.

They both understood the significance of Charles James Simms, a white man notorious for his extreme views on race. Both of Charles James Simms' adult daughters married men of color, and had been consequently disowned.

"The two men who attacked you were the deceased rancher's adult sons," said Freddie, "Robert and Calvin Simms."

"Oh, Christ." Kate rubbed her eyes. "I know the sisters, Charlotte Benton and Marissa Callywater."

"I'm aware of your relationships with Mrs. Benton and Mrs. Callywater, Kate," said Freddie. "I'm just not sure where their brothers fit into the scheme of things. They don't seem to be the type of people you and Paul would socialize with."

"Never," Paul agreed.

"Who did I...which young man did I shoot?" asked Kate.

Freddie sifted through a few more pages in the folder. "That was the younger brother, Robert."

"And the other, his legs." Kate shuddered. "He was trying to kill me. I knew while he was choking me, I had to do something before I totally blacked out, so I kicked his legs while they were locked. I really did mean to break something."

"An ambulance took Calvin Simms to Lassen-Flagg," said Cherry. "I could look into his status, if you're interested."

"Please pardon me for saying that I am not interested, Cherry. I'm so sorry. But I didn't use lethal force until the other man was already strangling Paul."

"So you left one alive, and killed the other?" Freddie asked.

"I did what I had to do!"

"You should tell her," Cherry interjected.

"The hell I should," said Freddie calmly. "Be my guest, Deputy."

"Calvin Simms wasn't going anywhere, Kate." Cherry read from her own notebook. "But it appeared to me that Robert Simms was prepared to use lethal force of his own. There were loaded firearms in the Simms's vehicle—a sawed-off shotgun and a thirty-eight. And Robert Simms was carrying a loaded nine millimeter holstered under his jacket."

"If they had all of that, then, I don't get it," said Paul. "Why wouldn't they just use the firearms? Why would they try to kill with their hands?"

"Because, they enjoyed what they did!" Kate concluded.

"Maybe they meant to use firearms as a back-up plan," said Cherry.

"I clearly didn't wish to harm either of these men," said Kate carefully. "I'm not the kind of person who itches to be a vigilante. The first thing I did was to tell Charlie Kat to call for a deputy." Tears were streaming down Kate's cheeks. "But I had no choice in this situation. They were trying to kill me, and the man I shot was strangling my husband." She pounded the table with a fist. "I *had* to protect my children!"

"When did you go for your gun, Kate?" asked Freddie, returning to his notes, as though recognizing a link absent from her story.

She blinked. "What do you mean?"

"Just what I asked, when did you go for your gun? You told me that you were pulled out of your vehicle, subject to being asphyxiated, and then you slammed your feet into Calvin Simms's legs."

"Yes."

"While Calvin Simms is prone, Robert Simms picks you up, and throws you into a rock, breaking some ribs. You return to your vehicle, where you encounter Robert Simms in the middle of his attack on Paul."

"That's right."

"So, you either had your gun *before* Calvin Simms pulled you out of the truck, or you somehow grabbed it on the way back to intervene in Robert Simms's killing of your husband."

Dakota was tugging on Kate's sweater. "Mommy, remember? I gave you the Big Boy, when you were going to jump on that man again."

"What did you say, son?" Freddie prompted.

"Mommy, she was going to jump on the man's back again," Dakota explained. "I could tell, because she already did, but he pushed her down on the ground, and hurt her even more."

"This Big Boy, son," said Freddie. "What is it?"

"Mommy's gun. I loaded it for her, after he took her from the truck. It was scary, because she disappeared, and then a man came back to hurt us. He was laughing while he was trying to hurt my dad, and Mommy used it to stop him from hurting us too."

Kate hugged Dakota close, realizing the crucial gap omitted from her initial recount.

"What were you trying to do, Kate, before your son gave you the gun?"

"I was thinking I'd stick my fingernails in his eyeballs, or maybe break his neck," she answered softly. "But he'd already cracked my ribs when he threw me against a rock. I couldn't do much of anything to stop him." She regarded Freddie somberly. "He was going to kill us all, you see."

73

Freddie sifted through more documents in the folder. "Both Simms brothers are listed as members of the American Nazi Party in northern California. It's real big and ugly up here, according to the Southern Poverty Law Center, though mostly because of the prison system, you know, white inmates and their gangs."

"Did the Simms have contact with any prison inmates?" Paul asked.

"Not to my knowledge," Freddie admitted. "But they've been on an FBI watch list for fifteen months. They're suspected to have been involved in three bank robberies in San Joaquin County."

"Why would they rob banks?" asked Kate.

"Apparently they had serious financial problems. Litigation against their two sisters over the ranch, and issues with probate."

"So, why would they want to attack us?" Paul wanted to know. "They obviously weren't trying to rob us. There was absolutely no financial benefit to either of them if we died."

Cherry reached into her notebook, and pulled out a numbered plastic zip bag containing a ragged-edged article torn out of the *Great Basin Register*.

"I'm going to make an educated guess," said Cherry. "We found this article on the bench seat of the Simms' truck, which leads me to believe it may have provoked the attack." Cherry held up Jake Weatherby's "Amerika Turns Heads."

"I don't understand," said Paul.

"It's an affront, that a mixed-race woman would paint what you painted, Kate," said Cherry. "As though you were publicizing the failures at Furly's Fort."

"Why would my depiction of Furly's Fort enrage the Simms brothers enough to want to kill my family?" asked Kate.

Cherry tapped a page in the notebook. "They were both arrested when the ATF and the Sheriff's department conducted the raid."

"In nineteen ninety-seven?" Kate was puzzled. "The Simms brothers couldn't have been old enough to get involved with a militia back then."

"Oh, they were up in Madeline, all right," Cherry assured. "They were underage when they were arrested during the raid, fourteen and sixteen. Because they were minors, and didn't have any prior criminal record, their public defender was able to strike a plea deal with the Feds for release under the supervision of the county juvenile probation department. And that's the extent of their punishment."

"I never should have painted it," Kate said hoarsely, her ribs painful, and piercing her with every breath. She felt as though she were on the verge of collapse.

"Are you okay?" Cherry asked.

"I told you, Cherry, my ribs were broken, when the…when Robert Simms threw me against a boulder."

"You need to see a doctor, Kate."

"Why, so I can be told something that I already know?" Kate challenged. "And then get charged for it?"

"You have every right to your personal opinion, Kate," Freddie interjected, "and so did the Simms, but they did *not* have the right to try to kill you and your family."

"Attempted murder with a hate-crime enhancement, that's a start of what we'll be recommending the D.A. charge Calvin Simms with," Cherry Parker announced, rising from the table. "And you reacted in self-defense."

"So, that's *it?*" Kate held out her hands. "I killed that boy, and I get to walk?"

"Yes, Mrs. Sumner, you *do*," Freddie confirmed. "Unless the D.A. thinks you should be charged, but frankly, I just don't see it happening." He stood, the folder in hand. "One of these days we need to have a talk, off the record, Kate."

Kate didn't respond to Freddie, as her eyes met Paul's gaze. He owned a haunted, grim look, and she remembered on that fated morning, not long past, when she was heading into town with the provocative "Amerika," and her husband's dire warning:

"Jesus Christ, Kate, that painting might be too controversial, especially in this Godforsaken country. Nobody's going to be able to understand it."

Now, Paul squeezed her hand, and she realized, after letting go of her poise, that she was trembling. Her husband and two sons hugged her in a tangle of limbs. Though her chest ached, it felt good to be buried in their sheltering arms, clinging to them tightly.

* * * *

Jake Weatherby was familiar with the features of the girl who entered the lobby of the County Jail. While she was processed through the metal detector, he couldn't immediately match a name to her face. However, he knew she was younger than eighteen, because he could always sense jailbait, a saving grace.

She was slender, and her sensational hair lay down her back in a single, red tinged braid. Her eyes were gray-blue, the color of cold, as though she could calculate his weaknesses the way a lion might evaluate a deer in peril of the fatal moment.

A name suddenly popped into his head: Kristina Sumner. She was the young woman who, a year ago, stomped an upperclassman to death at Susanville High in an act of self-defense.

Jake had read the article about the incident, written by Kara Kinnion, and felt he could have improved upon Kinnion's stilted, censored words. Jake wondered if he could've applied the same cold reasoning had a gun been held to his own head. He could only conclude that Kristina was uncommonly brave.

She was also on the top of the list of choices for the *Register's* apprenticeship program, considered a shoo-in for the position with her journalistic objectivity.

He was about to make a move to introduce himself to this formidable girl, when she gave him a hostile glare, and opened her mouth to speak.

"You are not to come within ten feet of me, Mr. Weatherby," she warned.

He could have sworn she snarled as an aftereffect.

"They're in that room." He motioned to the windows, which had the blinds partially drawn, though still allowing for the occupants to be observed.

"As I said, don't approach me," she repeated. He was properly impressed with her lilt of maturity.

She headed down a hallway, where she was presumably buzzed through a door, because Jake saw her enter the conference room, and rush to her family. This was the first time—but not the last—he would witness that expression of vulnerability on Kristina Sumner's face. She seemed almost childlike, until harsh rage replaced the girl's softened emotions.

I should have ethics, he berated himself. But he kept scribbling his impressions of the Sumner family on his notepad, unable to tear away from the seduction of his chosen profession.

* * * *

When the check for "Amerika" came into Gladiola Parker's possession at her gallery, she passed the paper document along to Kate Sumner, one hand to another.

The two women walked six blocks to the City Hall building, and returned the check directly to the County Clerk, Sharon McCormick. When the act was completed, they made their way to the Library on Main, where, under the protestations of the staff, Kate removed "Amerika" from the wall.

They carted the painting to a nearby fenced-in, vacant lot owned by Gladiola, where naked cottonwood trees loomed. Kate poured kerosene from a jelly jar onto the canvas. Under the watchful eyes of about fifty or so curious onlookers—including the *Register's* Jake Weatherby—Kate set the controversial work on fire with Gladiola's lighter. She and

Gladiola stood back, watching the illumination from the flames shimmer across snow-etched gravel.

* * * *

Dennis Caldwell might have been one of the gawkers at the fence, had he not been off duty, and suffering from a severe guilt complex.

He felt accountable for the attack upon Kate Sumner and her family. He took responsibility for the death of Robert Simms, and the crippling of Calvin Simms, who awaited his preliminary hearing, incarcerated in the County Jail, both legs trapped in casts and wheelchair-bound.

Dennis's girlfriend, Cherry Parker—the deputy who first arrived at the scene of the carnage—spent her off-duty hours talking to him in a low, patient voice, as though to persuade his rational side to reckon with his guilt.

There, on Cherry's wall of the mobile home she once rented from Dennis, and where they now lived together in sin, was another McLain painting, the complete opposite of "Amerika." This painting portrayed the Susan River in autumn, crisp with blazing color, the essence of Lassen County.

Entitled carefully on the wood framing of the canvas, Kate Sumner had penned, "America, with a C."

Chapter Six
Cork

Once he began the drive to the Spotted Horse Ranch from the Sheriff's station in Susanville, he hadn't realized the trip would involve nearly an entire hour of his time. Lack of sleep the previous two nights affected his driving, plus he'd stopped briefly at his girlfriend's place, where they'd had sex.

As he drove, Freddie Snake pondered on the issues he had with his steady girlfriend of two years, Jordan Kinney. Normally a decisive man, when it came to Jordan he seemed to lose focus and judgment.

The opportunity to sleep with other women presented itself from time to time. There were more females employed by the Sheriff's department now, than in Freddie's early years. Working undercover, he was endowed with tunnel vision and a psychologically inhibited libido. The female perps involved with meth labs were sellers or users themselves, or engaged in prostitution to feed their habit. The thought of having a sexual encounter with a target meant he'd be defiling his scruples, so he adhered to a work ethic designed for removing himself from impossible situations.

During the lengthy fling with Jordan, he'd been tempted once to stray sexually. The slip-up occurred about a year ago, just before a huge drug bust in South County.

She was a Drug Enforcement Administration agent, confident, attractive—and white. He couldn't recall her name—Linda, or Lydia? All he remembered were the shape and feel of her tits, muscular like the rest of her body. She had a firm ass, tight pussy and perfect teeth, and on the small of her back, a scorpion in black and red.

They'd been housed on the government's dime in a fusty motel in Doyle. That final night she came to his room discreetly and gave herself to Freddie with a peculiar violence, half animal passion and half explosive anger. He figured he gave her plenty of reason to hate him. He was difficult on purpose, an alpha, with the calculating type of demeanor that criminals sought to ally with in the shady rural business of the meth trade. He respected her professional abilities, which made sex with her so damn memorable.

At the conclusion of their simultaneous orgasm, she'd bitten his lower lip. With blood dripping down his chin and wincing at the pain, he sat up in the blood-spotted sheets and cursed her. She'd only laughed, and left him in that room alone. No affection—just a primal fuck. When the operation was completed, Linda—or Lydia—returned to San Francisco.

If he saw her again, he wouldn't remember her face, just the scorpion, stinger-tipped poison tail beneath his fingers as he bounced her up and down on his rigid cock.

But he'd rather forget about his indiscretion, no matter its residual heat, because the memory meant that he'd been unfaithful to Jordan. Freddie would have beaten a man black and blue for committing an infidelity against one of his sisters, a white man's curse, and not Paiute cultural behavior. Good thing Jordan didn't have any blood brothers likeminded as Freddie.

Focusing on the subject of the moment, this trip to the Spotted Horse Ranch was less business than a method of personal information gathering. As he had assured Kate Sumner, an off the record conversation would beget her no penalties. He was only fascinated by her history.

"I don't know if I want to talk," Kate reasoned, when he telephoned his request. "I certainly don't see any purpose for it."

Freddie thought back to the interview he had with Mrs. Sumner at the County Jail. She'd inexplicably excited him—not her fear, or rehashing of her past, but her animal confidence. After that episode, he'd had a wet dream involving Kate and his total submission. He finally admitted to himself that sexual energy was the sole engineer for this trip to the Spotted Horse Ranch.

Not that he expected to get laid. A fantasy was simply that, not based in fact or reality. The rise in his libido contributed to restlessness—hence, the visit with Jordan on the way out of Susanville. Freddie was safe, as he could never fuck a woman when the scent of another still lingered on his flesh.

* * * *

Mrs. Sumner was working in the kitchen when Freddie arrived, and answered the door sporting a flour smudge on her chin.

"You've got something on your face." On impulse, he reached out with his hand to wipe it.

She ducked, and rubbed the spot herself, embarrassing him.

"I'm not bedridden," she huffed, meaning that she could take care of herself. But the mention of "bed" threw him into an unfamiliar state of anxiety.

Kate was blessedly clueless and led him into the kitchen. At least she displayed the habits of a middle-aged ranch wife.

"I'll make coffee," she offered, as he followed her with a twinge of guilt into a kitchen rich with cooking odors.

She seated him at the spacious table, and set out a plate of cookies, steaming fresh from the oven. They were cinnamon, sugar, and butter Snickerdoodles. Freddie poked at one curiously, receiving a minor scorching for his trouble.

"I didn't know when you'd get here," she admitted, as she set up the coffee maker. "I've been following my daily schedule."

"Which is?"

"Cook, clean, wash." A laundry basket piled to the rim sat in a window seat beside a neat stack of folded towels. "That's after I get the kids down to the bus stop for school. And later, I'll lock myself in the attic until the bus returns."

His first thought was *mental issues*, but she was intuitive, and waved him off.

"No, I'm not crazy. The attic is my art studio." She was pokerfaced, but he could still read the sly humor in her gaze.

"How long have you lived in this place, Kate, if you don't mind me asking?"

The coffee done, she hit the pause button as she set out the particulars. Only after she'd pulled in a chair, did she reply.

"Well, let's see…I've lived here since…what, nineteen eighty six, I think. The fall before Sara's birth."

"Over twenty years."

"What a talented mathematician you are, Deputy Snake."

"Always have to be quick on the draw." He eyed her. "Kind of like you, you're pretty quick in your thought processes."

She shrugged. "I presume you've read about the man I killed in the late eighties."

"Yeah, what are you, an antiques collector? The report mentioned an ash bow."

"I used a Lakota ash bow and a hunting arrow. For the longest time, the wood floor carried the mark of the broadhead, and a nasty bloodstain. By the time my son Daniel was born, I'd sanded out the stain and refinished the floor, though the mark is still there under the rug."

"I'm wondering Kate. Can you describe it to me?"

"Describe what, Freddie?"

"You know, how you felt."

"How I felt, when?"

"When you decided to shoot him."

She sat forward, fingertips on the edge of the table. "When I shot which man, Freddie? The first, or the second?"

He was breathing a little too quickly. Perhaps she was executing a swift mental calculation: when her husband might return; the school bus schedule; the closest weapon at hand, which was a paring knife on a cutting board between them; and whether Freddie carried a sidearm. All of this, in seconds, but then, his respiration slowed, and he could sense her tension ease, though distrust remained in the room, like a foul odor.

"Is this what you came to talk to me about," said Kate, "what I felt like when I killed?"

"Not exactly. Well...yeah, I guess I am."

"Let me tell you, I felt the same as I do now."

"Now? What do you mean by that?"

"I'm like this all the time, on my toes, watchful. Now, you can define it as a mental defect, or a personality disorder, but you have to know my history before you judge me. You have to remember that my daughter Sara was kidnapped and assaulted by Chase Piper, or that one of Kristina's male classmates almost shot her in the head. *Must* I add in everything else? Or haven't you taken a good look at me, Deputy?"

She was vibrant, and he felt that sense of distraction again, awash in the light that seemed to pour off of her physical body, and cast out a heat that aroused him.

He was teetering on a treacherous moment, sitting there with a throbbing erection in his pants, and knowing she could just as easily kill him as swat a fly. He found that oddly exciting, though he could no longer hide his physical attraction from her.

"You have to go now, Freddie," she said quickly, standing, and putting her back toward a door that led from the kitchen directly outside to a porch. "*This* isn't all right. *You're* not all right, so you *have* to go."

He stood, concealing his hard-on with his coat. Shaking out the stiffness in his legs, he realized he'd been rigid since the moment he arrived.

"It's not what you think," he lied.

"I've known you for over twenty years, Freddie. You were pretty good about warning me a couple of times in the past, and I want to return the favor. Neither of us will find ourselves in this situation again, is that understood?"

"What situation?"

"Alone."

"Why, Kate? Think you might be tempted to do something?"

"The only something I might be tempted to do is stop you permanently before you ever touch me."

She turned abruptly, opening the kitchen door to the porch. Out of the weather sat a stack of split wood, and a pair of black rubber boots, and beyond, the endless distances of trees and mountains.

"You want me to go out his way?" he asked, careful to keep his hands out in the open.

"Yes," she said curtly, and he complied, setting his teeth and walking down the steps. She quickly shut the kitchen door, and he could clearly hear the sound of the deadbolt lock being turned.

* * * *

He sat at the long bar in the White Dog, and settled into a Seagram's, washed down with beer and a shot of tequila. Fortunately, there were only ten blocks to his apartment, a distance he could easily stagger if he had half a mind to.

Behind the counter, the bartender, Timothy Calhoun—also part owner of the White Dog—washed glasses and stashed them in oak cabinets, after squeaking them dry with a dishtowel. Freddie studied the man for a moment, and then turned to observe the only other person at the bar that weeknight, Midge Russell.

Midge had a top-heavy torso above skinny legs, dressed unflatteringly in leggings and a baby-doll blouse. She was thirty-eight, but appeared over fifty-five, with the rumbly voice of a heavy smoker. Every now and then she would depart the stool, wander out to the sidewalk, and lean against the wall, a prop for her flat ass, while she smoked a cigarette. When she returned, climbing onto her seat with a muffled grunt, the stench of smoke wafted off of her like a toxic plume.

Right now, Midge was staring back at Freddie.

"Need company tonight, Freddie?" she asked in her throaty, husky voice, and then coughed, spitting phlegm into a cocktail napkin. He counted five of these used napkins, crinkled into balls each containing a mucus surprise, arranged around her drink, a Tom Collins.

He smiled, likening himself to the Cheshire cat, hiding his vulgar intent and noxious deviltry behind a cordial grin. The thought of fucking Midge Russell left him slightly nauseous. To avoid any misunderstanding about his revulsion toward her, he cleared his throat to speak.

"Quite frankly, I'm not sure even with Viagra I could get it up for you, Midge." He tossed back the leavings of his tequila, and then slid from the chair to put on his jacket.

"I could change your mind." She winked.

"Midge." He stood teasingly close to her. Her horrid breath was sobering, and her deeply wrinkled face reminded him of an evil troll.

"My dick has a mind of its own. It's already made up its mind that you give it the willies."

"Deputy, I'm a whole lot of what you'd call fun," she said, slightly indignant.

"You're a whole lot of something, but a repulsive old hag ain't any fun, Midge."

With that, he left the White Dog, Timothy Calhoun's discreet snort of amusement on Freddie's heels.

The night air was cold, and he inhaled deeply as he walked trying to forget Midge Russell, or else he was certain he would puke.

Frowning, he recalled how that afternoon he'd avoided contact with Jordan, ignoring the numerous cell phone voice messages she'd left. They stacked up, along with unread text messages. Just past ten p.m., she seemed to have given up. He was relieved really, still struggling with his carnal thoughts of Kate Sumner. Masturbating did him no good, and only caused the fire to burn hotter. This alcoholic binge was designed to purge the spreading ache in his groin.

Apparently, drinking did him no good. While he walked, he brought up memories of Kate Sumner from her younger days in Susanville as a single woman, up to now, when she'd become this compelling, middle-aged warrior queen. His fixation made no sense, his dick shoving him on a single track toward disaster, and he hated himself for it.

Several blocks from the White Dog, a police cruiser pulled over and caught him in its searchlight. For a moment, blinded, the internal images of Kate Sumner dropped away, and Freddie could only blink for the officer. A window unrolled, and the driver released an expletive.

"Shit, Freddie, you're a walking liquor cabinet. I can smell you from here."

Ken Watson, a Susanville police officer, with the tone of amused disgust sounding like a sweet caress to Freddie's ears.

"Yeah, I am drunk," agreed Freddie, approaching Ken's window, and leaning forward conversationally. "Someone send you out to find me?"

"No, I just happened to see you on my rounds, that's all. And you're swaying," he pointed out, because Freddie seemed to lean one direction, and then find the correct stance just before he toppled over.

"Do you need a ride somewhere?" Ken asked.

"Nah, my place is about…hmm…" He trailed off. "Is this Maidu Street?" He squinted at the street sign on the corner. "Madrone? Shit, how the hell did I get over here?" He scratched his head, puzzled.

"You're in Uptown," said Ken. "Don't you live over near the College?"

Freddie felt foolish. "Guess I'm off course," he admitted. "Do you think you could redirect me?"

Ken motioned with his head. "Get in, I'll drive you home."

Freddie, stumbling slightly, went around the cruiser, and fell into the front seat. Just as Ken turned the car, the world began to spin freely in Freddie's head, and the contents of his stomach rose. Ken recognized the sound of gagging, and pulled to a screeching halt. Tearing open the door, Freddie plunged onto the pavement, and on his knees, vomited his stomach contents into the Madrone Street gutter.

* * * *

Freddie's eyes fluttered. Besides a pounding inside of his head, his mouth felt parched as cotton. He had absolutely no idea of the day, the time, or his responsibilities. He turned over in the tangled bedding, until he was able to get up on his elbows, head leaning against the headboard for support.

"You're pretty fucking pathetic," said his girlfriend, Jordan Kinney, in disgust.

Apparently she was in the room, though Freddie couldn't see her. Grunting, Freddie grasped the headboard and opened his sticky, red-rimmed eyes.

"I heard you were drinking like a rez Indian!" she continued in an angry tone. "Got all drunk, and then threw up in the street."

"You've got a lot of nerve," he complained weakly, "calling me names, since we're *both* Indian." He could sit up now, and stared down at his lap, the gap in his boxers revealing his limp genitals, just shy of being bare-ass naked.

Once he was satisfied he was in the bedroom of his own apartment, he stumbled to the bathroom, where he washed his mouth out with cold water. Finding his toothbrush, he applied a dab of paste, and began to scrub his teeth furiously until the residual taste of vomit subsided.

When he turned around, Jordan was standing in the doorway, holding out a glass of fresh water. Nodding his thanks, he drank the contents without pause. That prompted the urge to pee, so he quickly handed her the empty glass, and flung open the toilet. He aimed awkwardly, one arm braced against the near wall for support.

"Who is Midge?" Jordan asked, when Freddie was done urinating, and had flushed.

He moved past her, and collapsed in a chair at his wobbly kitchen table. The Formica top beneath his palms was covered with old crumbs, but he ignored the grittiness, and waited for his body to recover from last night's self-abuse.

"Midge?" His head was pounding, though rubbing his eyes didn't alleviate the sensation. "Where did you hear that name?"

"Last night. Ken Watson called me from your apartment, said you were shit-faced, and wanted to know if I could come over, and make sure you were okay. You kept pushing me away. You said, 'no Midge,' over and over."

He sucked air in through his teeth. "Yeah, I remember now, Midge Russell. She's a hideous old hag. She was hanging out at the White Dog. She's miserably ugly. She propositioned me, but I would never sleep with Midge Russell." He laughed, but stopped when his head hurt. "I think I told her I couldn't get it up for her."

"What a thing to tell any woman, even a hag." She paused. "Freddie, who is Kate?"

"Huh?" He automatically assumed a stance that conveyed nothing, a technique he'd learned during his time as an undercover member of the Lassen County Drug Enforcement Task Force. The irony was that he telegraphed the lie, especially to Jordan, who knew him so well.

"I tried to get into bed with you, Freddie, but you were sobbing. You called me Kate, and you kept apologizing to me."

"Shit, I don't know what the hell you're talking about." His maneuver was an inelegant and transparent manner of revealing his guilt.

To relieve the discomfort of lying to Jordan, he stood up, and began to putter around in the kitchen for something bland to eat. The only edibles in the fridge were an expired carton of milk, browning head of lettuce and a few slices of bread in a twisted plastic bag. He slammed the door shut, and returned to the dinette with a sigh.

Jordan left him to his thoughts, not satisfied with his response, and even deeply suspicious of his behavior. She made a pot of coffee, while Freddie dithered silently in his seat.

"I know someone named Kate," she finally said, bringing coffee, and toast from the remnants of the refrigerated loaf of bread. The carton of milk, sniffed at by Jordan, was added to the table, along with a box of brown sugar.

"Do you?" He squinted. "I'm happy for you."

"I know Kate Sumner. I seem to remember that you said you were involved with an interrogation a while back—"

"It wasn't a fucking interrogation!" he snapped. His face puckered up, as he stirred a clod of brown sugar into his coffee. "I just had to tie up some loose ends about a shooting."

"I know. It was in the paper." She found a jar of jam in a cabinet, and spreading a spoonful on her toast. "You can tell me about Kate."

He took a breath, knowing he'd given away the lie with body language. Suddenly, he no longer wanted to keep anything from Jordan, nor did she deserve to be deceived. He longed to spill his guts to someone he trusted, and Jordan was the closest person in his life who fit into that category.

"There's not much to add," he told her. "I had a wet dream. I can't control that, I guess. I went out to the Spotted Horse and talked to her, but she kicked me out."

"Why would Kate Sumner kick you out?"

"Because." He looked Jordan in the eye. "She knew I was only out there to seduce her, so I could have sex with her."

Jordan stared at him for a moment. A door slammed at a downstairs apartment, and a car honked on the roadway in passing, and still, her dark eyes were unfaltering. She finally took a deep breath.

"Did you?"

"Did I *what?*"

"Did you fuck Kate Sumner?"

"I wish I *had* fucked her." He groaned, and rubbed his eyes again, as though the gesture would solve his problems. "But she's crazy about her husband, and definitely not interested in me. In fact, I think she was looking around for a knife."

"Freddie, is there something I should know? Is there something else you want to say to me?"

He nodded painfully. "I think I need a breather Jordan, a break."

"You need a break? From what, from me?"

"That's right. I need a break from this relationship before I do it any more harm."

She braced her hands against the tabletop, and stood with dignity for such a petite woman. Rather than picking up her plate and flinging it against the wall—or, horror of horrors, into Freddie's face—she leaned close, and kissed his cheek tenderly.

"I can't say anything else. This should say it all." She then departed, closing the door behind her carefully. He watched Jordan from behind the window blinds as she backed out of the apartment complex, and drove away.

* * * *

Two days later, and fully recovered from the drinking binge, Freddie was seated in a conference room at the Sheriff's department's main office with seven other members of the usual Lassen County Drug Task Force.

This venue was slightly different, because Freddie usually headed these meetings, but now Sheriff Carl Weatherby was sitting in, itching for the helm. An official-looking fax communiqué was folded beneath his blunt fist.

Freddie gave his boss an irritated glance, which seemed to calm the Sheriff down.

Sheriff Weatherby was in usual incompetent form, and stammered on with a need to introduce new members of the task force before they pushed through the conference room door.

"What are you talking about?" Freddie asked. "*What* new members?"

"The Drug Enforcement Administration. We've got four agents on their way in from Reno."

Freddie paused, suppressing the inclination to cuss. Not only had Sheriff Weatherby withheld crucial information, Freddie might find himself in a peculiar face-to-face meeting with his ex-fling. But, he recalled that Linda—or was it Lydia—had been sent from San Francisco, so it was highly unlikely he was in any danger of facing a snarling cat today.

"You never told me this, Carl," said Freddie, trying to keep his cool. "Why did you decide to ask for DEA assistance?"

"I think it's the other way around. They need help from us." Weatherby scratched his head. "It's good to give help to the feds." And he shrugged.

You sloppy jackass, Freddie thought, gauging Sheriff Weatherby with sharp, calculating eyes.

Poor planning that the County Board of Supervisors had chosen to appoint Carl Weatherby when former Sheriff Adin Parker resigned. Freddie privately surmised that at least they could have selected a candidate with an IQ higher than seventy-five. He had difficulty believing that Sheriff Carl and Jake Weatherby, the *Register* reporter, were brothers, as Jake was mentally limber, while Carl displayed the thought processes of a rock.

Freddie was stewing in silent frustration, when the conference room door opened, and four agents, identified by their dark blue jackets marked DEA in large yellow block lettering, marched in single-file to find empty chairs at the table.

"Deputies, let me introduce Frank Ketchum, Warren Pinchot, Lawrence Healy, and Layna Dawkins," said the Sheriff, assuming the demeanor of one in charge. He read from the fax, matching each agent to a photograph.

At this point, Freddie was well beyond being irked at Weatherby, his attention riveted on Agent Dawkins.

Shit, it's her! He felt cagey, and yet, wondered about that scorpion tattoo.

The DEA agents nodded all around, and then Dawkins, who seemed to be in charge of the quartet, started right in.

"Gentlemen, we have access to intelligence, which, as I understand, is severely lacking in your department."

"I don't agree with that assessment," said Freddie calmly. The feeling was normal after years in this profession, to speak with a smooth tongue while his heart was hammering. "It's a back lot here in Lassen County. We find the users, bust 'em, and then the D.A. arranges plea deals to get the perps to rat out the labs and the dealers." He smiled condescendingly. "That's fairly simplified."

"If that's the case, Deputy," her eyes sharp as she met Freddie's gaze, "then why is there a three-hundred percent increase in street meth in Washoe County alone?"

"Labs in Nevada, Agent Dawkins. Did you ever get a look out in your own yard?" He sat back in his chair. "You should be breathing down Trevor Jurow's neck, not here," he said, referencing the Washoe County Sheriff.

"Intel notes a large-scale operation in the area of the Fort Bitterbrush Mountains." She scooted a file folder toward Freddie, but he deliberately ignored her.

"That on Nevada's side or ours?"

"Look at the report, Deputy."

With an obvious show of reluctance, Freddie opened the file, and worked through the stack of documents, while some of his own people drummed their fingers or heaved sighs. The report included a satellite view of a cluster of small trailers, with a key indicating it rested in the top of the Fort Bitterbrush Mountains, roughly closer to the border of California than to Nevada.

"I see," he concluded, closing the file, and passing it to the next deputy. "I suggest, Agent Dawkins, that you go forth and take them down."

"With all due respect, Sheriff," Dawkins addressed Weatherby, as she was evidently making no progress with Freddie. "I would rather work with the law enforcement body in the jurisdiction of the bust, rather than take the lab out on our own."

"The DEA needs cheap labor, eh?" Freddie mused, even before Sheriff Weatherby could speak.

"No, we need trusted people with experience and the ability to execute a plan," Dawkins said.

Her manner was asexual, and so removed from his previous memory, that Freddie released his hold on being difficult, and grabbed up the report once more.

"Let's put a strategy together," Freddie said.

The Sheriff, nothing more than a glorified paper-pusher, excused himself.

* * * *

The four agents and eight deputies developed out a strategy, after studying satellite photos and topographical maps, and weighing all possible contingencies. Freddie delegated tasks to certain deputies, from obtaining basic supplies to ensuring the necessary gear was available from the department's outfitting shed.

With the conference room clear, the space was left to Freddie, involved writing notes in the file. Agent Dawkins had packed her briefcase, and was now studying Freddie with cool blue eyes.

"Anything wrong, Agent?" he asked, glancing up at her briefly.

"Perhaps you don't remember me, Deputy."

"If you have a red and black scorpion tattoo right above your ass cleavage, I do remember you. Vividly."

"As a matter of fact, I have a tattoo just like that."

"And I would've had a scar on my lip, except your bite wasn't deep enough to require stitches."

She blushed, breaking their professional wall.

"What was that all about, Agent Dawkins?" he asked, grinning.

"Let's just call it a slip of the teeth, Deputy." She grasped her briefcase, and swung it against her leg. "Are you doing anything tonight?"

"Yes, in fact, I'm doing my girlfriend," he lied, standing, and pushing the chair in. "I'll probably get laid," he speculated. "You know, the usual thing us men are all about, and women too, though your gender doesn't often admit it."

"I admit to enjoying those activities," she said carefully.

"So does my girlfriend."

"If you change your plans, I'll be at the Blue Ox in Westwood for dinner." She took a business card from her wallet, carried in her back pocket like a man, and wrote a telephone number on the back. She slid it across to Freddie, who only stared at it guardedly.

"That's my personal cell," she told him. "If you want to discuss anything, you know where you can find me."

When she was gone, Freddie put one finger on the card, and pulled it toward him. After reading it, and committing her name to his active memory—Layna, neither Linda nor Lydia—he tucked the card into his back pocket.

* * * *

He was driving toward Main Street, having come from Sheriff Merrill Lane, and up South Greeno Street, when he spied the dark green GMC Yukon belonging to Kate Sumner's family, the replacement for the crashed and bloodstained white Chevrolet Suburban.

The Yukon was gliding down Main Street, filthy with road dirt. As the vehicle approached, he noted Kate Sumner at the wheel. In a quick study through the Yukon's tinted windows, he confirmed there were no passengers. On sudden impulse, he turned onto Main, and followed the Yukon through town.

She drove as far as the edge of Susanville, and turned left on Old Johnstonville Road. Freddie, having missed the turn light, could only watch helplessly as the Yukon headed off. Cursing through his teeth, he thumped the steering wheel impatiently, until the light changed in his favor.

He drove past the concrete plant and recycling center, and a new home improvement outlet, until Old Johnstonville Road cut through a legion of small properties. His eyes were hunting for the green Yukon, but the SUV was nowhere in sight.

On a hunch, he made a U-turn, and drove toward town once more. This time, he turned into the hardware outlet, nosing around a fence that had partially blocked a view of the lot from the street. There, beneath a wind-blasted, leafless sycamore encased within a concrete border, was the Yukon.

Freddie parked beside the green SUV, and studied it for some time. The truck was empty, an indicator that Kate Sumner was probably inside the store. Climbing out of the Crown Victoria, he stood beside the GMC, until he saw her exiting the store, pushing a flat cart of stacked two-by-fours before her. When she arrived at her vehicle, he stepped out, hands in the air.

"Hello, Kate," he greeted.

She wasn't smiling.

"Do you know what a two-by-four will do to a man's skull?" she asked bluntly.

She opened the back of the Yukon, and began to load the eight-foot sections into the vehicle. They slid neatly beneath the bench seats, all the way to the front console, with just enough room to once again close the rear doors.

Freddie joined her, to help hustle the lumber.

"What are you doing here?" she asked, making a point to keep a wide margin of space between them.

"I...followed you," he admitted. "I happened to be leaving a meeting and saw your truck."

"This would be considered stalking, Deputy." She shut the rear doors. "I really suggest you get a life, but don't include me in it."

She pushed the now-empty cart toward a designated drop-off area, and shoved it through the concrete retainers.

"Do you need to talk about anything?" she asked, returning to her truck. "Because I have to pick up Paul at the dentist in Uptown in about ten minutes."

"No," he assured her softly. "I only wanted to see you again, that's all."

"Look, Freddie." She adjusted her plaid wool scarf. "I'm stumped as to why you have this fixation on me. I've known you for years, and you've never come on to me before."

"I know. I'm a fool."

"I'm hardly a girl of fashion, and I'm definitely not beautiful." She tapped her chin. "And I'm not even a girl, I'm headed toward grandmother-age."

"You're fucking hot, Kate. I don't know if your husband even knows it."

"I'm in love with Paul. And he's crazy about me, and he tells me he loves me, that I'm beautiful, every day of our lives together."

"I'd do the same, I'd tell you every day how crazy I am about you."

"I'm a mother and wife, Deputy Snake, and very happily married." Her voice was absent of any irritation, but her eyes were piercing. "I'm off-limits to you, and you know that."

"I remember when I first saw you down at the Bow River colony," he said, ignoring her statement. "You were, what, twenty years old?"

She scowled. "I was twenty-one, I think."

"Why I didn't go after you then, I'll never know."

"What makes you think I would've returned your affections, Freddie? Do you realize how arrogant you sound?"

He was standing close to her, and he could feel the heat rise off her body, before the cold wind whipped her scent away. His lips were parted, and he imagined leaning in, and touching her.

At the moment he formed the vision, she cringed, repulsed, as though reading his mind. He reached out to grasp her braid, to heft the weight of it, and she jabbed the back of his gloved hand with the point of her keys.

He grunted, and shook his hand painfully.

"Stop!" she hissed.

"Kate, I'm—"

"Stay away from me, Freddie. I don't want you, your advances are unwelcome, and if I have to resort to violence to protect myself, I won't hesitate, no matter how long we've been friends."

"Kate—"

"Be honest with yourself. Find an ex-felon, if you think violent behavior is attractive. May I suggest something? Date a cop!"

He removed his glove, and was examining the risen welt between the tendons on the back of his hand. "I can't help wanting you."

She jingled her keys. "Get a grip, or I'll be filing a restraining order. And that's one move before I feel compelled to protect myself and my family, do you understand?"

She climbed into her SUV. He could hear the mechanical *click* as she pressed the lock button. She started the engine, and drove a neat curve out of the lot, without ever glancing back at him.

* * * *

At eight p.m., Freddie entered the front doors of the Blue Ox in Westwood. Ducking briefly into the restaurant area, he determined Agent Dawkins wasn't dining.

He walked into the bar of the Blue Ox, already heavily populated with locals and Correctional Officers. He doubted he would find Agent Dawkins in the mix. When he spotted her, seated on a stool along the far end of the oak bar quite to herself, his heart filled with fire. Approaching her, he noted she was leaning over an open book, and nursing a gin and tonic.

A disheveled elderly man occupied the stool beside her. Freddie whispered in the man's ear, slipped him a ten, and claimed the stool once the man reluctantly slid off. Nicely settled, he tapped the counter beside the book.

"What are you reading?" he asked.

She glanced up sharply, expecting another bearded face, and seemed astonished to see Freddie.

"Deputy Snake." Her smile was bright. "I didn't hear from you, so I guessed you were with that horny girlfriend."

He shrugged. "I broke things off recently." The bartender approached, and Freddie ordered a draft beer.

"You must gave done something terribly crass to be dumped by a woman."

"She didn't dump me. I broke it off."

"Still." She batted her eyelids. "You must have screwed up."

"Of course. Isn't it always the man's fault?" He lifted the book to study the cover of a science textbook. "What's this?"

"A primer on forensic entomology." She shuffled through pages, and showed him glaring photographs of crime scenes, including the accompanying insect life that devours a corpse. "I'm supposed to go to Quantico."

"An offer from the FBI? I'm impressed. When did this go down?"

"Three months ago. I'm actually trained in biology, and I have a masters in forensics as it relates to the disintegration of the human body, plus I studied botany as a minor."

"Wow, you're certifiably intelligent." The bartender set the beer in front of Freddie, who slid several bills across the counter. "So, what did you see in me?" Freddie asked, lowering his voice.

"Recreation. We both had a good time, right?"

He touched his lower lip. "Except for the biting. I didn't know you were a biter."

"Neither did I. I've never done that before."

"Uh-huh." He drank some of the beer.

"I suppose you could say you brought out the animal in me, Deputy."

Their eyes met for a moment, as they locked eyes, and then, he grinned.

"You know, the reason I didn't call, was because I really didn't expect you to be here," he informed.

"I didn't expect you to come. After all, except for our professional association, the rest was casual sex."

"I wouldn't call what went down in Doyle casual sex."

"Sure it was, a matter of coming and going. Besides, we never kept in contact." She finished her drink. "You didn't even know my name, Deputy."

"Why do you think that?"

"Because you always referred to me as Agent Girlie. Don't think that I couldn't understand you. Clearly."

"Well, you certainly proved to me that you're more than capable, Agent Dawkins. More so than most of the men I work with."

"Tell me about this girlfriend you broke up with."

"Hmm, we dated for about two years."

"Two years! Oh, so when we paid our dues in Doyle, you were hitched already."

"I wasn't married."

"No, but you were involved in a relationship understanding, and that makes you slime, Deputy."

"I'm curious, Agent Dawkins. What does that make you?"

"Excuse me?"

"For walking into my motel room. For removing your clothes, being the aggressor. I didn't bang on *your* door, Agent, and by the way, I meant to imply the word 'bang' as a sexual innuendo."

"Okay, I'll admit, you're kind of attractive in a dangerous...I don't know, dirty way, the type of man that a girl's parents warn her about, charming and slippery."

"Uh-huh. The type who makes you scream when you come."

"That would explain why I bit you, Deputy, I needed to draw blood. Bestial of me, yes, but I was strongly compelled to do it."

He sat close to her, her hair brushing his cheek. With one hand, he pulled her hair back, exposing her tender pale neck. He leaned in, his lips hovering over her skin, inhaling the fragrance of her body. Without kissing her, he moved his mouth to her ear, and whispered,

"Would you consider revisiting that bestial activity with me?"

She backed off, blue eyes searching for his humanity. Layna Dawkins was an attractive woman. Her physical element combined with a sharp intellect, and exceptional law enforcement skills.

He recalled the intuition she possessed, serving the close of their case the previous year, when they made that huge bust at the Greeves Ranch outside of Doyle. Agent Dawkins predicted the perps' behavior, and their mass abandonment of the property, instead of digging in for a shootout.

"They're not related," she had explained. "If they were family, you'd expect them to stay together, but none of these men has any investment except for what money they can secure from their trade."

Tonight, she conveyed a vulnerability he had never seen before.

"If you say you'll kiss me when we make love," she contended, "I'll let you go back to the motel with me."

He touched her hair, lifting it off her cheek. This time when he leaned close, he tasted her skin, and pressed his mouth to her earlobe.

"Anything you want," he whispered the promise.

Measuring the width of his daring—or his insanity—he followed Agent Dawkins' Crown Victoria from the Blue Ox in Westwood, to The Red Barn, a small motel near Chester, three blocks from the Main drag of Highway 36. He was surprised that she had chosen to book a room so far from Susanville, even to the point of being in the next county.

"I know you're wondering," she said, as he followed her to a one room cottage-like building in a row of identical cottages, all trimmed with white pin lights.

"What am I wondering?" he asked, as she locked the door behind them.

"You're wondering, why did she get a room so far away from everything we're doing?"

She removed her jacket, and her sweater, and only then, did Freddie note her slim muscular figure magnified by her long-sleeved T-shirt, despite the unisex black slacks, which only accentuated the curve of her ass.

He held her close, and put one hand behind her neck, beneath her hair, savoring the softness of her bare flesh.

"The thought occurred to me."

Their faces were inches apart. He could smell fresh air and wood smoke on her skin, a trace of the gin, and the realization captivated him.

"The answer is: What we're doing should be kept geographically far away from our professional association."

His lips were on her cheek, then down her neck.

"No!" She grasped his face with both hands. "You promised."

He kissed her on the mouth. There was a fragile tenderness in the act, an unfamiliarity that defied the significance of the past.

* * * *

When Freddie awoke following their numerous acts, his watch gave up the time as 3:18 a.m. Telling himself he wasn't going to spend the night with her, he rolled over and stuck his nose against her neck, smelling her skin. The scent of their lovemaking seemed to be on every square inch of their naked bodies.

Layna stirred, turned her face and found his lips. The motion awakened her, and she smiled at him through her sleepiness.

"Deputy," she called him.

"Shhh, go back to sleep." Strange to talk with their lips pressed close.

"I told myself we were going to stay casual."

"Too late." He broke away, and sat up, fishing his clothing off of a chair.

She propped up on one elbow, watching him. "You kissed me."

"That was your doing."

"But we didn't kiss before."

"What do you mean? Of course we did."

"Not like this. The way you kissed me tonight...well, you were a hungry man. It makes you different, in a sense."

He was nearly dressed. "Why?"

"Your tenderness humanizes you."

He laced his boots, and grabbed up his jacket. "Sleep on that, Agent Dawkins."

"Layna," she suggested. "At least, in this situation, you could call me Layna."

"Oh, no." He laughed. "I might call you Layna on the job, and that wouldn't do."

She switched on the bedside lamp. "Freddie," she spoke, and he paused at the door.

"Yes?"

"You drive safely, Deputy Snake."

"You sleep well, Agent Dawkins."

With care, he locked the knob, and closed it the door. As he ducked beneath the icicles of the overhang, he could hear the metallic slide as the chain engaged.

Freddie was almost in Susanville, when he remembered Jordan Kinney and Kate Sumner. What had pushed these two women to the forefront of his thoughts was baffling. He had passed both the Spotted Horse Ranch gate and Jordan's mobile home without thinking about either.

He laughed softly, recalling the last few hours. He could hold the memory close; treasure the tenderness, countered with the day-to-day inflection of hardened lives and equally difficult choices.

Beneath his fingertips, the scorpion had revealed itself, while the woman, Layna, bent over him with luminous blue eyes. If he weren't so wise to the world, he would have considered the word "love" to define his feelings for her.

* * * *

Later that morning, after a brief respite in sleep at his apartment, and then a brisk shower, Freddie was back at the department headquarters, reviewing his notes from the meeting.

His desk sat in a corral of partitions, serving to shield the view without losing track of office noise—the hum of the computer system, clacking of keyboards, and soft conversation punctuated by occasional laughter, or expletives. He could always tell by the drift of air past his feet, whether the main doors were opened.

No surprise, when the warm air shifted briefly to cold, and Victoria Blackwood, receptionist and dispatcher, appeared at the aperture in his khaki-colored workspace. She wore a twisted smile on her mouth.

"Deputy, there's a Mr. Sumner here to speak with you about his wife. Do you want me to show him to your cubicle?"

"Yes, of course," Freddie said through gritted teeth. The young woman was always polite, and yet impossible too because she wasn't naïve to human nature, and let you know it in a less than subtle way.

Victoria left him with a soft chuckle, and then returned briefly to drop off Paul Sumner.

Freddie pulled out his extra chair. "Have a seat, Paul."

"Thank you."

Sumner was aging gracefully in the typical manner of health-conscious, middle-aged white men. Fit and lean, his dark hair was infused with a smattering of gray. Although he wore glasses, the eyes behind the lenses were clear and youthful.

"Can't say as I blame your wife for finding you attractive," Freddie told him, a continuation to the impression of vitality Paul Sumner emanated.

"If you're trying to get on my good side, just don't," Paul warned. "I was hoping to have a conversation with you that might prevent further legal action, you know, something that might blot your record. I really don't want that to happen. You're an exemplary deputy, and this issue in your personal life really has no place in ruining your career."

"Thanks, I appreciate that." He stared at Sumner now, intrigued by the man's complete lack of hostility. "Aren't you going to try to punch me?"

"Punching you in the nose won't solve this, Freddie, and quite frankly, I think you'd be more likely to kick my ass, than having it fall the other way."

"Right you are."

"Aside from this current issue, I happen to like you, and becoming violent with you wouldn't be conducive to preserving our friendship."

"Although I probably deserve a good ass-whipping for wanting your wife."

"You can desire her, but it's unbecoming to actively pursue her."

"You lucky dog."

"I agree with you, I am a lucky dog. And Kate is an absolutely stunning woman. I still lose my breath every time I look at her." Paul smiled. "I actually *am* surprised that this doesn't happen more often."

"I think it doesn't, because Kate isn't a facilitator. She's not the type to fool around."

"Then it's even more surprising that you can't seem to stay away from her." He folded his hands, elbows resting on the arms of the chair.

"Rest assured, I will leave her alone, Paul."

"I heard about Home Club, Freddie. She said you might have tried to kiss her."

He sighed. "Yeah, I guess I did, I don't know, I'm glad I didn't. I think she would've buried one of those two-by-fours in my skull. What do you think?"

"She did tell me she was sorry about the key in the back of your hand."

"Tell Kate…tell your wife that I'm sorry. I *am*. I've got a grip, just like she advised."

Paul stood, and they shook hands. "Freddie, I want you to know that I still consider you a friend."

"Thanks, Paul. I don't deserve it, but thanks."

Sumner had gone, and Freddie sat alone inside the cubicle. For a moment, he stared blankly at the screen of his computer terminal, and then he opened one of his desk drawers.

From beneath a road atlas of Lassen County, he very carefully pulled out a plastic page protector containing a news article, the newspaper yellowed from age. He removed it from its safe plastic niche, and spread it on the desktop, the print and accompanying photograph still easily discernible.

"Local Woman Kills Intruder," the article claimed. The photograph, taken twenty years ago, revealed a twenty-four year old Kate McLain.

What had struck Freddie at the time was the photo's composition, snapped by the late *Register* reporter, Colonel Jackson Hayes. Hayes might have been a professional photographer, for the way in which Kate McLain had been portrayed, almost a Madonna With Child theme. Perfectly fitted into the rectangle was Kate, holding her little daughter, Sara White Owl, in a protective embrace. There was an expression of wary ferocity across Kate's features, dulled by the newsprint pixilation.

Freddie had glimpsed Hayes's original, which used to hang in a frame above the old boy's desk at the *Register's* office, until Hayes' death. The photograph, like Hayes's outdated typewriter, was relegated to the *Register's* basement. Freddie supposed the boxes waited in the dry habitat for their final dump run.

For a moment, he considered going to the *Register* to retrieve the original from the basement, and then, realized the insanity of even thinking it.

The woman in the photo had roused Freddie's interest then, the untouchable Katherine McLain—and not due to preconceived ideas about her death blows, no, quite the opposite. She was the incarnation of womanhood, white or Indian. He supposed she represented all women, militant and confident, a secret attraction to any real man.

He caught up the article and crumpled it tightly inside of his fist. When he was done, when the fragile paper had been minimized, and all possibility of resurrecting it gone, he tossed the tiny ball into the trashcan.

* * * *

The target huddled in the highest saddle that joined four peaks of the Fort Bitterbrush Mountains—Burke, Klickitat, Washoe, and Childers. The wind whistled through the rocks, and scoured the snow-tinged slopes with an incessant voice, withering with either cold or heat in all seasons.

From his perch below the southern peak of Klickitat, Deputy Snake crouched among the boulders and scrutinized the collection of trailers and battered RVs through a pair of field glasses. To the north, two deputies and DEA Agent Ketchum stood their observation, and to the east and west, respectively, were Agents Healy and Pinchot, each assigned a pair of deputies. As afternoon sank toward evening, all awaited the high sign, a white signal flare, which would rise from Freddie's position.

"The vehicle noted from the aerial photographs isn't in place," said Deputy Irwin Moss, Freddie's assigned partner. He also observed the meth lab through binoculars, while Agent Dawkins monitored the access road.

There were two routes up to the summit. One, a beaten and risky narrow fire road made by Cal Fire bulldozers in 1983, during a large wild land fire, and the other, a ranch track, pock-marked with hoof prints from range cattle making their way to brief, high altitude pasturage during the best feed midsummer had to offer.

The task force avoided all known roads, and instead, had ridden cross-country on quads, outfitted with food and regulation containers of fuel strapped to the racks. The trip was executed over beautiful, rough terrain, but they'd managed to haul the quads on two trailers, as far as the back wire of the Triple-H Ranch, cutting twenty miles from their trip. Still, the remaining fifteen miles had been steep and treacherous, with Agent Pinchot nearly overturning his quad on a rocky slope.

"Dangerous, to go that way," said Freddie to Agent Pinchot, as the latter braced one leg to prevent the four hundred pound quad from rolling down the mountain. Freddie yanked the compromised quad around, with the assistance of the exhausted Pinchot, and put him back on the right route, a barely discernible flood line from a prehistoric seabed between ancient lava flows.

Secured in the rocks, and the quads hidden on the opposite side of the mountains, Freddie felt the wind slam his back, while he remained as motionless as possible. For this reason, he chose fleece, wool and cotton for his layers, avoiding anything nylon that would snap and shimmy in the wind.

"Moss is right," Dawkins agreed. "Parlhorst's brown Ford is nowhere in sight."

Devin Parlhorst was the mastermind of the meth lab outpost. His arrest would potentially start a cascade effect in both Lassen and Washoe Counties, as the supply lines pinched.

During the initial meeting two days ago, Agent Dawkins agreed to the quads to support the stealth of the mission.

"How do you suppose," she said, "once we cut them off at the pass, so to speak, we get their felonious asses off the mountain, Deputy Snake?"

"Helicopters, Agent Dawkins. The feds can come up with those, right?"

He'd given her that fixed grin, perhaps raising all of her innate suspicions about a man who made passionate love while denying he ever fell in love.

He seemed to feel Layna's physical electricity from her pocket among the boulders. Freddie dropped the binoculars for a moment, turned halfway around, and smiled at her, before putting his law enforcement persona back on.

Just before the sun faded, and they lost all assistance of natural light—not to mention the misery of spending a winter night in the mountains—a brown bull-like Ford truck traveled slowly up the cow-trampled ranch track. The tires raised a thin line of dust in a wind that flattened all trace of motion into the immensity of the terrain.

"That would be Parlhorst," Deputy Moss confirmed.

"I'll wait until the target's secure, before I signal," Freddie said.

The truck pulled up to one of the trailers, lit from within by sallow lights fueled by diesel generators. Two figures got out, and disappeared into the trailer, briefly casting a wedge of light across the ground.

Freddie was already on his feet. Their redoubt, a mere three hundred yards from the meth lair, meant the point of action could be reached on foot. He waved his companions on, and they sped down the slope, while Freddie, following the plan, shot a single white flare into the sky.

"Why a flare?" Frank Ketchum, the more argumentative of the DEA agents, had asked during the planning phase.

"Radio static," Freddie had explained. "You'd better presume these perps are listening to police band, and even a secured channel will give us away with active static."

Fortunately, the wind was nearly gale-force on the saddle, blowing away from the trailers. As soon as the white marker arced into the sky, Freddie could see the team erupt from rocky strongholds, and head down the hill as though aching for engagement.

They ran among the trailers, kicking open doors and collaring the occupants, including Parlhorst, a vicious criminal who came out brandishing a loaded shotgun. Freddie took a shot at Parlhorst's arm, and put a slug through his deltoid, knocking the shotgun to the scoured earth. Except for Parlhorst's cursing, and the muttering of those cuffed and shackled on the ground, the only sound was the endless wind.

The shot came from the outermost trailer, the official report later read. Nobody heard the crack of gunfire, due to the turbulence of the wind, and besides, the encampment had been presumed secured.

As he was radioing for helicopters standing by in Doyle and Hallelujah Junction, Freddie was spun about and knocked to the ground by an invisible assailant.

He gasped for air. Between the shoulder edge of his Kevlar vest and the top of his shirt, he could feel warmth spread, like urine. That was his thought—he'd somehow peed on himself, but the implausibility brought him to a place where an all-encompassing pain gripped him, and squeezed the breath from his chest.

Agent Pinchot and two deputies, Steele and Harris, approached the trailer with guns drawn. A couple of shots zinged out of the door, but their combined gunfire flushed out the shooter, as a young man embracing an AR-15 with an infrared scope collapsed down the metal steps, and keeled over dead in a steady stream of his own blood.

Agent Dawkins was on her knees beside Freddie, radioing for the Medevac transport. Behind her, the edge of the moon sailed into view, spilling ghost light onto the saddle, casting shadows from the collars laid out on the ground.

Freddie could barely breathe. Sputtering rose in his chest, and a compressing tightness, as he began to drown in his own blood. Meeting her eyes, he remembered:

"Cork," she told him, that night in her cottage at The Red Barn, after they first made love.

The scorpion had lounged underneath his caress, as they lay close, so words couldn't escape.

"What?"

"A tree," she explained, "its layers, they die and become cork, the new bark a part of the old. I want to be like that with you, our new layers fixed forever."

"Freddie." She leaned close now "They're on their way." She pressed a hand to the wound, but the blood kept coming.

The wind was savage, and he reached up with a trembling hand. He traced the outline of her cheek with two fingers, before his hand dropped to the unyielding earth.

"Agent Dawkins." He grimaced from the pain. "Layna."

He was very tired. A trickle of blood leaked from his right nostril. In the wash of cold moonlight, he could identify the color as it flowed across the scourged land and filled the rocky seeps, up to the ridgeline where the sage grew in ageless tenacity.

Chapter Seven
Sleepwalking

When he stood in front of Judge Rob McFarlin for sentencing on a Tuesday in April, the emotion former Susanville police officer Wade Clark felt most keenly was pain, though not his own. Pain was a sentiment he learned to suppress to survive his chosen profession.

The anguish was being channeled through the mouths of his victim's survivors, the children, to be precise, who had been allowed to speak candidly at the hearing, in order, as Wade supposed, to tip the scales of justice toward heavy-handed punishment.

In this Wade was passive. There was nothing in the natural world that could bring Stanley Haskins back to life, once Wade's three-quarter-ton truck lay atop the dead man and his crushed car.

Wade had time, at least, to reflect upon the chain of events that led him to Susanville. As he sat down beside his attorney to await the judge's decision, those milestones tumbled about in his head like the pandemonium of a landslide.

He could almost feel the hot breath of Sheila Haskins, Stanley's widow, sitting in the gallery behind the defense table.

Mrs. Haskins hadn't spoken her thoughts, though her children had expressed bitter torment in losing their father prematurely. Instead, Sheila had written a thickly folded letter, passed along to Judge McFarlin by the bailiff. Taking a glance, the judge uttered his intent to retire to chambers to deliberate on the letter before entering his decision.

For Wade, the tension of waiting drove his thoughts back to the start of all his troubles.

* * * *

A catalyst for Wade Clark's extreme decision to move to Lassen County had been the unrelenting persuasion of his buddy, Bill Marconi, who'd caught the fever fourteen months before.

Believe me, it's like Heaven up here, Marconi insisted by e-mail. *You can buy a house for a fraction of what it costs in the Bay Area. Good pay scale and benefits, as long as you don't work for the County.*

Wade and Bill had served together on the Palo Alto police force, but neither could afford to live in Silicon Valley. Bill roomed briefly with a sister's family down in Gilroy, while Wade rented a shabby, questionable apartment in Pittsburg. The irony was being a cop by day in an upscale community, but at night, boxed in with the meager furnishings of an affordable living space.

Bill tired of the routine, and took a job in Lassen County with the Susanville police, moving to the opposite side of the state.

You can make the jokes about rednecks and hicks, but it's my kind of town, Bill wrote.

Meaning that Susanville was inhabited—and probably run by—law enforcement.

Wade vacillated, until three neighbors in his apartment complex were shot to death walking from the car to the front door. Wade had been on his shift in Palo Alto at the time, and when he returned home, bloodstains from the crime splattered the concrete pathway across from his front step.

That night, he made an inquiry through the web site of the Susanville P.D., and submitted an application for employment. Within three agonizing days, the department had replied favorably, and so began Wade Clark's journey north.

* * * *

In the early days in Susanville, and even as a civilian, Wade stood out. Add the uniform, a clank of gear across the belt, and he was a genuine hunk, with hazel eyes and broad shoulders. Women loved him, though his inherent shyness delivered him from most awkward situations.

He easily opened up with children. Their innocent awe inspired him to demonstrate to them life's opportunities. Though Wade had mentored troubled youths at Contra Costa County Juvenile Hall in his spare time, their futures had seemed bleak. He found it distressing, especially as a cop, to accept that many of those youth wouldn't amount to anything except numbers in the State prison system, habitual offenders constantly cycling through the system.

But Susanville was a different venue, vandalism the most heinous crimes committed by juveniles. Family cohesion was strong in the County, parental involvement the norm not the exception.

As a member of the Susanville Peace Officers Association, Wade joined in youth activities such as fishing derbies and hike camps, and the occasional campfire sing out, when the group campgrounds up at Eagle

Lake were rented by the SPOA. Various church youth assemblies banded together for singing hymns around a roaring bonfire.

* * * *

"Watch out, it's like that movie, *Children Of The Corn*," Bill warned.

He'd met Wade at the White Dog Bar & Grill after their shifts, for a beer, and Monday Night football on the bar's big-screen television. Among the packed tables and merrymaking, they clinked bottles to toast the unbelievable atmosphere of Lassen County.

"You mean everyone's suddenly going to reveal an evil side?" asked Wade, amused. While he spoke, he tried to ignore a red-haired woman seated at an adjacent table. She had her eye on him, and this attention gave Wade a sense of discomfort. His unease was compounded when she seemed to be considering a physical approach.

"I don't think there *is* a bad side to this town," said Bill, who'd also taken note of the woman, and gave a low whistle. "What a babe," he commented.

The "babe" had risen to her feet, and was making her way toward their table.

"Hello, gentlemen," she greeted.

"Hi there!" Bill returned, grinning brightly.

"Hello, ma'am," said Wade, feeling the familiar pain of shyness descend. Wade could scent her heady perfume, sweet warmth that went straight to his groin. He blushed the moment he felt aroused.

"Aren't you a cop?" she asked Wade, standing close enough, he could hear her confident tone above the boisterous drinking crowd.

"Yeah." He nodded, the odd reserve choking.

"I'm Lucille Jennings. But you can just call me Lucy." She held out the kind of immaculate hand tended weekly in a salon.

"I'm Wade Clark." He shook her offering. "This is Bill Marconi." Getting past the introductions was the toughest part, and he pulled out a chair for her. "Do you want to sit with us?"

"Thanks, I'd like that." She settled into the chair, and Bill rose from his.

"Don't worry, I just have to take a restroom break," he explained, departing.

"Nice guy," Lucy said, placing her hands on the table. "Are you two good friends?"

Wade explained their affiliation, the origin of their friendship from the Palo Alto police force, and now, in Susanville.

"I haven't been here long," he told her. "Maybe six months."

"I figured that. I saw you at the big to-do up at the lake." She smiled. "No girlfriend?"

He shook his head. "I've dated, but there's been no one steady since college." He tapped the beer bottle nervously with a knuckle. "I can work with anyone in a professional capacity, but I kind of freeze up in certain personal situations."

"I figured, well, a guy like you." And she paused.

"What do you mean?"

"Officer Clark." She leaned close to keep her comment discreet, her words breathy in his ear. "You're very hot, didn't you know?" Her lips brushed his cheek. "You should be getting laid on a regular basis."

His eyes changed in the half-light of the bar, unnerved by her bold approach.

"I'm sorry," she apologized, immediately sensing his reticence. "That was entirely too forward of me."

"Look, Miss Jennings—"

"Misses," she corrected.

"What?"

"I'm *Mrs.* Jennings. Recently separated, not yet divorced."

Wade rose to his feet. He seemed to attract aggressive women, or those who with unresolved relationship baggage.

"Goodbye, Mrs. Jennings," he said meaningfully, one hand proposing her departure.

Sighing, she stood gracefully, and with a nod, joined her former companions, without so much as a glance back at Wade.

When Bill returned, Wade was seated again, staring at the football game with an expression of distaste across his face.

"Not your type?" Bill grinned, pulling in his chair.

"Married never was."

"C'mon, man, she looked like she was into cooking."

"Maybe. But if I'm going to cook with a woman, I don't want to share the meal."

Bill only laughed.

* * * *

Wade might have dwelled on that event in a string of failures when it came to women. At least his good fortune was having Bill Marconi as a friend.

"She wanted a little piece, is all," Bill observed, dredging up the episode once more. "What would be the harm in it?"

"It's a small community here," Wade reminded. "I don't want to piss anyone off."

"You're a wise man. A hell of a lot wiser than I am."

To amuse himself, Bill had taken a weekend job as security for a youth rodeo held at the AlpineGlo Ranch in unincorporated Susanville. He invited Wade to join him one Saturday.

105

"It's extra money," Bill reasoned, "and the police department doesn't have any clauses that rule out moonlighting. Besides, you should see the women at these things. They're drop-dead gorgeous."

Wade needed the distraction, so he accepted the job with Bill's referral.

The AlpineGlo Ranch nestled against the base of Dennison Mountain, where the desert plateau met the foot of the peak. In July, fields of baled hay formed a picturesque backdrop to the ranch's quaint, nineteenth-century house, and the well-preserved barn and out buildings.

Today, the huge field of hay stubble abutting the barn was neatly filled with parked vehicles, and rigs hitched to stock trailers. The grounds were a flurry of riders, horses, and parents chasing down small scurrying children.

"See what I mean?" Bill said, as they approached the ruckus, pointing at a group of college-aged girls busy braiding the tails of their show horses. "Lots of real pretty faces."

They walked to the barn, and Bill introduced Wade to Stanley Haskins, the rancher, who opened his property to the local rodeo on the third Saturday of each month.

"It's a hobby," Stanley insisted, shaking Wade's hand firmly. He was a pleasant middle-aged man with a slim build and strong grip, dark hair graying at the temples and sticking out from beneath his hat. "But my wife Sheila's into it for real."

As though on cue, a woman approached. She was at her ease in riding boots and Levi's, slim and muscular, discerning eyes roving the gathering like a guardian dog with sheep.

"Stan!" Sheila Haskins barked. "Are you making me into the villain again?"

Wade could see from the way her gaze softened she adored Stanley, and wondered just whose energy indebted the community to the AlpineGlo rodeos.

"Follow Bill," Sheila told Wade. "He'll show you the ropes."

"The ropes" meant where to cruise the grounds, what to look for, and who to eject. Wade strolled around in the ninety-degree heat, eyes concealed behind a pair of sunglasses, head protected from the sun by a billed cap emblazoned with the Susanville P.D. emblem. He wore a walkie-talkie at his hip, and used it to talk to Bill and the other security workers, a pair of off-duty deputies from County.

"There's a bunch of drinkers over here," one of the deputies, Dennis Caldwell, called over the hissing frequency.

He dictated the location, and they converged on a party being conducted inside somebody's trailer. After confiscating the alcohol, they escorted the rig and its occupants from the ranch.

"I'll take that," Bill suggested, in reference to the bottles of liquor. "Maybe it'll be good for later."

Caldwell just stared at him blankly. "Oh, yeah?" One by one, Caldwell dumped the contents of the four bottles into the turf, tossing the empties into a nearby garbage bin.

"Isn't that in violation of some environmental law?" Wade asked.

"City boy," Caldwell scoffed.

"It's a waste, either way," Bill added.

"Maybe the ground squirrels will like it," retorted Caldwell.

The other deputy, Cherry Parker, shrugged, and then walked off with Caldwell, laughing together like a couple of rowdy teenagers.

That was the only true excitement of the day. The remainder consisted of minor scuffles between teenaged males, and a loose dog chasing calves by the chute.

"Well, hello there, Officer," a woman's voice intoned.

Wade turned, and there she was, Lucy Jennings, her freckles hidden beneath the shade of a pinch-front hat, eyes simmering behind a pair of sunglasses. She tipped the hat to him in greeting.

"Hello, Mrs. Jennings," he responded politely.

"My, Officer Clark, so formal." She clucked her tongue.

"Have a nice day, Mrs. Jennings." He moved on.

Later, when Sheila Haskins dispensed their pay envelopes, she complimented Wade for his handling of Lucy Jennings.

"You did the right thing, son," she assured. "Lucy Jennings is a floozy, pure bad news."

Wade was positive Sheila Haskins couldn't be older than thirty-five. Due to his own approach to age thirty, he figured she wasn't in the correct age bracket to refer to him as "son."

He asked Bill about Sheila Haskins when they walked together through the mostly empty lot, the envelope from Mrs. Haskins in his back pocket.

"Sheila Haskins?" Bill laughed. "Man, she's closer to fifty. You see that big boy who rode the Haskins' bucking bull?"

"That was a bucking bull?"

Wade scratched his head, because the so-called bull—a doe-eyed Brahman steer—had been so complacent when mounted, it required a smack of the rider's hands to set it off, bucking halfheartedly a few times, then ambling across the dusty arena.

"The boy was Steven, the Haskins' youngest, and he's sixteen. Guess the age of their oldest child."

"I couldn't." Wade finally brought out the envelope from his pocket, and tore it open.

107

"Twenty-five," said Bill, knowing Wade wouldn't even venture to guess.

"So?" Wade counted out five twenties onto his palm, a hundred bucks, not too bad for a pleasant afternoon, and an easy gig.

"Come on, man that makes the woman at least forty-five."

Wade grinned at Bill's persistence. "Just call me the next time, Bud, I'll be happy to work this place with you."

* * * *

The AlpineGlo Ranch evolved into monthly pocket money, even in winter when sleigh races were held in the formerly summer dusty arena. The pay was slimmer during the coldest months, as there wasn't such a large turnout. Wade was satisfied to take home fifty bucks when he wasn't committed to anything else in his spare time.

Home for Wade was a cottage on North Greeno Street in Susanville, built in 1945, and fully restored before it was placed on the real estate market. With two bedrooms and one bathroom, the cozy house stood in an encircling embrace of sycamores.

During the first months of residency, Wade dutifully mowed the lawn and trimmed hedges. In fall, there were endless sycamore leaves to dispose of. When winter came, he shoveled the stone pathways and concrete sidewalk, and read sci-fi books in front of the wood stove. On the back porch, he kept a stack of split and seasoned lodgepole pine purchased from a local woodcutter.

He lived a good life, a bit lonely, but sweet. Except for the monthly rodeos out at AlpineGlo, and the scattered SPOA events he volunteered for, his days was blessedly uneventful. No shootings at the neighbors', or street races along Main. As Bill Marconi had described in a long-ago e-mail, Lassen County was *drowning in its own boredom.*

Alcohol consumption was on the upswing once winter settled in, but the Susanville P.D. worked in conjunction with the County Sheriff's department, and there were plenty of officers to go around. Occasionally there were alcohol-fueled brawls to break up, especially prevalent at the Rodeo Club, a bar on the outskirts of town. But many townies were involved in preparations for the Solstice Festival, which included a complex pageant, and the number of youth-involved crimes declined rapidly.

There were, however, plenty of domestic disputes to go around— children severely neglected, or spousal abuse, generated by the cold hand of winter, which kept people indoors.

Wade had his share of calls to homes where one spouse was figuratively boiling with rage, and the other battered and bruised. Arrests weren't that common, as simply mediating often calmed both parties down. Police were allowed to provide an emergency restraining order when there were no other remedies.

* * * *

One of these calls came from the newer subdivision on the northeast slope of town, surrounding Ruby Mountain Casino, and adjacent to the Indian Rancheria. Wade was on duty that night and arrived at the address within minutes of the request being just down the road citing a speeding motorist in Shanty Alley.

He knocked on the front door, identifying himself as protocol dictated. A woman opened the door. She was alarmingly familiar—Lucy Jennings, with a bruise welting beneath her left eye.

"Please come in, Officer." Her tone indicated that in this situation, she would consider him a stranger.

"How did that happen?" he asked in reference to her face. His eyes roved the room carefully. Unlike his older cottage, which contained a quaint foyer, the newer homes in C.O. Row opened directly into the living room.

"That bastard!" she exclaimed, motioning to the rear of the house.

Wade wisely called for backup, even as he unsnapped the holster of his sidearm. Beyond the hall, the shadow of a man loomed. By the profile of the silhouette, the man was holding a weapon of some sort, though Wade didn't want to find out with Mrs. Jennings in possible crossfire.

"Ma'am, please step outside," he urged, pushing her away, because she had pressed up behind him.

"Outside, are you crazy?" she snarled. "This is my house, and it's fucking cold out there."

Wade pushed her to the door anyway, despite her noisy protest, and unholstered his sidearm, urging the armed man to come out with hands up.

There was a clattering of a broom being dropped onto a wood floor. The shadow became a man who emerged from the recesses of the house with arms held high.

Wade was stunned for a moment. The person Mrs. Jennings had referred to as "that bastard," was revealed to be the Lassen County District Attorney, Davis Mimms.

"Sir, turn around and put your hands on the wall above your head," Wade instructed.

Mimms leered at Wade. "You've got to be kidding."

"No, sir, I'm not." He assisted Mimms by pulling the man around and pushing his face up against the wall.

While he cuffed the D.A., another unit had pulled up to the house. Officer Ken Watson soon joined Wade.

"Mrs. Jennings," Wade spoke, in front of the second police officer, "is this the man who hit you?"

"Yes!" She wiped tears from her face with the back of a hand, but she was infuriated, rather than afraid. "That son of a bitch."

"Hey, no one calls my mother a bitch and gets away with it," Mimms hissed. "You're the bitch."

"Do you need a paramedic?" Watson asked Mrs. Jennings.

"No, God damn it. Arrest him. Just take his ass to jail."

Ken Watson had called for a female officer, Marlene Parsons, to interview Mrs. Jennings, and photograph her injury.

"So, how does this work?" Wade asked, as he drove an enraged D.A. Mimms to the city jail, for booking.

"What's your problem?" Mimms asked. "Are you insane? You'll regret arresting me, you prick."

"Is that a threat, sir?"

"What makes you think you can arrest me, and keep your pathetic job?"

"I don't know, Mr. Mimms, you tell me." Wade turned into the lot of the Station. "As I was asking, how does this work, do you prosecute yourself, or is there an assistant D.A. who can handle it for you?"

"Fuck off!" Mimms postured, but Wade, unruffled, only grinned as he led the muttering District Attorney into the booking room.

* * * *

Details of D.A. Mimms's arrest never made it into the local newspaper, but as Bill Marconi stated, "Friends grease each other's palms." Davis Mimms golfed with the *Great Basin Register* owner, Jonathan Barringer, so it implied there was cronyism at work.

Wade, who'd received credit for the collar, was called into Police Chief Sam Pilger's office at the end of a shift, about two weeks after the arrest. Pilger, Wade knew, was an occasional golfing associate of Barringer and Mimms.

"I've gotten a lot of flack from this," said Pilger.

"Are you telling me I shouldn't have arrested the D.A.?" Wade asked bluntly. "Because that's what the victim wanted. And I have two other officers who will state the same."

Pilger waved him off. "I've already spoken to Watson and Parsons."

"What's the deal here, Chief?" Wade persisted. "Are you going over my head, because Mimms is your friend?"

Chief Pilger cleared his throat. A quarter-inch above Pilger's shirt, Wade could see the top of a scar from open heart surgery, which made tough old Pilger seem frail, despite the goatee and military posturing.

"No, you did it by the book," said Pilger. "I just want you to be sure, Officer Clark. You might suffer some backlash. That's my warning."

"From you, Chief?"

"My duties extend to the people, which is far beyond golf, Officer Clark. Davis Mimms's family has roots here, and you don't. I'm saying that Mimms will fight this, and I want you to be prepared." He shuffled papers in a file. "That's all, Officer Clark. Keep up the good work."

* * * *

"Chief Pilger supported you?" Bill Marconi was amazed.

"Why not?" Wade asked.

"Because the Chief is in cahoots with Mimms."

They sat in Bill's living room, in a newer house up in the Row, Lucy Jennings's neighborhood, drinking beer and watching the pro-football playoff games on satellite television. Three other cop friends were also there—as Bill said it, "friends among cops are the best kind."

"I don't know much about anything," said Wade, "except for the golfing connection."

"I've been reading up on it. Haven't you heard?"

"Enlighten me."

"Chief Pilger was having an affair with a County building inspector."

Wade was puzzled. "Pilger is gay?"

Bill laughed, as did Thomas Jefferson Parker, a city cop, whose artist wife didn't subscribe to satellite television.

"Aren't you an ignoramus," Parker said. "Pilger's little inspector just happens to be a young babe, Aurora Campbell."

"Yep," Bill confirmed. "Campbell's father worked with Pilger, a long time ago."

"And Campbell is young enough to be the Chief's daughter," Parker added.

"I thought Chief Pilger was married," Wade said. "He wears a ring."

"That's because he and the hottie got hitched," said Parker, finishing his beer.

"I guess that's their business," Wade concluded.

"No, this is a small town," Parker corrected. "It's everyone's business." He laughed harshly, and then got up to clear his bottle to the kitchen.

"You guys make too much noise," Harold Beckett complained. Harold's countenance was walled in gloom. While in uniform, his morose demeanor intensified.

"Look, watch the game, will you?" Kyle Soschak snapped. Kyle's manner was much like a harried chicken, even to the skinny calves sticking out from beneath the hem of his pants. "I mean, God. You can see it without having to hear, can't you?"

111

Thomas Jefferson entered the living room once more.

"I've got to go," he excused. "I promised my wife I'd give her a good time tonight, if she let me watch the games." Finding his jacket in Marconi's coat closet, he zipped it up against the cold of the evening.

"Looks like someone's got a ring through his nose," Soschak teased, but Thomas Jefferson only laughed.

"Yeah, that's right," agreed Thomas Jefferson. "I *am* a bull, and I've got a beautiful pussy waiting for me at home." He scratched his head. "Let's see, Kyle. Whatcha got at home? Hmm, no wife? No woman?" He snorted, and went out the door.

"That's low," Kyle muttered, and then was immediately distracted by the game's action.

"I should go, too," said Wade.

His companions tried their parting shots, though Wade only smiled at their ribbing. He found his coat in the closet, and departed, walking through the cold to his truck.

Bill followed him down the icy walkway, and shoved a boxed pizza into Wade's hands.

"That should keep you fed," Bill said.

"Thanks for the good time," said Wade, climbing in and starting the truck.

"Just be careful," Bill warned. "I've got a bad feeling about this thing with Mimms." Snow began to fall, the flakes gathered in his short cut.

"I will," Wade promised.

* * * *

All the way to his Uptown cottage, Wade was focused on the slick roads. He forced away thoughts of Mimms, and the issues the arrest had spawned.

When he pulled up his driveway, the stovepipe was spewing smoke. His first thought was an intruder inside the house, though there was no sense for a thief to have stoked a fire in the wood stove.

But as soon as he came through the front door, and saw Lucy Jennings seated in his favorite chair, he knew she was in trouble.

He laid the boxed pizza on the foyer table.

"Mrs. Jennings, you shouldn't be here. I didn't invite you."

"Officer." She leaped to her feet. "I can't stay home, he's looking for me."

He studied her obviously frightened expression.

"Who's looking for you?"

"That bastard. That Davis Mimms." She was shivering.

"Call the police, then. Maybe I should call, since you broke into my house."

"I didn't break in, your back door was unlocked."

"Look, Mrs. Jennings, if you're afraid, you can appeal to the Chief for protection."

"I just need to get out of town. Can you get me out of town?"

"Where would you go?"

"Sheila said I could stay at the AlpineGlo." She pointed to a small suitcase standing beside Wade's leather chair. "I'm ready, I just can't drive there myself."

"You walked here?"

"Of course. Do you think I'd start my car? That son of a bitch probably has a bomb wired to the ignition."

"Mrs. Jennings, you had a relationship with the man. Didn't you know what you were getting into?"

She stared at him, aghast.

"Are you saying what I think you're saying? Are you implying that I would actually fuck that man?" Her face became redder, and her freckles stood out. At the peak of her rage, she began to laugh.

"Are you all right, Mrs. Jennings?"

"Oh!" She laughed further, and then held up her hand. "Yes, but you have it all wrong, you see."

"How is that?"

"Davis Mimms isn't my lover, Officer Clark, he's my political opponent."

"What do you mean?"

"I filed paperwork. I intend to run for the office of the District Attorney."

"What was Mimms doing up at your house that night?"

"He was attempting to intimidate me." She sighed, shaking her head.

"But you didn't mention any of this when I responded to the call."

"Trust me. It's not domestic abuse. It's assault. Mimms struck me when I refused to back out of the campaign."

"Maybe you'd better tell me who you really are, Mrs. Jennings."

She sighed heavily. "I didn't grow up in Susanville. I'm from Fort Jones, originally, up in Siskiyou County. After I married, I lived in Bakersfield. I told you that I'm separated, and that's the truth, I am, it's just that the divorce hasn't been finalized. My soon-to-be ex is a car salesman of the worst caliber. He slept around, and that's why I filed for divorce. I came up here to Lassen County, because my sister lives up here."

"Who is your sister?"

"Sheila Haskins."

"Wow. Did you know that Mrs. Haskins called you a 'floozy, pure bad news?"

Lucy laughed. "Of course, she would. She doesn't have one nice thing to say about attorneys."

"You're a real lawyer."

"Yes, of course. That's why I intend to run for the D.A.'s office, to get that scum out." She eyed him curiously. "And I think my sister was trying to keep you away from me. I can be bad news, though I'm not a floozy."

"You did try to pick up on me at the White Dog," he reminded.

"Yes, I did, but believe me, that's generally not my M.O. It's just that I think you're quite beautiful, for a man, for a cop, and I wanted you to know it." She smiled. "It's a tribute to you, Officer Clark, that you walked away. You proved to me that you're exactly how I envisioned you."

He stood, and peered out the window, though it was too dark to see anything.

"I know I'm going to regret this," he said, "but I'll take you to the Haskins'."

"You won't regret it," she assured, gathering up her suitcase.

"I hope not, Mrs. Jennings."

They loaded into the truck, and Wade backed out to the street. The sequence of events that followed soon burned into his memory, as he'd had to relate it over and again to sundry law-enforcement agencies.

The truck slipped briefly on the icy street, so he engaged four-wheel drive, and headed toward Main. Behind them, another pickup truck roared to life, headlights and fog lamps piercing through Wade's rear window.

"They're following us," Lucy said, gripping his arm.

"*Who's* following?"

"I don't know. I just know that someone's after us."

"And maybe you're just paranoid."

The other vehicle accelerated, confirming her suspicions.

Lucy fumbled about in her purse for a cell, and telephoned Sheila Haskins. The conversation consisted of one brief sentence from Lucy, and then Sheila had her moment, while Lucy was forced to listen. When the conversation was over, Lucy stuffed the phone into her purse.

"Sheila says she'll have Stanley meet us at the gate, and once we're through he'll lock up."

"Good. Now, call the Police. Call the Sheriff's department."

"Yeah, right. I don't trust them."

"Mrs. Jennings, you're with a cop right now."

"Yes, but you're different, Officer Clark. You wouldn't even talk to me because I was married."

"Well said, Mrs. Jennings. But if we die here, I may kick myself for not sleeping with you anyway."

"Ooh, Officer Clark, and here I thought you were an honorable man."

"I don't think honor is enough to get us out of this."

He yanked open a jacket pocket and pulled out his personal cell phone, rarely used, but the battery was apparently dead, for no amount of pressing *ON* would revive it, and he let it drop to the seat.

The truck followed them down Main, to the next light, where Wade hung a right. Their pursuer ghosted along, despite being led in circles, as Wade wove a circuit through town. At one point, they lost their tail, and sped back to Main.

"Now's the time to go to the police, Mrs. Jennings."

Wade intended to turn into the station, but Lucy pulled the steering wheel the opposite direction, causing Wade's truck to shimmy on the icy street.

"What the hell are you doing?" he asked, when he regained control of the truck.

"No, please don't," she protested. "I think you lost them. Let's just get to the AlpineGlo."

They certainly seemed safe, as there were no headlights reflected in Wade's mirror. But the mystery truck soon caught up to them at the casino turnoff. Well past the police station now, Wade turned left, figuring he could muscle through to the AlpineGlo.

The road climbed the grade, past the casino, then the hospital, and the college. Beyond the outpost of lights, the road was white and banked high with snow by the plows on either side. The pursuing truck, lift-kitted and capable-looking, roared up the incline, headlights closing in.

Wade downshifted, feeling all four wheels grip the road between sheets of ice. At the turns, the second vehicle would fishtail briefly on patches of thick, snow-laden ice, and then catch up easily on the straightaway. Wade knew the other truck didn't have four-wheel drive, and they owned the advantage especially once they hit the access road for the AlpineGlo.

"You should call nine-one-one," Wade advised. "I don't think this is going to end well."

"Do you have a gun?" she asked, both hands on the dash's grab-handle as Wade negotiated the turns. With her hands occupied, Lucy apparently wasn't planning on calling for reinforcement.

"Always." He could feel the slight weight of it holstered against his left side.

"Good, I have one, too." She let go briefly to pull a forty-five semi-automatic from her purse.

"Lucy, is that thing loaded? Do you even know how to use it?"

"Of course, dammit. I had to take a class to qualify for a carry permit."

The turn for the AlpineGlo was close, but the chase vehicle caught up, and slammed Wade's rear bumper hard. There was a sickening moment as Wade's truck skidded across the road, and onto the shoulder, churning snow. They bounced off hidden rocks, and slid back onto the asphalt, clipping the other truck with their fender, sending the pursuit truck reeling into the left wall of plow-heaped snow. It hit the bank full on, and spun out, hitting Wade's truck again, shoving it brutally off the road.

Instantly, they were airborne, the spinning wheels trailing snow and mud, the sky arcing over them, clouded, and a few stars showing through the gaps. Below, he could see the AlpineGlo's buildings, the yellow-lit ranch house, and the headlights of Stanley's Subaru at the mouth of the access road.

"I'm gonna be sick," Lucy was groaning, hands clenched around her seat belt strap.

As they plummeted down the slope, he recognized Stanley seated behind the wheel, staring up at them in the reflected light with his jaw dropped in disbelief. Wade realized in horror that the truck was going to land on Stanley's car.

They slammed onto the Suburu, and continued to skid along the snowy road, the truck's wheels locked into the Subaru's mashed body. What halted their momentum was a wire fence, which caught the two vehicles and forced them backwards, sliding to a stop in the gash of broken snow.

Wade smelled gasoline. Fighting the deflated air bags, he unbelted, and dragged Lucy out with him. There was blood on her face where she'd cut her lip on her teeth, but she was conscious and clung to him tightly.

Above them, the pursuit vehicle had come to its rest off the road, upside down in the snow.

He managed to get Lucy well away from his truck and Stanley's car, tight in a locked embrace. She seemed to be going into shock, but first Wade had to get to Stanley Haskins.

He tucked Lucy into his jacket, leaned her against a fence post, and ran toward the crash as fast as he could, calf-deep in snow. As he gained on the truck and car, the air erupted violently in an ear-splitting explosion that threw him backwards, onto the ice-rutted road.

* * * *

"That's when everything went black," Wade told Chester Watkins, the Assistant District Attorney, who was known to hate Davis Mimms so fanatically he'd been trolling for a new position as far away as Florida and New York.

Soon the truth was revealed, that the two men in the truck following Wade were known associates of Davis Mimms. Hard proof was flimsy at best. Both were killed when their truck spun off the road, coming to its rest on the roof, and crushing the occupants against a pile of rocks beneath the snow. With their deaths went the chance that Mimms could have been directly incriminated.

Wade's lawyer, Jack Potter from Quincy, advised his client's silence, though Wade felt he had nothing to lose. He was on paid administrative leave, and on the verge of job termination. His house was on the market, because he feared defaulting on the mortgage once his income stopped. Though the SPOA had provided some funds for legal counsel, Wade's modest savings had been depleted in picking up the slack.

Without any official duties to attend to, he felt disconnected. He stopped shaving, wore jeans and plaid flannel, and took to sitting along the Susan River, staring across the canyon at the nothingness offered up by the spindly woods.

He was about as cooperative as a man can be when his entire world has crumbled.

"At least follow my advice, Wade," Potter pleaded. "You could spend up to a year in State prison."

But Wade stuck to his one-track stubbornness.

"I have to account for everything I've done," Wade addressed the court, choosing to ignore paid counsel. "I killed a man. I'm responsible for the death of someone irreplaceable to his family and community. I deserve whatever the court dispenses."

That was all he had to say to Judge McFarlin, and then, Wade awaited the verdict.

The judge deliberated for exactly sixty minutes, and returned to the bench, regarding Wade with a no-nonsense expression.

"I took the letter from Mrs. Haskins into consideration," the judge stated. "She claims that you, Mr. Clark, have been punished enough. Conversely, there is no punishment meted out by this court that can reach beyond your personal culpability in the death of Stanley Haskins."

Wade nodded. "Yes, sir," he agreed. His face was burning, and there was a lump in his throat.

"Therefore, Mr. Clark, I sentence you to one year probation." Judge McFarlin pounded the gavel.

All Wade could do was sit there, enveloped in a kind of numbness, as Jack Potter congratulated him.

"Thank you," Wade said, "but I haven't won anything. I killed someone."

As he left the courthouse, two women stood outside beneath the greening elms surrounding the grounds. One was Lucy Jennings, and the other, Sheila Haskins.

Wade just stood there dumbly. He hadn't shaved in three weeks, despite having to sit in court before Judge McFarlin, and his beard was scraggly. He wore an old leather jacket, a pair of scuffed leather boots, and faded jeans. He felt like a tattered bum.

"Mrs. Haskins," he started, and choked up. He owned no words for his offense.

"Mr. Clark." Sheila tipped her chin, the way she would have tipped her hat had she been wearing one. "Didn't I tell you once that my sister was pure bad news?"

"Yes, ma'am, you did."

"Well, you mightily saved her sorry ass." Sheila smiled. "And for that, I thank you." She nudged Lucy gently. "You wanted to come here with me, so say your piece."

Lucy's eyes met Wade's.

"I'm so sorry," she told him. "Everything that happened that night was my fault, and yet you were charged instead."

Wade nodded, recalling his meeting with Chief Pilger, when he's been requested to turn in his badge and sidearm:

"You'll probably never work in law-enforcement again," Chief Pilger had advised Wade, just after he was charged with misdemeanor vehicular manslaughter in the death of Stanley Haskins. "It's my regretful duty to inform you that the Department has suspended you with pay in regards to your employment as a Susanville police officer. And," Pilger had sadly added, "if you're convicted, it's a given you'll be terminated."

Even Bill Marconi was stumped as how to handle Wade's predicament.

"You're in a world of shit, Buddy." He offered Wade an extra room, as needed, once the North Greeno Street house was sold. "I'll never let you down, even if you've let yourself down."

"Thanks," Wade said now, in front of the courthouse, to Lucy Jennings. "I was thinking I'd leave, as soon as escrow closes."

"I wish you wouldn't go, Mr. Clark," Lucy begged. "I'm still running against Davis Mimms on the ballot come June, and I'm confident I'll win."

"I wish you the best," Wade said sincerely.

"You don't understand, there'll be a job for you," she persisted.

"There's nothing here for me anymore, Mrs. Jennings, but thanks anyway." And he walked away.

* * * *

As soon as Wade was out of earshot, Sheila turned to Lucy with a red face.

"You really fucked that man over, but *good,"* Sheila hissed at her sister. "Forget that, you really fucked us *all* up permanently."

She jogged off, catching up to Wade just before he stepped off the sidewalk.

"Mr. Clark." She grabbed his arm, pulling him around to face her.

"Mrs. Haskins, I'm extremely sorry." His hands were in the air, and tears poured down his cheeks.

"No, it's not that, Mr. Clark, it's not your fault!" she nearly screamed at him. "And it's so Goddamned awful, all of it, that I sure would hate for you to leave. In fact." She tucked her hands into her pockets to assure him she wouldn't be manhandling him again. "I need to ask you a favor, if you'd be so indulgent."

"A favor from me?" He seemed dumbfounded, and cleared his throat. "I'd do anything, Mrs. Haskins, anything at all. I could never do enough, you see."

She smiled, slowly, until all the creases in her face that were usually hidden by her seriousness accounted to her age.

"It's a win-win, and I think you'll like it."

* * * *

Each month, at the AlpineGlo, there's a rodeo, a local wonder. Children and young adults, chasing calves from a chute or riding the AlpineGlo's own 'bucking' steer, and the trick riders, coming from miles around Lassen County to share in the glory of carefree exhibitionism. They win nothing, except the adulation of their peers, and the exuberance of the crowd.

To keep them all in line is Wade Clark. He is the foreman of the AlpineGlo, with the physique of a man, and the temperament of a saint, and along with his wife, Sheila Haskins Clark, patiently united in the singular purpose of mentoring the youth of Lassen County.

Chapter Eight
Purtenance [PUR-tn-uhns]—noun—the liver,
heart and lungs of an animal

For fifty years, the annual Spring Parade had served the citizens of Susanville as a deep-rooted milestone. Folks dressed their houses in facetious trappings, including the ever-present pin lights to net the coveted Susanville City Award for Excellence. No matter what direction one faced on a chilly late winter afternoon, a shimmer would be cast from the stateliness of Uptown, to the rickety lanes of Citrus Flats.

Few who lived in this upcountry hamlet required an excuse for preening and strutting, but the Spring Parade gave them legitimacy.

The parade was springboard for the Susanville Strings Concert, and Mt. Lassen Pageant, a counterfactual rendering of settler Anton Parker's first winter in the Honey Lake Valley (1854-55), when Parker resorted to cannibalism. Written in 1955 by a Parker family member, the script failed to mention Anton Parker's penchant for man-eating—or his subsequent womanizing. The celebratory event, a hybridization of Christmas and New Year's, would abruptly cease if the truth were ever revealed.

The fakery had been spoon-fed to the masses for over five decades, white lies perpetuated by the *Great Basin Register,* and reflected in the Native lineage of Parkers, whose celebrated matriarch, *Nama'dzadzibua*—had been Anton Parker's concubine. The historical debauchery of old Anton was furiously resisted, despite physical evidence to the contrary. The general belief was of an Anton Parker, beneficent and kindhearted historical figure, the savior of the Honey Lake Valley, a far easier sell than accepting Parker as an oversexed playboy.

* * * *

How I Wethered That Last Snowfall
By Velma Harris, Staff Writer, Great Basin Register
Have you looked outside lately? There's snow, folks, covering the roadways, mountainsides, and yes, even your backyards! It's almost springtime, and here we are, stuck in winter.

If you forgot to clean your stove or chimney flue, it's time you got on it. Did you know that during the winter months, one of the leading causes of house fires in Lassen County is attributable to dirty flues? I myself had my flue cleaned in October, reminded, of course, by the many plumes of smoke from the outlying areas, as residents burned pine needles and other unwanted vegetation.

And a spark arrester is just as critical as a clean flue, so have that inspected, as well as the integrity of your brick or stone chimney, especially in your attic where cracks can go unnoticed. Remember the Two C's: Clean and Clear, from perimeter pine needles to the state of your flue or chimney.

Paul Sumner looked up from his newspaper, and over his shoulder at his wife, Kate, who was holding back laughter behind the flat of a hand.

"First off, Kate, stop snuffling," said Paul, placing the paper over his breakfast bowl. "You'll get something from your nose into my oatmeal."

"Ah, can I say it?" She peered around covertly, but they were obviously alone in the kitchen. "That Velma is a lousy writer. She 'sucks,' as Charlie Kat would say."

"I don't get it." Paul whacked the paper with his hand. "How did any of that drivel explain how Velma Harris spent this recent snowfall?"

"And this spelling, 'Wethered.'" Kate pointed at the title. "W—E—T—H—E—R? A wether is a castrated male sheep. Did she do something with a sheep?"

"Maybe she tried, but if it's castrated, it probably wasn't interested."

"Let's not forget last week's edition," she reminded.

"Oh, right, Velma Harris's article entitled 'Senior Center Gets New Redwood Dick.' The woman needs an editor. There's a big difference between a dick and a deck."

"Apparently not in Velma's world."

"Maybe she's still upset about her divorce," Paul mused.

"I think she's upset because her husband left her, before she could up and leave him. Some people have to make the first move, just like they need to have the last word."

Paul tossed the paper aside in disgust. "I'm tempted to subscribe to the *Reno Gazette*."

Kate simply scoffed. "The *Register's* a free paper, Paul, so what do you expect, professional journalism? Besides, you've been browbeating me with that threat for years, so go do it."

She snatched the paper off the table, and took off for the stairs. If Paul had been lighter on his feet, and prepared to abandon his coffee, he'd have taken off after her. Instead, he simply shook his head and opened the *Sports* section.

On the second floor, Kate slowed to a standstill, and gazed into the bedroom of their eldest live-in child, Kristina.

The space was immaculate, bed perfectly made, and awash with pale light through filmy curtains. The desk was arranged carefully and without clutter, centered with a shining Apple eMac computer Kristina had received for Christmas the previous year.

Behind the desk, and on the wall, hung a corkboard, pinned with news articles clipped from the far-off *Santa Cruz Sentinel*, denouncing the Bush administration. The dailies came regularly in cartons, mailed each week by Kate's eldest son, Daniel, as reading fodder for the ambitious Kristina.

Kate recalled the conversation between father and daughter:

"I'm going to be a journalist," Kristina had declared, with clear-eyed determination.

"You're going to be poor," was Paul's advice. "You'll sleep in a hostel room with nine other women as poor as you are, and you'll eat beans from a can, cold and with a knife."

"Not at all," Kristina calmly insisted. "I'll be internationally mobile, not ultra-famous really, just well-paid."

The irony in the foundation of Kristina's confidence seemed to sit squarely on her role in the death of Tucker Parker.

Kate let the *Register* section slip into Kristina's garbage can, rustling the plastic liner. A computer printed essay sat on the desktop beside the keyboard, marked with "100%"—a grading by Kristina's AP History teacher.

The subject matter, an evaluation of the current U.S. administration's foreign policy, lacked fire. In essence, the paper breathed journalistic integrity, a literal standing back and assessing of the facts, without emotional entanglement or dramatic phrases.

Held beside Velma Harris's tangential mishmash, was like comparing a sleek racehorse to a moth-eaten jackass.

Kate realized she was allowing her eyes to wander around her daughter's room. This scrutiny violated every tenet of her parenthood, and she wisely backed out the door, but not before grabbing the discarded *Register*, and tucking it into her jeans pocket.

* * * *

The interview was proceeding smoothly in Kristina's opinion.

On a Thursday afternoon, and just after school, she'd driven her father's maroon Ford diesel pickup truck south to Milford for an interview with the oldest living active rancher in Lassen County, Jack McKinley, who recently turned ninety-three.

Mr. McKinley was a grand old bird, displaying the rheumy blue-edged gaze of an elder, and possessing more fluid physical activity than many people half his age.

"Are you still involved with the business aspects of your ranch?" she had asked, which prodded a bit of chin scratching from the old crank.

"'Course, Miss Sumner, I always manage to work out a plan for each year."

Jack had fought at the Normandy invasion, and endured the Battle of the Bulge, one of the fortunate few who survived World War Two bodily intact, but slightly mentally skewed.

The manifestation wasn't immediately discernable. Jack was incredibly sharp minded, but he had a switch that would trip, and he'd briefly detour into a diatribe about the rise of fascism. If one wanted to ramp up Jack's excitement, all they needed to do was nod and smile.

Kristina was making Jack toe her line. There were no mental slip-ups, and engaging him verbally in the practical aspects of his ranch was the cure.

"You're not going to print any of that crap, are you?" a grating voice spoke up.

In the archway between the dining room and sitting room of McKinley's antique ranch house, stood a gangling white man, Jack's great-grandson, Terrence Hobart. Fresh from the barn, the distinct aroma of swine rose from his manure-addled overalls.

"Dammit to Hell, Terry," Jack grumbled. "I know I've warned you about the shit. You have shit on you. I can smell it. It's on your pants, and your dang boots."

Apparently Jack McKinley was lucid enough to express irritation.

"Grandpa, there's a lady present," Terrence reminded the old man, pointing his chin toward Kristina.

"Don't mind me," she said, not mincing words.

Terrence nodded, sizing her up. Kristina imagined the cogs whirring drunkenly in the man's head: is she eighteen? Perhaps Terrence's hope rose with the smell of the girl's clean scent, fading fast in the heady stench of swine manure.

"Take it outside." Jack waved a hand, dismissing his grandson.

"Sure, Grandpa, but wait. Who do you have here?" His eyes, copper-colored and peculiar, dispossessed of shyness, were gathering Kristina in for the kill.

"I'm sixteen," Kristina spoke up, sophisticated enough to read Terrence's intent written all over his stupid face. "So back off!"

Terrence's eyes drew a blank. He rubbed his face, frowned, and made his exit straight for the back door, the boots encrusted with swine shit crossing the kitchen linoleum in record time.

Jack McKinley was laughing into a coughing fit. Kristina thought at first the old man was going to die, but after a huge gasp for air, he recovered.

"You're a sharp one, Miss Sumner," he said approvingly. "You should go into business for yourself. Don't sit around wasting time in this fucking place."

"You're referring to Lassen County, I presume."

"Hell, yeah. Though I don't think you're necessarily wasting your time with me." He pointed toward the back of the house, in the direction Terrence had fled. "You'd do better than that boy, even though he's my blood. He's too spooky." He looked self-satisfied. "Know what else?"

"What, Mr. McKinley?"

She had already wrapped up the interview, and was tucking her tools into her satchel—tape recorder, note pad and digital camera.

"He doesn't know that the ranch has been left in a trust to his cousin Wilma," Jack said softly, an unaccustomed tone for the old bird, who liked to deliver an opinion in record decibels.

"I'm guessing you don't want that information in my article."

"Right on, Miss Sumner."

They shook hands to seal the understanding.

"I'll walk you out," Jack offered, "'Cause I have a feeling Terry's hanging around."

Sure enough, as McKinley escorted Kristina to her father's truck, there was Terrence Hobart standing beside a shed where split wood was stored. He was pretending casual, but those odd copper eyes followed, somewhat unnerving, even with old Jack at her side.

* * * *

When she arrived in Susanville, Kristina stopped at the *Register*, and checked in at the front desk with Melissa DeLaCroix. Alone in a silent back office, Kristina proceeded to log onto an available computer. Seated at a well-lit desk, and with headphones in place, she began to prepare a transcript from her taped interview with Jack McKinley.

She had been retained by the *Register* on an apprenticeship program, and exclusively extended to high school seniors. Kristina, with her precision and intelligence, had arrived at the program one year premature, under the recommendation of her English teacher, Lainey Rojas.

"I know you're not a senior, Kristina," Ms. Rojas had reasoned. "But I think you have the qualities they need." She had smirked, and added, "*Definitely* what they need."

Kristina privately wondered who at the *Register* was responsible for her appointment. She was told the choice had been related to the packet of five essays submitted with the application, showcasing Kristina's objectivity. She could produce the flair of rodeo and the excitement of politics just as easily as she could delve into the local art scene and the city's taint of corruption, at ease with personal detachment.

Engulfed in the headphones, and her eyes on the computer screen, Kristina was startled by the sudden entrance of Jake Weatherby.

She yanked off the headphones. "Can I help you, Mr. Weatherby?" she asked, disguising her shock behind a steady gaze.

"Uh," he mumbled, face averted and eyes on the far wall. "Nope."

He retreated to a desk exclusively his, and shuffled a few papers. His face was red, and hair disheveled, and turning on his computer terminal, he treated Kristina as though she were invisible.

Shrugging, Kristina replaced the headphones, and continued typing the transcript. The presence of Jake Weatherby was soon dismissed as she turned all focus upon her work.

* * * *

"That girl's missing a heart," was Jake Weatherby's opinion, when he sifted through the packets. "She's perfect for journalism."

Eighteen proposals had been submitted to the *Register's* office by the tri-county high schools, some just hours before the deadline, but Kristina Sumner's pieces had caught Jake's eye.

"This place is small potatoes, Miss Sumner," Jake had spoken candidly, when he telephoned her with the *Register* staff's decision to award her the honor. "Your work is much too refined."

"You should learn not to negotiate against yourself, Mr. Weatherby," she replied.

Jake was given responsibility of supervising Kristina in the *Register's* office, though Kara Kinnion retained the editing of Kristina's copy.

The supervisory job lent him mixed feelings. On one hand, her writing style was mature and professional.

"How someone your age can do what you do," he'd wondered out loud, and then scratched his head, as though perplexed.

But there was an element to the girl that bothered him.

He couldn't nail it down until he remembered their brief exchange at the County Jail the month before, when Kristina's mother killed Robert Simms allegedly in self-defense.

"You are not to come within ten feet of me, Mr. Weatherby," she'd said, her figurative hackles raised and ears laid back.

Never in his life had a female intimidated Jake. This devil-child had the ability to make him squirm with a mere glance.

His discomfort was sharply enhanced by a physical attraction to the girl. He could look himself in the mirror over the sink of the men's room at the *Register*, and repeat "Jailbait," in a chant, and he'd be back out there, seated near her, a hard-on threatening in his slacks.

Jake felt like a wretched thirty-one year-old pervert, lusting after fresh meat, and the misery was damaging him. She didn't appear underage, and could have easily passed for a college grad student, or a fresh-faced journalist.

He'd had been dating Tammy Hart, the owner of The Beadery. Tammy owned a tendency for nonsensical small talk, but was halfway intelligent and could keep up her end of a conversation if the content was superficial. At least Jake was getting laid on a regular basis. He hadn't figured out what sex was "regular" enough to take the edge off his appetite.

Right now, he was sweating. The Sumner girl was typing away, an automaton on the computer keyboard, eyes half-closed as she translated the squeaky cassette interview into a viable body of print. She was completely oblivious to Weatherby's presence, and his sweaty palms. After some time, her keys still ticking away, he managed to get a good look at her, causing him deeper turmoil.

"Shit," he swore softly, and closed one of his desk drawers with a grunt.

The typing halted. The girl had removed her headphones, and was staring at him inquisitively.

"Did you say something, Mr. Weatherby?"

He pushed back his hair, which had an irritating habit of falling into his eyes.

"Yes, I did. I said, 'shit.'"

She studied him for a moment. Her eyes were large in her face, the irises a deep blue that appeared gray in most light, and their enormity was unsettling.

"Oh." She nodded, gathering up her gear and tucking it all into her satchel. "That's what I thought you said."

"Are you…are you finished yet?" he asked, a stack of papers in one hand.

"I'm sorry, am I keeping you from something?"

Her tone was sincere, but he had trained himself to suspect her intent since that County Jail interlude, and therefore handicapped by a tendency to read into everything she said.

"What would you be keeping me from?" he wanted to know.

She shook her head. "I don't know, Mr. Weatherby. I'm sorry I asked." She hoisted her satchel over one shoulder, and dug her keys from a pocket of her jeans. "Have a nice evening, Mr. Weatherby." She switched off the terminal, and departed the room in the rhythm of hurrying feet.

Jake, released from the tension of her presence, collapsed into his chair, sighing loudly.

She returned, and spotted him leaning back in the desk chair, feet propped on the edge of his workspace.

"Sorry." She smiled ruefully. "I forgot to e-mail it." Throwing her bag onto the desk, she switched on the terminal, and waited for the login page.

"What did you forget to e-mail?" he asked, deeply curious, and leaving his feet on the desk anyway.

"I interviewed Jack McKinley for an article Kara Kinnion suggested, and I wanted to e-mail the transcript to myself for editing purposes."

"I hope Kinnion didn't hand over some ridiculous guidelines she wanted you to follow," he muttered, rolling his eyes.

"She did, but I decided after reading them they were too restrictive, so I just ignored them."

He swung his feet down, and sat up. "You did?" He was amazed that Miss Sumner would defy the managing editor.

"Is that necessarily a bad decision, Mr. Weatherby?" She tapped away on the keys.

"Well, it's not as though Kinnion would fire you." He laughed impulsively. "Not like you're a paid employee."

"Don't worry," she said with evident satisfaction. "She didn't give me a list of guidelines."

"What?"

"Well, you asked, and I figured I'd play you." She eyed him warily. "Loosen up, Mr. Weatherby, I was only joking. You're kind of nervous, Mr. Weatherby. Is everything all right?"

"Shit," he repeated his earlier theme.

"Anyway, thanks for being here, Mr. Weatherby, I really don't like being alone in this place." She was obviously unruffled by his foul language.

"Why not?"

"Ah, you know, old buildings, old history. That, incidentally, is something I'd love to write about."

"What's that?"

"California, Mr. Weatherby. Ghost stories."

"I thought you were aiming for serious journalism."

She clucked her tongue. "At the *Register*?" Kristina seemed to thrive on the aggravation in Jake's demeanor.

Finished with her e-mail, she once again shut down the terminal. "Good night, Mr. Weatherby." She exited the office, her footfalls retreating.

127

This time she was gone for good, because Jake could see her pass the clouded glass windows of the office, designed to let in light, and repel prying eyes. He'd know that girl anywhere, her silhouette causing a knee-jerk reaction as she passed.

Alone, Jake Weatherby leaned into his palms, and groaned.

* * * *

The weather pattern changed in the days following. High pressure drew in warm winds that began to melt evidence of that last storm. Any snow tucked into shadow below the elevation of seven thousand feet disappeared into the earth. Watercourses were no indicator of the melt, as the parched soil absorbed every drop.

At the Spotted Horse Ranch, it was business as usual in reference to the stock. The Sumners raised American Paint horses, and the brood mares were foaling in sync with the season. This point in the breeding cycle required Kate and Paul to be available at all hours. As a result they were often awake and supervising laboring mares without a break for sleep.

With two parents focused on the horses, the children were entrusted to carry on daily activities. The eldest was placed at the helm to keep an eye on the younger siblings.

This was Kristina's first year as a licensed driver. She embraced the responsibility of substitute parent, and shuttled her little brothers to school in the morning and home in the evening. Their normal routine was to meet the rural school bus, but with Kristina's responsibilities tied into the *Great Basin Register*, and her parents preoccupied with horses, she was now required to use her father's older diesel pickup truck for the daily run.

She brought Dakota and Charlie Kat with her to the *Register* after school. The boys sat together at an unused desk, and finished their homework, while Kristina produced her articles.

The staff, delighted in the novelty of the boys' presence, brought in treats like donuts and cookies, and six-ounce cartons of milk pilfered from the Richland Middle School cafeteria.

Jake often barged in on the trio quietly at work in the office. The boys would be doing their homework, nibbling away at a treat above a catchment of old newspapers, while Kristina hovered over a terminal.

Jake's first inclination had been defined irritation, expecting the two boys would be tripping mischief, but as the week closed, and another began, they proved their consistency and well-bred discipline.

He commented about this, on the eighth day of sharing the office with aloof Kristina and her quiet brothers, their dark heads leaning close as they split an old-fashioned donut Kara Kinnion had given them.

"You're good kids," he said. He expected some concurrence from Kristina, but she only replied,

"What do you expect from us? We've all been beaten."

Jake sat there, flabbergasted.

"Are you saying your parents beat you?" he finally spoke.

She considered him with a cold, inscrutable gaze.

"What do *you* think, Mr. Weatherby? Why else would children be so well-behaved?"

Charlie Kat pivoted in his chair, and stared open-mouthed at his sister. "Kristy," he reproached.

"Listen, Charlie Kat, have you ever been spanked?" she asked, raising her brows.

"I refuse to dignify that question with a response." Charlie Kat returned to his portion of donut.

"That's just like Charlie Kat, he got ahold of that phrase somewhere, and God! He can't stop using it."

Jake gauged that Kristina's entire presentation was calculated. He studied her, but she was absorbed in typing, completely ignoring Weatherby's presence.

"Your parents don't beat you," Jake finally said.

Kristina didn't waver, but the younger boy, Dakota, turned to smile brightly at Jake.

"Why would you make up something like that?" Jake asked.

Kristina glanced up at him. "Because. I enjoy being provocative."

"Even when it could get your folks in trouble?"

"Mr. Weatherby, you've seen the good fight. Nothing could get my parents in trouble. We've all been blessed. We're survivors."

Apparently finished at the terminal, she switched it off, and gathered up her books and jacket.

"Come on, Dakota, Charlie Kat. It's time to go home."

The younger boy dutifully followed his sister, but Charlie Kat paused beside Jake's desk, and shrugged.

"What's a brother to do?" he asked Jake, his tone suggesting he was at his wits' end with Kristina.

Jake leaned forward. "Absolutely nothing. She's got to work it out for herself."

Kristina stuck her head back around the doorjamb. "Charlie Kat! Are you coming?"

"Hold your horses, Kristy, I'm coming."

Charlie Kat winked at Jake, and gave him a high-five, while Kristina observed, her features unreadable.

"Now would be good," she stressed, though her face didn't match her voice.

As always, Jake followed the progress of Kristina past the windows, her silhouette guarded by the uneven heights of her brothers.

* * * *

The end of foaling brought relief to Kristina's schedule, and she once more returned to the *Register* alone. The table was pitifully empty without the two boys huddled beneath the light, sharing afternoon treats.

"What happened?" Jake asked, arriving in time to witness Kristina logging off of her terminal.

"In reference to what, Mr. Weatherby?"

"Your brothers."

"The foaling's done." She pulled on her jacket, unconsciously arching her back, and apparently catching his poorly disguised glance.

"Are you *looking* at me, Mr. Weatherby?" she asked sharply.

"There's not much to look at." He dropped his gaze to the terminal he was working on. "I've got a girlfriend."

She scoffed. "Since when does that mean a man's eyes don't wander?"

"Since you're under eighteen, Miss Sumner," he grumbled. Opening his briefcase, he withdrew several court documents he'd procured earlier that day, and spread them out on the desk.

"If I were eighteen, would you still be such a jerk?"

He looked directly at her. "Yes, Miss Sumner, that's my nature. I'm an asshole, so just fucking leave, will you?"

His face was flushed, and he had the beginnings of an erection, but his physical response made no sense. He disliked this girl, due to her difficult, bitchy attitude. She was maddening, and head-trippy, and he was weary of her high maintenance rancor. He made a mental note to demand Kinnion take Miss Sumner off his hands.

But she hadn't budged from the room. "Why?" she asked.

He slapped the papers on the desk, and sighing heavily, folded his hands.

"Why *what*, Miss Sumner?"

"Why would you still feel compelled to be an asshole if I weren't underage?"

"Well, then, maybe I wouldn't be. If you were over eighteen, I could say a thing or two with honesty, and maybe set you straight."

"What do you mean by that?"

"Someone should tell you like it is, Miss Sumner. But I can't be that someone. I would probably use the most inappropriate words possible to impress upon you why I feel like being an asshole in your presence."

"Why can't you just be honest with me?"

"Because I'm almost certain your father would shoot me if he thought anything improper was going on. Not to mention, I'd have the cops on my ass." He returned to the computer screen.

"I'm a virgin," she stated, though that hadn't even entered his mind. He'd been working diligently just to keep himself squared to reality.

"I don't doubt it, Miss Sumner."

"Nobody's ever asked me out."

"Maybe it's because any prospective date's terrified you'll kill him."

"I—I'm not a killer, Mr. Weatherby." Her voice was small, a flipside of Kristina Sumner he'd never have reckoned.

"I just look at facts, Miss Sumner, and I'm sure young men your age are crapping their pants when you head their way, wondering if they'll be next."

She dropped her gaze, and nodded. "That's true," she agreed, another blow to Jake's estimation of her. "A lot of guys think I'm a bitch." She met his eyes. "Do you know what Tucker Parker used to call me?"

Tucker Parker, he thought, frowning. He'd heard that name..."Isn't that the boy you killed?" he asked impulsively.

"Yes."

"Okay, so I'm game, what *did* he used to call you?"

"The Ice Queen."

"And why would he call you that?"

She shrugged. "Because I wouldn't...I wouldn't let him touch me."

He was instantly alarmed. "In what way?"

"Touch me, he tried to grope me, and when I pushed his hands away, he called me that."

"What predicament did you allow yourself, that he was able to grope you?"

"There wasn't anything improper, Mr. Weatherby. It was P.E., we were out on the grass playing field hockey."

"Didn't you tell your teacher?"

She made a face. "Ms. Larkin? No way! She hates kids."

"I take that as a 'no,' Miss Sumner." He crossed his arms. "What did you do about it?"

"I...well, I broke his arm. He just wouldn't stop trying to grab me, and I gave him plenty of warning. Afterward, he was going around telling everybody he'd broken his arm in a hay baler, but *I* broke it; it was not a machine that did it to him. You think they would've figured out that no one bales hay in January."

"Why do you think he tried to shoot you?"

This conversation was fascinating, but also repellent, mostly because Jake was attracted to her. A distant rage was beginning to form toward the deceased Tucker Parker.

"He wanted to shoot me because he knew I wasn't afraid of him, Mr. Weatherby."

"What about his parents? Didn't they mourn the loss of their son?"

"I suppose…after the police cleared them of wrongdoing, for leaving a gun around for a minor to access."

As though she couldn't resist, she smiled, her lips trembling and curling up in a smug grin.

"You know, you should get into acting," he observed. "I mean, hell! You're really very good. No wonder you got away with killing Parker. You even had me believing you." He shook a finger at her. "I think it was the smile that gave you away. It's almost like you have this…I don't know, a private thing going on, Miss Sumner. It's uncanny."

"It's not an act, Mr. Weatherby," she insisted. Her face reddened, and her eyes took on an expression of pain, as though beseeching him to take her side.

"Boo-hoo, Miss Sumner." He began to slowly clap his hands. To the sound of his sarcastic applause, she grabbed up her belongings, and ran out of the office. Sitting back in his chair, he watched her bobbing profile dart past the windows.

Staring at his computer screen, all he could see was Kristina's face, that softening of love, when she rushed into the arms of her family at County Jail. Whatever hard, merciless shell she'd slid in place over vulnerability was the true guise, and Jake kicked himself for acting like such a jerk when the girl needed a sympathetic ear, and a shoulder to lean on.

Five minutes later, Steve Whitaker, the sports writer, drifted in with an armload of files.

"What's with the kid?" he asked Jake.

"What kid?"

"The Sumner kid. She's sitting in her truck out in the parking lot, crying."

Jake shot to his feet. "Are you sure?"

"Well, yeah. I tapped on the glass, but she told me to go away."

"Is she still out there?"

"I guess."

In a hurry, Jake made his way out of the building, and around to the back lot, where, sure enough, the maroon Ford sat parked. He could see the shape of her head through the tinted back window.

He approached the driver's side, and tapped on the glass, startling her. She jumped, and then quickly wiped her face, as though embarrassed to be caught crying.

She unrolled the window about two inches. "What?"

"Miss Sumner, are you all right?"

"I'm okay."

"Don't try to pull a fast one on me. Look, I wouldn't want you to drive in this state."

"I would never drive like this, thanks all the same, Mr. Weatherby." She smiled, honest from mouth to eyes. "I'm sorry, Mr. Weatherby."

"Me too. Did you ever just talk to someone about all of it?"

"Yes, my parents, especially my Mom. And the police sent me to a shrink for a while."

"You seem kind of damaged, Miss Sumner."

"I just feel alone. Not at home. My family is very supportive, but at school I'm by myself. Like I said, no boys ever ask me out."

"You're not missing much," he promised.

"Yes, I am, I'm missing dates and proms and dances. I'm missing rallies at school, and Homecoming Week."

"You don't strike me as the type of girl who'd find meaning in any of that. Besides, you can go stag to those events."

"Nobody just goes alone. And I don't have any friends."

"None?" He was baffled. "Not even girlfriends?"

"None."

He scratched his head, frustrated. The wind was cold, and he could feel the chill raise his nipples, but aside from that minor discomfort, Kristina Sumner's deep issues heavily weighed on his conscience.

"Do you want to go have coffee or something?" he asked.

"Why?"

"We could talk. It'd be in a public place, Miss Sumner, so you wouldn't have to worry about anything."

"I don't worry about anything with you anyway," she told him, looking straight into his eyes.

"That's good."

"I mean you're old, like my dad." She was grinning, and he could see she hadn't meant it.

"We could walk." He pointed toward Main, and the Half Moon café.

"All right."

"I'll meet you inside. I have to get my coat."

"I can wait here. I don't want to meet up with Steve Whitaker again. I was kind of mean to him."

Jake retrieved his coat, and met Kristina at the truck, and together they walked two blocks to the Half Moon café. Up and down Main, they could see white pin lights blazing. The American flag was displayed on the front of nearly every home and business.

"It's like a movie set," he commented.

"What do you mean?"

"Small-town America only looks like this in movies. Until I came to Lassen County, I'd never seen this sort of exhibitionism."

She shrugged, as though it flag waving were a compulsion exclusive to Susanville.

He opened the door of the Half Moon for her. Once inside, they ordered snacks and coffee, and tucked into a booth in plain view.

"You know, I heard that coffee can stunt your growth," he teased.

"My Mom's ex drinks it all the time, and he's six feet tall."

"I know. But...it's just small talk, Miss Sumner."

"I'm not too good at small talk," she admitted.

"All right. I'll change course. Tell me a little about yourself."

She broke the ice, and talked about politics, defying Jake's Republican stance on executive power and world domination. She tended toward liberal opinion, and owned a persuasive manner of talking him out of his rigidly conservative ideals.

He eyed her thoughtfully. "I think the reason you don't have any friends is because you're an intellectual."

"You consider me an intellectual."

"I've read your pieces, and yes, I *know* you are. And how many kids your age have such deep political conviction?"

She shrugged. "I wouldn't know. I never really talk to anyone."

"I'll bet your teachers love you."

"Sure they do. I hand in my work on time."

"I saw your GPA, it's...now tell me, how can somebody get a four point eight? That's like getting one hundred-fifty percent on something."

"AP classes. It's called a weighted grade. Susanville High implemented the formula last year."

"Oh. Of course." He sighed. "I suppose they do things now they never did in my day, you know, the ancient past."

"I think it has to do with competition, Mr. Weatherby. There are more students graduating from high school, and less openings at university. I have stiff competition."

"You don't have any competition in Susanville."

"If you rated me against an urban student, I'd get buried by the scores."

"That's why you have to do more, Miss Sumner. Stanford admissions must see those four point eights all the time. They're looking for spectacular, the sublime. Maybe working at the *Register* could do it for you."

"Well, there's the *Register*, and there's church volunteer work, and some other work I do in Gardnerville with the Washoe tribe. My mom has connections, friends in Nevada. And being a member of a federally-recognized Indian tribe has its perks, too." She paused. "Plus, when I took my AP tests last year, I did very well on the scores, so I'll be able to apply those toward the general education requirements."

"You should go to a reputable college or university. Don't stay in Susanville."

She leaned forward at the mention of education, and he recognized the passion in her eyes.

"I love school, and I love to write. And I really appreciate this position with the *Register*, too, Mr. Weatherby. I know I'm often in dissent with you."

"More of an irritating presence, Miss Sumner." He laughed gently.

"I do have a smart mouth. That's one reason I'm by myself a lot. There's another reason, of course, why I don't have friends, and you were right, Mr. Weatherby."

"What, the boy?"

"Yes, the killing." She paused, and stared at her hands.

"Go on, it's off the record, and I swear I won't write about it."

"I had some friends before that, mostly boys. My parents breed Paint horses, and I attended a lot of their equestrian events, the auctions, AlpineGlo rodeos."

"I've seen plenty of girls at those things, Miss Sumner."

"I know, but girls!" She shivered. "I never knew any girls I liked, except for my sister Sara. But that's because she's more like me."

"What about your mother? Do you get along?"

"Yes." She nodded. "We're all in the same boat, Mom, Sara, and me."

"I don't remember that Sara White Owl ever killed anyone."

"No, but she was kidnapped and attacked by an ex-boyfriend, and my sister didn't just sit still for any of it." She set her elbows on the table. "What is it about us, Mr. Weatherby?"

"What do you mean?"

"We lure violence. My mom's had a strange life, and Sara's had her brush with death twice. And me, with Tucker Parker." Her cheeks flushed. "We're minding our own business, but the world's out to get us."

"I dispute that the world's 'out to get you,' but I do offer that the women in your family, Miss Sumner, are extremely...well, I'll be blunt, attractive and intelligent. You're standouts. Not pushovers, by any means, just extraordinary."

"Thank you, Mr. Weatherby." She toyed with her empty paper cup, and then looked at her watch.

"I'm sorry, it's getting late," he apologized. He stood, and gathered up their trash.

"Mr. Weatherby, you know, thanks, really, for the coffee and the muffin."

"It's okay. My pleasure. You seemed so heartbroken."

They made their way outside, and began to walk toward the parking lot behind the *Register*.

"About the conversation, Mr. Weatherby. Thanks for listening."

"You're welcome, anytime. I take a fatherly interest in you," he fibbed. Maybe he could transform the truth into an admirable notion, and purge the halfwit tendencies of his libido.

"You're a liar, Mr. Weatherby," she spoke, but only loud enough for his ears. "Your interest isn't fatherly at all."

He imagined the passing traffic was tendered every word, each subtlety, and all of his guilt.

"God!" he groaned, his voice breaking. The expression of fear in his eyes must have confirmed her hunch.

"Don't sweat it, Mr. Weatherby. Actually, if I ever get married, I hope it's to someone like you."

"Don't patronize me, Miss Sumner," he said through his teeth, perspiring beneath his clothes.

They arrived at her father's truck. She turned to him, and placed a hand on his arm.

"I'm not patronizing you, Mr. Weatherby, I'm sincere. You've been very kind to me."

He withdrew from her touch. "I don't have a hidden agenda. I just…I care what happens to you. I feel your pain. And that's it."

"Please accept my gratitude, Mr. Weatherby. I really appreciate what you've done."

"Horse shit!" he scoffed, helping her load into the truck by opening the driver's door, but aside from that gesture, not touching her.

"You know," he said softly, "if I were your father, I'd shoot me." He deliberately implied his feelings for her, though he was terrified to go further than innuendo.

"If I were my mother, I would, too." She smiled.

That was his memory, her genuine smile, and how she turned smoothly out of the parking lot. He stood in the cold wind, and watched the maroon Ford disappear onto Main, before he returned to his own car, raging at himself all the way home.

* * * *

136

The following day was a test of endurance for Jake. He flitted between the serious aspects of his current stories—an arson fire at the County Fairgrounds, a two-headed calf at the Four Dot Ranch, and Richland Middle School's production of *Annie Get Your Gun*—and his protracted conversation last night with Kristina Sumner. He was so wound up with conflicting emotions that he caught himself counting down the clock to the release time of students from Susanville High.

Kristina entered the *Register's* back office in predictable fashion, satchel over one shoulder, and bundled in a wool sport coat. Slim and precise, she looked every part the young professional. She greeted him without her normal detachment, though she retained a demeanor of respect.

"Good afternoon, Mr. Weatherby," she spoke with a happy lilt, as she set the satchel onto the work space, and began the login sequence on the *Register's* computer system.

"Hello, Miss Sumner."

He'd been out in the wind all morning—first in the wake of the City's fire inspection team as they combed the burned hovel of the Livestock Center in the course of their arson investigation. He then drove to the Four Dot, chasing around old Jeff Parker while trying to photograph an unsettling two-headed Hereford calf. Checking the time, Weatherby drove hell-bent for Richland, to interview Gloria Wassel, the director of the after-school drama program, to produce a blurb on their upcoming production.

"How was your day?" he asked, hoping his friendly tone wouldn't be misconstrued.

"I had a very good day." She motioned to her own face. "Have you been outdoors?"

"Yes, though unfortunately everyone knows it." He described the events of his day.

She sat in a chair. "I can just see myself working at some Midwest paper, like the *Cleveland Orb*, or the *Milwaukee Times*, pursuing stock auctions, and fat corn-fed girls at beauty contests."

"There are moments, Miss Sumner, when even a seasoned journalist has to pay his dues." He tilted his head. "What do you see yourself doing after college?"

She paused, fingers over the keyboard. "I think I told my parents I'd be traveling through foreign lands, be well-paid, though not necessarily famous."

"That depends on how much ambition you have."

"I've always admired Kate Webb. She was a real trailblazer for women in field journalism."

"She came from New Zealand, and Webb's generation is tough as nails from the deprivations of World War II. Is that what you want to be, an investigative journalist?"

"I think it would suit me, except for the part about deciding whether or not to have a family."

"Sometimes you just have to make choices as they come, Miss Sumner."

"What were your plans after college?"

"Are you asking if I stayed true to my aspirations?"

"Yes, I guess I am."

"I did my graduate thesis at Cal, earned a JD degree. I could have been an attorney, but I couldn't settle myself as a silver-tongued genius, even though I passed the Bar exam on the first go-around. I've always loved to write, and it was important to me that people read what I wrote. I wanted to work for *Newsweek* or *Time*, but I ended up in Denver working on a weekly, the *Mile High Progressive*. There was the *Phoenix Sun*, and the *L.A. Times* and the *Sacramento Bee*, and then I found myself in Susanville, right back on a weekly."

"The *Register* isn't exactly the *Sac Bee*."

"I was inspired. My brother's the Sheriff, and all the blog traffic got me to thinking I'd found a rare hotspot of news."

"Did you strike the mother-lode, Mr. Weatherby?" she asked, batting her eyelids, and cracking a sarcastic smile.

"So, I was wrong." He grinned sheepishly.

"You know, talking about your brother the Sheriff?"

"Please, I know you're wondering."

"Why are you two are so different?"

"Same father, different mothers. Carl is fifteen years older than I am. He grew up in Tucson, and then I guess my father moved to New Mexico after the divorce, and that's where he met and married my mother."

"That's a relief, Mr. Weatherby. If it means anything, I don't think you're like your older brother at all. You have a lot of integrity."

"Well, I hope I can offer the *Register* some integrity, and that's how my articles are seen." He sighed. "But you, Miss Sumner, you need to shoot high once you're done with college, and while you're in school, you should intern with a solid media outlet in the vicinity of your university."

"Mainstream press has become a vehicle for this administration's agendas."

"You're right, but it always has, Miss Sumner, from day one of this country. Find another angle, other stories, ones that are meaningful to *you*."

"I will. And thanks, Mr. Weatherby."

"You're welcome."

They smiled at each other from across the room. Jake counted to five, slowly, before their eyes simultaneously averted, and they settled down to their *Register* business. Still, the room fairly danced with the shift in their relationship, a truce exceeding basic camaraderie.

* * * *

After six o'clock, Kristina finished the research article about septic-sludge processing in Lassen County. She had already edited the piece, and e-mailed it to Kara Kinnion for final scrutiny.

Standing, she stretched unselfconsciously, for she was alone in the spacious room, Mr. Weatherby having departed a couple of hours earlier to investigate an incident he'd caught wind of on the police band. The light through the clouded glass windows was colored by the sunset, and she paused for a moment, entranced by the beauty of its shimmer.

"Miss Sumner."

"Mr. Weatherby," she replied, caught by surprise.

Jake entered the office with a paper bag in one hand, and a briefcase in the other. He wore a camera around his neck, and his coat gave off a definite chill from the outdoors.

"I didn't think you'd still be here."

"I just finished, I was going to leave."

He set the bag and briefcase onto his desk, and removed the camera and jacket.

"Are you hungry?"

She nodded. "A little, yes."

"I have a turkey sandwich." He motioned to the bag. "I'd be willing to split it, if you're interested."

"That's very generous." She pulled in her chair, while he produced half of a sandwich.

"Want some?" he asked, lifting a can of diet cola.

"Sure." She accepted the paper cup of the soda, and lifted it in a mock toast. "Thanks."

"Did you finish your article?"

"Yes, and I'll never think about septic tanks quite the same way as before."

"Believe it or not, the sludge is great for alfalfa."

"I do believe it. I've seen what grows in this area." She nodded to him. "What about your adventure?"

He frowned. "Oh, yes, that. An accident. Some drunk coming out of the Rodeo Club in broad daylight ran into a big-rig. Guess which vehicle won."

"So...did he die?" She could feel herself recoil in prospect of the answer.

"Lucky guy, he survived. Actually, people who are drunk often live through a crash, because they're so relaxed at the time of collision. But I don't think he'll be leaving the drunk tank anytime soon."

Kristina finished the sandwich, and began to clean up her desk.

"Thank you, Mr. Weatherby. You were kind to share your meal with me."

"Kind? Miss Sumner, I was hoping to be able to share it with you. I really enjoy your company."

"I like talking with you, too."

She paused, biting her lip, because there was a threshold she could never cross, no matter how much she liked this man. To hide her rising emotions, she caught up her satchel and keys.

"I kind of took my time finishing up," she revealed. "I was hoping to say good night."

He eyed her curiously. "I'm glad you did, Miss Sumner. This office isn't the same without you."

They both smiled spontaneously.

"Well, good night, Mr. Weatherby."

"Nonsense, I'll walk you to your truck."

Grabbing up his coat, he pulled it on, leading the way to the parking lot, where she unlocked the cab, and climbed in.

"Drive safely, Miss Sumner, and I look forward to seeing you tomorrow."

"Thanks, Mr. Weatherby." *Jake.* Thinking his name, her eyes changed, and she felt herself leaning toward him, though she couldn't break the taboo.

At that moment it was a toss-up, but apparently Jake grabbed the reins on good sense, and closed the door.

With a grateful smile, she started the engine, and drove away, his reflection in the driver's door mirror a target for her eyes as his likeness dwindled into the night.

* * * *

Kate saw the strangeness on her daughter's face, even as she came through the door—a somber cast of shadow, and subdued nature unlike Kristina's usual upbeat and confident demeanor.

"Hi, Mom." Kristina kissed Kate on the cheek, bent over her mother as Kate fed a log to the wood stove, shutting the door with a *clank.*

"Hi Kristina. Did you eat?"

"Um, yes. Thanks. I picked up a sandwich in town." She carried her satchel up the stairs, her posture one of defeat.

Kate walked straight to the master bedroom, where Paul was drying off from a shower.

"Something's happened," she declared behind the closed door, but still, in a soft voice, because Kate understood the sharpness of their daughter's ears and mind.

"What happened?" He was naked and chilled, and searching through his armoire for briefs without benefit of his glasses.

"Here you go." She handed him what he was searching for from another drawer.

"Thanks. Now, what were you saying?"

"Something has happened," she said distinctly.

"To whom?"

"To Kristina."

"What happened? Is she okay?" The alarm seemed to endow him with a sudden dose of adrenaline.

"She *looks* okay," Kate explained, "but she *isn't* okay." She was growing impatient. "It's her aura."

In the past, Paul would have snorted at his wife. He might have even called her a "hippie," but that was before evil shed its bitterness upon his family. Kate found he was more likely to listen to her understanding of the nuances of human body language.

"Did you ask her?" he inquired.

"No, but I intend to."

Glasses on now, and fully dressed, Paul seemed to recognize his wife's rising angst.

"Let me do it," he warned. "She'll talk to me. With you, she might get defensive."

"All right." She kissed him for good luck.

* * * *

Paul climbed to the second floor, and paused outside of Kristina's door. He could hear the sound of her tapping away on the computer keyboard. He hated to disturb her momentum, but he rapped on the door anyway.

"Come in," she invited, and he opened the door.

His daughter was seated at her desk, the room lit only by the computer monitor and the desk lamp, which beamed onto a neat stack of papers to the right of the keyboard. Never in disorder, nor ever cluttered, Kristina's bedroom could have leapt from the pages of an interior design magazine, with its pastel walls and discreet lighting complementary to the color scheme and furniture. Along the window was a built-in seat, an original construction, now revived with pads covered in fabric with a festive country-flower design.

"Hi Dad," she said, and smiled. "Let me guess, Mom wanted to talk to me, but you volunteered."

He sat on the edge of the bed, with its wedding ring quilt.

"You're psychic."

"No, it's just that I saw Mom's face when I came home. She knows me, Dad. She knows when something's up. I just expected one or the other of you two, that's all."

"You're right about your mom, she knows you." He eyed her computer screen curiously. "What's that you're writing? Is that for the paper?"

"This?" She stared at the words pensively. "No, it's a poem."

"I didn't know you wrote poetry. It seems kind of whimsical for a young lady who wants to be a journalist."

"It's for English class, but I admit, I was inspired. Would you like to hear it?"

"Yes, of course."

So, Kristina, in a clear, soft voice, began to read.

"Cottonwoods, arisen from water and earth,
exuded the rank odor of death.
Their scent of spring and green rebirth,
belie my faltering, guilty breath.
That evil portrays a placid face,
and hides its killing, wicked side.
Beneath the brief and tender buds,
as flames consume my rage and pride."

He shook his head at the profound nature of the lines. "Kristy, have you…wow, are you by any chance… uh, in love?"

"Oh!" Tears came to her eyes. He could see their rise and spillover, as she wiped them away impatiently. "How could you know?"

"It doesn't take a genius, baby, to see what I see in you. Remember, I love your mom, I've been there, I've felt the pain, I've had those days when everything is beautiful and rarified."

"It can't be right, Dad. I mean, he's old and stuff."

"I don't have to tell you the difference between right and wrong, do I, Kristina?"

"No, Dad, I know what's right and wrong. I would never put myself or anyone else in a risky situation, either legally or spiritually."

"And I would never tell you you're too young to love, Kristina. That would be like telling you that how you feel about Mom and me has no merit. But I think you know the rest."

She sat next to him on the bed, and he put an arm around her shoulders.

"He's…do I have to say who he is? It isn't like he's done anything. He's never been a slime-bag to me, Dad. He's never done anything improper. He probably doesn't even know how I feel."

"Do you want me to get involved? Should I be involved?"

"Yes, Dad, you should, and I want you to."

He waited for her revelation.

"It's Mr. Weatherby, Dad," she told him in a voice of resignation.

"Jake Weatherby? From the *Register*?"

"Yes. It's not his fault. He's done nothing to make me care. I've always been a complete jerk to him, and he's been very helpful, kind, but always proper, Dad."

Paul brought up an image of Jake Weatherby in his head, a clean-shaven, handsome young man, serious at his craft, willing to tackle projects that walked a thin line between impropriety and good journalistic sense. That Jake Weatherby should be the younger brother of Sheriff Carl Weatherby seemed inconceivable. They were separated by at least ten or fifteen years, and both looked and behaved nothing alike. Carl was a rotund, rather sloppy character, with a reputation for brown-nosing, while Jake was trim and energetic, and quite, as Kate once summed it, "the ladies' man."

To even think for a moment that Jake Weatherby might have a hand in stirring up his daughter's emotions was beginning to irk Paul.

"He said he'd shoot him, if he were my father," Kristina told Paul.

"What did he mean by that, Kris?"

"I guess he meant that he wouldn't jeopardize my childhood, ever."

"You've become a young woman, Kris. You're not quite a child any more. But in many ways, you have to remember that you're still a child by law."

"I know that, Dad. Mom always talks about ripples, and being connected to everything else in our world and our lives."

"Yes, that's true." He grinned. "That's one of the reasons I love your mom so much."

"I understand consequences too."

He smiled, and touched her cheek. "You're like your mom, so much, Kristy."

She turned and hugged him tightly. "Do you want me to quit working at the *Register*?"

"What do you think about it?"

Paul had learned this concept from Kate, to hold his opinion close like an astounding hand of cards, before revealing them. If the party to whom the question was directed came up with an answer within the boundaries of his personal ethics, those cards would never have to be slapped onto the table. Usually, it was an effective practice.

"I think I should finish the program, Dad. After all, it'll look good on my college applications. And I know I'll hit bumps in life all the time. I just have to learn how to handle them."

"I agree."

They hugged once more. Paul was recalling Kristina as a small child, so serious and exacting, a mixture of himself and Kate. He didn't doubt ever that she could handle herself.

As he stood to leave, she caught his hand.

"Dad?" She looked up with those huge eyes, more gray than blue, like water under inclement skies.

"Yes?"

"I love you, Dad."

"I love you too, Kristy."

* * * *

Kate Sumner, not her husband, telephoned Jake Weatherby at the *Register* the following morning, early, while Kristina was in school. She requested a meeting, somewhere public, yet discreet enough for a reasonable conversation.

He knew why she'd contacted him, and he was prepared to face Kate Sumner.

"How about the grounds of the Court House, about eleven?" he suggested. "It's not too cold. We could walk around the garden area and have a talk."

"All right."

She was there at exactly eleven o'clock, walking briskly toward him, dressed in a thick wool coat, and her long hair in a braid. If not for his foreknowledge of her age, he might have assumed her to be a college student, though as she closed on him, he caught sight of a few gray strands mixed into the mostly dark, red-tinged hair.

They shook hands, and began to walk slowly around the maze of concrete benches and dormant flowerbeds. The breeze was chilly, and stirred the naked limbs of the stately elms.

"I'm sure you know why I'm here, Mr. Weatherby," Kate opened.

"Mrs. Sumner, I haven't done anything illegal or immoral with your daughter," he said, throwing caution to the wind.

"I appreciate your candor. Apparently Kristina wrote a poem last night."

"I know all about it, *The Cottonwoods*. She e-mailed it to me."

"What else has she e-mailed to you?"

"Nothing, Mrs. Sumner. She doesn't even send me her articles, but I don't edit her, Kara Kinnion does."

"Then why would Kristina send you a poem?"

"She mentioned it was for English class, and she wanted an unbiased opinion."

Kate unfolded a sheet of paper that had been tucked into her pocket, and read the text. Jake, eyes half-closed, followed along with his lips moving silently.

"So you know it," Kate said sharply, "you know it well!"

"Mrs. Sumner, I'm not an idiot. Yes, oftentimes I've been a fool, but not an idiot, and I certainly wouldn't do anything with your daughter. Quite frankly, she's underage."

"So, maybe if she were eighteen?"

"Yes, *yes*, Mrs. Sumner, if she were eighteen, yes, it would be a different matter."

Kate could not bring herself to dislike this man, this charmer, whom she knew was not only dating Tammy Hart, but likely involved in a sexual relationship with poor Tammy as well.

"Are you in love with my daughter?" she asked pointedly.

He looked her in the eye. "Yes, I am, Mrs. Sumner."

That took the wind out of Kate's indignation—that he could stare her straight in the eye and lie would be one thing, but to speak the truth with conviction was entirely another.

"Mr. Weatherby." She shook her head fiercely. "Your life experiences exceed my sixteen-year-old daughter's by many years. Let's set aside the fact of illegality, and focus upon what's moral."

"Loving another person is not immoral."

"Yes, but loving a child, and you being a man, *is!*"

"Kristina is far more mature than many adults, Mrs. Sumner, and she certainly doesn't look like a child."

"She's sixteen, and you can't touch her," she said quickly, her voice in a hush, like water on stones.

"I haven't touched Kristina," he said firmly. "And rest assured, I will not touch Kristina."

"She's still a child."

"Mrs. Sumner, do you recall yourself at age sixteen?"

She hesitated. Jake wondered what she was thinking. He knew something of Kate's past, a matter of public record, which had been detailed at some length in the *Great Basin Register*. Not only the killing of an armed intruder in her home many years ago but also the series of events that connected Kate to her early life.

Perhaps she was remembering her call to adulthood in deflecting a rape attempt at age thirteen, or the violent deaths of her foster parents, and being forced to accept the stark realities of life well before she was eighteen.

"Yes, I do," Kate conceded. "But Kristina hasn't lived a life faced with my choices."

"Kristina has been gifted many opportunities and situations that most adults never experience."

She seemed to consider his statement, while nodding slowly.

"I will say this, Mr. Weatherby. If you so much as lay a hand on her before she's eighteen, I won't hesitate to involve law enforcement. If you conduct yourself properly, for the next year and a half, I would theorize that you might be welcomed into my family. But—"

She held up her hand, the paper still tucked inside the V of her thumb to palm.

"If you behave like a fucking gigolo with Tammy Hart, while you claim to love my child, I will hunt you down and make you into a eunuch. Is that understood?"

He stood with his hands in his pockets, nodding. When he finally spoke, there was a raw tone of irony in his voice.

"You know, I saw Tammy last night. Curious that I would see her, and then receive this e-mailed poem, is beyond me, Mrs. Sumner, and completely separate.

"So, I visited Tammy in Uptown, and I broke the news to her, that I was a rakish such-and-such, an emotional cheater, a lying bastard, and that I didn't deserve her. I thought she should know. I figured I'd break it off now, and she agreed. I didn't say toward whom my feelings were directed, because, after all, I understand discretion. Anyway, Tammy was understandably very pissed off.

"Afterward, I went home, and logged into my computer. I go to sleep late, you see, I'm listening to the police band, and conferring with journalists out of the area, etcetera. Watching CNN and Fox News on the dish. Then I received this e-mail. It was the poem, Mrs. Sumner, and it was beautiful. Remarkable. Precious. I can't say more, I only know that I can wait. For what, for whom, I can't say, but I can wait. It's not a long time. A long time would be defined as 'forever.' Eighteen months, this is not a long time."

If Kate were impressed, she hid it well. Instead, she merely shifted her feet, and asked, "How old are you, Mr. Weatherby?"

"I turned thirty-one on January tenth."

"Thirty-one, hmm. Let's see, a little math here, and *voila!* My daughter is half your age, Mr. Weatherby. Doesn't that concern you?"

"Mrs. Sumner, as I stated, I can wait."

This was all he was willing to say, and now their impasse as they stood there regarding one another, Kate with bared suspicion, and Jake in admiration of the woman's power.

"Anything you'd like to add?" she asked, her arms folded.

"Yes, I'd like to say that I know you don't trust me, but I will make it right, Mrs. Sumner. I'm honorable, and I respect Kristina, and her parents."

She let her arms down, and almost her guard, yet her wariness seemed to circle them like a vicious guardian spirit.

"I'm eternally vigilant," she explained, "because I've been conditioned. The world is an amazing gift, like life, but its putrefaction is overwhelming, and I cannot allow its stench to touch my family. Do you understand?"

"Yes, I do. I really do." He realized, had he not loved this woman's daughter, and then very likely, he would have loved her.

And then, her revelation:

"I knew all about Tucker Parker's assault upon my daughter," said Kate softly, "because Kristina doesn't pull any punches, she told me right away. But I also sensed that she could take care of herself when the boy wound up mysteriously with a broken arm." She inhaled. "It's not so much a fear of the unknown, Mr. Weatherby; it's defiance toward what I *do* know." She tucked her hands into her jacket pockets. "Eighteen months, Mr. Weatherby. You have eighteen months. Use it wisely."

As she walked away from him, Jake sought her age. Truthfully, the years lurked there in her face, a slight sunken-in appearance beneath the glow of exuberant health. But her stride contained a strength he had seen in Kristina many times. He felt something lift inside of him beyond his physical being, which he could only describe as elation.

* * * *

The euphoria wrapped around Jake's heart remained. He was seated at the usual computer terminal, waiting for Kristina. To be the bearer of this secret was notable enough, but to realize he was poised on the brink of her family's approval was phenomenal.

So, he idled, working on a couple of articles, watching the clock, and he was just finishing up, when she arrived at the office.

"Hi," she said, her face pale and drawn. She logged into a computer, and tried her best to be formal, but he stood and shook out his legs.

"I spoke with your mother," he opened.

"Oh!" She seemed upset, but was holding it together. "Why on earth did my mother speak with you?"

"She mentioned that I have eighteen months to get my act together," he said, summarizing the conversation.

"What does that mean?"

"She means you'll be a legal adult in about a year and a half, Miss Sumner."

She nodded. The air of misery seemed to be clearing. After a while, she was actually smiling.

"My mom must really love me."

"Need you even wonder if she does? Because it was evident to me that she loves you more than life, Miss Sumner."

"I never attributed indecency to you as a fault, Mr. Weatherby. I offered no blame but my own. I only admitted to my feelings."

"The rest goes without saying, Miss Sumner. You are an exceptional young woman, and this is not at all one-sided on your part."

A few tears, impatiently brushed away. "But to condone this?"

"She doesn't condone any of it, not for another eighteen months. She said that the world, despite all of its beauty, is a place of rot and decay."

"That's Mom," she said simply.

"I just thought you'd like to know." He sat back down.

"Thank you, Mr. Weatherby."

"You're quite welcome, Miss Sumner."

There was a companionable silence between them, torn by an incoming call for Kristina from the front desk.

"Yes? All right. Hello, Mr. McKinley? You sound strange, Mr. McKinley. Thanks, I'm fine, yes, I edited the interview. I mailed it weeks ago, didn't you receive it? That's strange." She glanced at her watch. "Well, it's almost four o'clock now, Mr. McKinley, but I guess I could bring you a copy. Okay, I'll be there within the hour. I can't stay long. Yes, thank you, I will."

Jake perked up. "What's going on?"

"That was Jack McKinley, you know that World War II vet I interviewed? He claims he never got a copy of the interview."

"Why would you send him a copy of the interview when it's already been published?"

"I felt he should have the clean unedited version I submitted for publication, sort of for posterity."

"Did Kinnion like it?"

"Yes, though she omitted the more provocative questions from the part that was actually put in the paper."

He laughed. "She's a bitch for certain details, isn't she?"

Kristina gathered up her satchel and keys. "No," she whispered conspiratorially. "She's just a bitch."

He was instantly on his feet. "Do you want me to go with you?"

She seemed anxious.

"Only if you want me to," he added, giving her an out.

"It's not that. I'm not worried about you, and yes, I'd like you to go with me, if you don't mind. Mr. McKinley has this really scary great-grandson who works on the ranch. He gave me the creeps when I was out there, and I don't like the idea of going back and seeing him alone again."

"Why? Did he say anything obscene to you?"

"Not really, he just came in and stood there, looking at me. When I said I was sixteen, he fled."

"You're sixteen," Jake said, thoughtfully.

"Yes, I am, Mr. Weatherby, actually, sixteen-and-a-half." She shrugged. "My eighteenth birthday will be August fourteenth, two thousand eight."

"I've just made a mental note of it."

"Maybe…" She seemed uncharacteristically shy.

"Yes," he said boldly, "I'll be there to celebrate it with you."

She smiled brightly.

They walked out of the back office together. Jake made the point of telling Melissa DeLaCroix, the *Register's* receptionist, that he was escorting Miss Sumner to Jack McKinley's ranch down in Milford. This was formality, and openness, abdicated of the worry of being thought a pervert by Kristina's parents. All right, so he *was* a pervert, but at least he was an honorable one.

They drove in Kristina's father's truck, a good choice, given that they were being chaperoned by the mere illusion of Paul Sumner's presence. Jake literally sat on his hands, and kept his mind from wandering where it legally should not.

"I wanted to tell you," she spoke, as they rolled southbound, out of town. "My English teacher, Ms. Rojas, really like the poem."

"Oh?" He smiled. "So did I."

"They're like that, they truly are. Cottonwoods, they smell, kind of like a wet dog does, all rank and earthy. Their odor rises up in the spring when they come back to life. You can actually smell the components of soil and water."

"I know the smell. I remembered it right away, as soon as I read it." He recalled the line. "But you spoke of death, not just of rebirth."

"All life is death, and death is life. It's a Native symbol, the circle, no beginning and no end."

"Like the Biblical Alpha and Omega."

"Yes, that's right."

He noticed her glance at him in the reflection of his window. He felt broody, gazing out at the passing mountains, the short western rise of desert into field and forest. As he looked through the glass, he again focused on her faint reflection upon its surface, and he spoke her words, now deeply ingrained in his mind:

"Cottonwoods, arisen from water and earth,

> *exuded the rank odor of death.*
> *Their scent of spring and green rebirth,*
> *belie my faltering, guilty breath.*
> *That evil portrays a placid face,*
> *and hides its killing, wicked side,*
> *Beneath the brief and tender buds,*
> *as flames consume my rage and pride."*

"I'm Indian, Mr. Weatherby, one-fourth Quinault, a tribal member. I told somebody once, that I am my mother's daughter."

"I see you've been in that circle you wrote about," he said gently.

"Yes, Mr. Weatherby. Yes, I have."

They passed Janesville, and the Caltrans rest area, and the waters of Honey Lake spread in a gray sheet beneath a clouded sky.

"*Deyuliyi*, the Washoe called it, for death by bitter waters," she explained. "No one could drink it, but there it lay."

He was unexpectedly struck at how the lake reminded him of the color of her eyes. He felt prose rise up, similar to the inexplicable feeling of joy after his conversation with Kate Sumner.

"I love you," he told her softly. "And I'm sorry. But I do, I love you."

"I know." She nodded, her hands gripping the steering wheel. "I love you, too."

There was the ranch gate for McKinley's, with its arch marked by a lopsided wooden M. Kristina turned right, and the road climbed a seven percent grade, before it leveled off, twisting through stands of lodgepole pines, dipping down briefly into a creek bed where ancient Fremont cottonwoods stood naked in the stripping wind. He might have unrolled the window and breathed deeply for their scent, had he not been aware of their slumber.

The ranch buildings came into view, clumped at the edge of an upland meadow, and a huge barn. The field had recently been plowed, so that when she parked, and they emerged from the truck, Jake could smell the fresh earth against the back of his throat.

He pretended to chase her, and Kristina ran away, giggling. Catching up to her, he met her stride, and they continued toward the main house, jogging side-by-side and close, but without touching.

She reached up to knock, though the door was already unlatched, and fell open beneath her hand.

"He came to the door the last time," she said, an edge of concern to her voice.

"That's really weird." Jake pushed the door, which swung inward on silent hinges. "A lot of people leave their doors unlocked, but never open."

"Hello?" Kristina called out. "Mr. McKinley, are you home?"

"Look, Miss Sumner, let me go first," he proposed, moving past her. "All right."

Jake was uneasy about a ranch house left adrift to the wind. He felt protective over Kristina, wanting to shield her in case something terrible had happened to the old man.

"I hope Mr. McKinley is okay," Kristina went on. "It seems like I only just talked to him on the phone."

Jake walked slowly through the ranch house, to the kitchen entry, where he froze, Kristina bumping into his back.

"Mr. Weatherby, what's the problem?" she asked, pushing against him gently.

"Move in!" a voice commanded, but it wasn't Jake's voice.

Jake turned and shoved her shoulder hard with one hand. "Run, get out of here," he hissed.

"What?" She seemed puzzled.

"I said, move into the room, you and the girl, *right now!*" the gruff voice insisted.

"Go!" Jake growled, and then the air split with the roar of a gunshot, tearing a bullet through the kitchen archway. They could see it blast the wall across the hallway.

"It's a forty-four, I told you to *get in here!*" the voice bellowed.

Jake moved inside, still trying to shove Kristina backward, but the gun was fired again, this time at Jake's feet. The cavern left in the linoleum smoked a thin wisp.

"Fucking get *in* here!" the shooter roared. "I've got FMJ ammo. You know what that is, motherfucker? That's steel-jacketed shit, and what it'll do to you sure ain't pretty. Might even take out the girl after it puts a hole through you."

"Oh no, Kristina." Jake licked his lips, his face pale. She moved into the kitchen to stand beside Jake. There, in a chair, and tied with a telephone cord, was Jack McKinley. His face was bloodied and bruised from having been beaten, but he was still alive and aware.

"Mr. McKinley!"

Kristina reached out to him with her hands. She obviously wanted to go to the old man, but Jack's great-grandson, Terrence Hobart, waved a husky revolver around the room, and was acting like he wanted to use it on somebody.

"Folks," Terrence addressed jovially, "now that you're here, you can join us in the process of locating my great-grandfather's last will and testament."

Terrence made it sound like a party, but there was shakiness to his voice that frightened Jake—not for his safety, but for Kristina's very existence. The man's copper eyes were roving around as though he'd shorted a circuit inside of his head.

"Is that what this is all about?" she asked Terrence defiantly. "You want Mr. McKinley's will?"

"Wow! Give her a prize, she's a fucking genius!" He pointed the gun at Kristina meaningfully.

"I told you, Terry," Jack spoke up, through the haze of pain and effects of the beating. "I ain't got the will here at the ranch."

Terrence shoved the gun butt against the old man's temple.

"And I told *you*, Gramps, I'm going to kill you, if you don't fucking tell me where it fucking *is!*"

He pulled the gun away, and grabbed Kristina by the shoulder, wrapping one arm around her neck in a loose L-choke, and pressed the gun to her ear. The posture was shades of Tucker Parker, and Jake could see the expression on Kristina's face he'd witnessed at the jail, like a thin wire of piercing rage slowly tightening around her heart.

"Now, you two work it out," said Terrence. "I'll be out back with this little girl, and when you're ready to tell me where it is, you can just bring it to me."

He forced Kristina through the back door at gunpoint, and then they were gone.

She hadn't made a sound.

Jake worked fast locating a steak knife, and cutting Jack loose from the cord.

"Are you okay, sir?"

"As okay as I'll be, given I'm pushing a-hundred." Jack was unsteady, so Jake made him remain seated.

"A phone," said Jake, "have you got a telephone?"

"I did. Terrence made me call Miss Sumner to get her out here, and then he cut the line at the box."

"I have a cell phone," Jake said doubtfully. He pulled it from his pocket and powered on, but there was no available signal.

"That's why I keep my land line," said Jack. "Signal's sketchy around here."

"The will, sir, do you have it?"

"I told the truth, Son. I don't keep it here. My lawyer has it. That boy can't be trusted."

"Give me some paper, Mr. McKinley. I'll make it look like it's official. And a typewriter, if you have one."

"Sure, I got both'n the study, Son, the typewriter's on the side, and I got all kinda paper in the desk, white paper, colored paper, you name it, graph paper…"

But Jake was already off like a shot, heading for the study, and hopefully, Kristina's redemption.

* * * *

Terrence pulled Kristina toward the dam at the top of the meadow, where a creek spilled through, the same creek that served the sleeping cottonwoods. She evoked their pungent scent, even as she stared at Terrence from the giant rock where he'd shoved her down.

He now hovered over her with the gun, smoking a cigarette.

The water, what remained in the winter-tired creek, fell like silver into the black depths. Small fish darted in the shallows, and far below, was the suggestion of rocks long drowned in darkness.

"You banging that fellow?" Terrence asked bluntly, the cigarette dangling from his lips as he clumsily extracted the spent pair of shells, and reloaded the empty chambers.

"I am not doing anything with Mr. Weatherby," she said calmly. "He is my superior at the newspaper."

He shut the action with a click and a spin. "I saw the way he looked at you. Come on, you're fucking him, aren't you." He waved the tip of the gun to compel her to talk.

"I'm a virgin, Mr. Hobart. I'm a high school student. And Mr. Weatherby has good ethics."

This statement was an intellectual stab at Terrence, but then, a man who'd stepped way over the line was less than receptive to the subtleties of the English language.

There seemed to be a malicious twist to his features. "Virgin, eh?" This evidently excited him. "Wonder what I could do to work that outta your system."

She felt a familiar stab of rage, and then, the anger drained away, and left her with a sense of peace. She had already decided that she was going to die here beside the shaded pool where the small fish coursed their fleeting lives. Maybe he'd shoot her in the head, and she'd fall into the singing water, her bones never found.

At least I told him. I said that I love him.

Telling the truth about her feelings was all that mattered.

* * * *

Jake emerged from the back of the house. First, he guaranteed the door slammed audibly, and then made a great show of heavy tread as he advanced toward the dam where Terrence stood, flashing the gun. Walking with both arms in the air, Jake held a packet of papers in one hand.

Terrence flicked the burning cigarette into the water. Jake could clearly read Kristina's face, and Terrence's act of sullying the water seemed to annoy her.

Jake knew after these many months of their association that she wasn't the type to panic. He prayed she could hold onto a feeling of calm, because it would offer a mindset to better focus on a solution to their current situation.

Terrence nodded his chin at Jake. "Whatcha got there?"

"I don't know, something your grandfather gave to me."

"Huh! Funny, I beat the fucking crap outta him, and he doesn't budge. Now all I have to do is take a virgin to water, and he's ready to hand over everything."

Jake's eyes flickered to Kristina, and then back to Terrence.

"Well?" Terrence challenged. "Ain't you gonna give me the papers?"

"Let her go, Terrence, and *then* I'll give you the papers."

"Oh-ho!" Terrence laughed loudly. "What do you think I am, a fucking dumb-ass?" He poked the air with the gun to accent every syllable.

During their exchange, Jake could see Kristina was working slowly with her hand to pick up a rock from the edge of the boulders where she sat. The pocked lava stone, etched by lichen, was almost too heavy to lift, but he noted her determination. Jake shored up the conversation, killing time to allow Kristina's strategic advantage.

"No, actually Terrence, I think you've put up with a lot from old Jack McKinley. I mean, room and board, a promising hog farm. What else is there?"

"Are you fucking joking me, man?"

Terrence lit another cigarette, the revolver jammed into his fist while he worked the lighter. He snapped the lighter shut, and slid it into his pocket, the burning cigarette stuck between his lips.

"Well, where's the love, man?" Terrence asked. "Hand it over!"

He wiggled his outstretched fingers, while the other hand trained the gun on Jake. The papers flapped in Jake's fingers, as both men reached for the prize.

Kristina, forgotten in the moment, launched herself onto Terrence's shoulders, and proceeded to viciously pound his skull with the rock.

Terrence screamed, and proceeded to shoot wildly of his sparing cache of six cartridges while Kristina removed hair and flesh with each blow. Bullets pinged off the rocks. Another caught Jake in passing, the shock of it pushing him backward.

In slow motion, he felt the rush of the wind, and the startlingly cold embrace of the water as he fell into its gullet. Looking upward toward the sky, through clear green and trailing bubbles, he could see the outline of Kristina as she furiously made the rock one with Terrence's head.

* * * *

On a daily basis, and with unbearable difficulty, she found herself staring at the empty space that had once housed Jake Weatherby's desk.

The piece of furniture had occupied the specific area for so long, that slightly darker carpet could be seen, the rectangular shape of the desk's base, inscribed by an impression caused by its weight into the pile.

All along she had assumed the walnut piece was the property of the *Great Basin Register*, but, in light of Mr. Weatherby's egress, the desk had been hauled away.

In early June, the light outside the clouded glass windows was painfully bright. Kristina Sumner spent most of her time in this retreat with the grinding swamp cooler. As the school year waned, she clutched at memories of their time together, which strangely kept her mind away from the most problematic of issues.

After the violence down at the McKinley Ranch, Kristina had once again been placed with a psychiatrist. On this round, it was a doctor recommended by the Lassen County Sheriff's department, claiming its obvious jurisdiction over the incident in Milford.

The psychiatrist was female, based in Reno, and contracted by the Sheriff's department on a case-by-case basis for deputies and their families—in the most profound of situations, on behalf of crime victims.

Despite her history, Kristina Sumner was a victim, twice over.

The sessions lasted eight weeks. Kristina embraced psychotherapy with a sense of honesty, and willingness to heal, unlike the previous period following her killing of Tucker Parker.

She stubbornly drove herself on the one hundred eighty-mile round trips. At that first session, Kristina sat down with Dr. Maria Edruggio, and dictated her own terms.

"I'm going to tell you my story, but you'll do nothing about it, except listen. I expect nothing less, but I also expect complete privacy. The moment I sense that doctor/patient confidentiality has been compromised is the moment I walk away."

"You don't trust anyone, then, do you Kristina."

"I trust a specific handful of people, and least of all you."

"Why?"

"I don't know you. We haven't established a relationship."

"And yet, you're willing to share."

"Share, yes, but not to incriminate."

"Are you afraid of losing control?"

"I can't be afraid of losing what I've never had to begin with."

"All right, Kristina. All right."

Released from strictures, Kristina began to tell her story over the eight-week period. Her sixteen years of life were compressed into eight hours for the sake of practicality. When she was finished with her words and with her thoughts, she would never visit Dr. Edruggio again.

But at least she could move forward in a way she had been unable to before.

* * * *

The sequel to her life came at night, during sleep, in the form of dreams. Rather than upsetting her newfound balance, these dreams offered comfort to her loss. Crystal clear and faithful to the truth, she welcomed the harbinger of joy that played the reels in accurate repetition:

The rock, clutched by her aching fingers, dug a corresponding slot into Terrence Hobart's head. Riding his shoulders, deafened by the man's screams, and the reports of gunfire, she was determined to break open Terrence's skull like cantaloupe.

Flying bullets marred the boulders in the dam. One errant slug seemed to push Jake backward, into the water. She wanted to lunge, and reach out her hands, as the water swallowed him whole.

Seconds later, Terrence fell unconscious onto the earthen pathway along the top of the dam. The gun skittered from his grip, and bounced into the pool, its load already spent. Kristina gave no thought as to whether Terrence lived or died, she simply ran for the water, and dove into the deep green shadows, while the gun wavered into the darkness.

The cold compressed her chest, as she searched through the gloom to find him. There, resting on the bottom was Jake Weatherby, a trickle of blood snaking toward the current, twining like smoke. His eyes were opened. This she noted as she closed in, kicking hard, lungs ready to burst, the cruelty of death leaving unseeing eyes open. His fingers were outstretched, as though he had been taken completely by surprise. Her own hands reached out, and then, just as she was about to lace fingers through his—

He blinked.

In rapid succession, he blinked several times more. Bubbles emerged from his parted lips.

With a mighty surge, she wrapped her arms around his torso, and pushed off the bottom to propel them both to the surface, where they broke water with a simultaneous gasp. He was choking and coughing, but at least he was alive. She reflexively sobbed as they made their way to shallow water, where they climbed onto a flat boulder, warmed by the thin sunlight.

He was bleeding dashes and drops. A black hole impressed his shirt, and blood oozed from tattered edges. She pushed with one hand, and the blood came through her fingers. But although it didn't clot, neither did it spill unchecked.

Yanking up the tails of his dress shirt, she realized he'd received a superficial flesh wound, a tear through skin and the thin layer of tissue above the muscle along his right flank. He was in no danger of dying.

She sobbed at the knowledge that Mr. Weatherby was going to live.

* * * *

There was order to the madness in the aftermath of Terrence Hobart's terrorist act.

The old rancher, Jack McKinley, limped out of the house, telephone cord in hand. He proceeded to subdue Terrence, leaving his great-grandson moaning in a daze, and bound to a post embedded in the concrete of the dam.

In light of McKinley's beaten face and advanced age, he was nevertheless salvaged by good health and a strong dose of rage. In Paul Sumner's truck, he drove Jake and Kristina the thirty-odd miles from Milford, directly to the Lassen-Flagg hospital, where the Sheriff's department was summoned.

She sat behind a curtain in an examination room, impeded from viewing Jake by a mere stretch of gaily-patterned cloth. Her parents had joined her by then. Kate held her daughter's hand, while Paul, after speaking briefly and quietly to Mr. Weatherby beyond the curtain, returned to sit on Kristina's other side.

Beyond the curtain wall, they listened to the physician tend Jake's wound. A deputy sat beside Jake's bed, and took a statement, while the stitching commenced. She could hear Mr. Weatherby's speech, and the virtue of his words. When he was through, the story would then belong to Kristina, a symbolic of passing of personal merit.

As she sat in silence, she wondered about his pain, the digging of the needle, the edges of his wound once touched by her fingers, and his blood on her flesh. Before the suturing was complete, the deputy had moved Kristina and her parents to another room, and beyond the range of Jake's ears.

* * * *

Kristina didn't see Jake again for several weeks, kept from straying far from school or home through the request of her parents. She rode the bus to and from school, her face toward the window, her cryptic reflection eyeing her in the glass.

There was a divide between her conscious self, and the internal resignation attributable to this disconnect. Her work at the *Register* had been put on hold—no articles, and no distractions from this life, her momentum temporarily suspended.

At the close of the first week, she began to visit Dr. Edruggio. But she longed to speak with Mr. Weatherby, if only to know his thoughts, and the utterings of a steadfast heart.

* * * *

Terrence Hobart survived with a jittery weakness on the left side of his body, due to being bashed with the stone, and the force behind Kristina Sumner's indignation.

Kristina knew this, because a county prosecutor had contacted her parents to keep them apprised of the case.

After a lengthy recovery in the jail ward at Renown Medical Center in Reno, Hobart had been transferred to the Lassen County Jail to await charges of kidnapping, false imprisonment, attempted murder, and aggravated assault.

Visited by his defense attorney, an appointed counsel from the Public Defender's office, the first thing Hobart spoke of wistfully, was the girl and her rock.

"I wish she'd 've put me outta my fucking misery."

* * * *

Jake Weatherby visited the Spotted Horse Ranch four weeks later, driving out to talk with her parents in private.

Kristina, up in her second floor room, lay on her bed and faced the ceiling, remembering his blood. She raised her hand to stare at her fingers where she had touched the hole in his flesh. Her skin was now so clean, unmarred, but the memory of his blood on her flesh had carried her.

A knock on her door, and Kristina sat up.

"Come in."

Her father entered. "Kristina, Mr. Weatherby asked if he could speak with you alone."

"And?" She rolled onto her feet, standing.

"Mom and I agreed. He's waiting for you in the kitchen."

She couldn't get down the stairs fast enough.

He was standing near the window seat, hands in his pockets. She searched for a change, a declination from his former assertions of love, and took comfort in the fact that he looked the same as before.

"Hi, Mr. Weatherby," she greeted, wanting to call him Jake."

"Hello, Miss Sumner."

"It's really good to see you." Her body agreed, a sweet ringing energy zipping from head to toe. "Did they fix you?"

"Believe me, they tried."

She understood the meaning beneath his words. "No, I meant about your bullet wound."

"Yes, a fine job, as a matter of fact."

158

"May I see it?"

He lifted the edge of his shirt, revealing a quarter-sized portion of skin, neatly incised by a red scar. The revelation was brief, and then he hid it away.

"That's good," she approved. "I'm glad it healed."

"I keep reminding myself that it was a large caliber bullet, and the outcome could've been far worse."

"Right, I remember the holes in the wall and floor. Besides that…well, how have you been?"

"I've been…" He inhaled. "Missing you, wondering about you, Miss Sumner. I'm happy to see that at least you look intact."

"I hope the cops weren't too hard on you."

"Eh, no more than expected."

"What was 'expected?'"

"They wanted to know whether or not I've been having a physical relationship with you."

Butterflies fluttered around her heart. To hide the sudden sweet rush through her body, she shifted her feet.

"My parents wanted to know too?" she asked.

He smiled. "No, your parents know you better. They never even asked."

"What did you say to the cops? Weren't you angry they accused you of wrongdoing?"

"Why would that make me angry? It's entirely natural that they would ask me that. It's entirely natural that I'd want to have a physical relationship with you."

"Oh."

"Don't get me wrong, I'll admit, I have been tempted. But I do know what's right, and I never had any misguided intentions with you."

"You've always been a good friend to me, Mr. Weatherby."

"Anyway, I told them basically to fuck off."

"You didn't!"

"You're not that sort of a girl, and it isn't that sort of a relationship."

"You're implying—"

"A pureness of heart, yes, I am."

She waited, knowing there would be more. Hot tears began to rise.

"And I came here to tell you, to tell your folks too, that I've decided to take a field reporting job with the Fox affiliate in the Bay Area." He grinned ruefully. "But no worry about my being in cahoots with conservative media in Liberal Country, Miss Sumner, because I think you've cured me of my stuffiness."

She was stunned. She might have been hit with a club and taken no notice, compared to the brunt of his words.

"You're going away," she said softly.

"Yes, but I'm not leaving you," he assured, one hand over his heart.

"Is it a different thing?"

"Miss Sumner, I characterize it like this: I am determined to sit on my hands. I believe in my morality, that I could probably not touch you, though God knows, I *want* to. But you see, I made a promise, and I intend to keep it. If I keep hanging around here—keep hanging out with you, I'm bound to do something really stupid, and stupid won't open any doors to the future."

"I understand."

"I leased a place in Berkeley, a cottage. I couldn't get away from an urban version of small town."

"Will you put a flag out front?"

"Already bought it."

"Will...will you think about me?"

"I'll never stop." He gazed at her, their eyes locked. "And maybe if you want to, you can apply to Cal or UCSF, I don't know. You can move out to the Bay Area, if you want to, when you're eighteen and going to college."

"Yes."

"On the same token, don't make your decisions because of me, you go where you want to go, and do what you want to do, for yourself, Miss Sumner. Right now, you should be a teenager. You should date boys your age. And if you decide in seventeen months that you still want me, I'll tell you where you can find me."

"I have a better idea," she offered. "On my eighteenth birthday, you can come to me, come here, because I'll be waiting."

"Kristina." His voice broke. He so rarely called her by her given name, consistently "Miss Sumner." She could count only twice when he'd called her by her first name—once at Jack McKinley's, and the second time, right now, each time filled with wonderment and longing.

"May I say goodbye to you?" she asked.

He wiped tears from his eyes. "We've always been honest with each other. I hope you know that you can say anything you want to say."

"I actually meant, might I hug you goodbye?"

She was so hopeful. The only time she had ever touched him was when she wrapped her arms around him, and they kicked to the surface; and when he bled beneath her loving fingertips.

"No, Miss Sumner, ah...I would have to say that's a really bad idea."

"Why?"

"Damn, your eternal querying. You were so maddening in the beginning, but I admit, right now it adds to your charm."

"You didn't tell me why I'm not allowed to hug you."

"Because, I won't be able to continue sitting on my hands."

"It's a wise choice, then. As you said, wanting to be physical is natural." She paused. "For me, too."

They seemed deliberate in keeping a looming space between them.

"I remember, how you told me the Washoe word for death," he reminded.

"*Deyuliyi?*"

"Yes, *deyuliyi*. What's their word for life?"

She hesitated, pondering. She had learned enough Washoe to converse particularly well with the people she knew at Bow River, even the Elders, who understood the nuances of an ancient language.

"I don't know if there's an exact word for life. Maybe it's because they simply lived. They formed descriptive for everything that abounded in their lives, even the scores of definitions for kinship. But I don't remember a specific word that I can attribute to life, unless it's water. They have a deep connectivity to water in life and lore. And then, the Elders speak often of *Tahoe*, the origin."

"Thank you, just the same." He turned to leave, but then faced her again. "Not that I intend to influence you, but I want to tell you, before I don't see you for a while, how very much I love you, and how very much you mean to me." He took a deep breath. "You're special, Miss Sumner." He seemed to want to say more, but was hindered by tears, and the restrictions of her age.

I love you too, she had wanted to say. She had yearned to let it out, because she felt it, deeply. But she was afraid of making him a slave to his hands, rather than a master of his fate.

So, she only nodded, and watched him walk out the door. Moments later, he was driving away in his Corolla, raising a line of dust on the access road.

* * * *

Following his brazen confession, Jake left Susanville for good, and Kristina resumed her work at the *Register*. Nearly three months had passed, and she was not happy, but accepting of what she couldn't change.

161

Chapter Nine
T'kill Ya

From his window in the shabby room of the Lassen Peak Inn, Charles Raines could just make out the lighted digital signboard of the Plumas Savings. The haloed yellow lights registered a temperature of eighteen degrees Fahrenheit, and falling. Eye-searing sleet evolved into thickly falling snow, evidence the signboard served no useful purpose. Eventually the board, like the street below, was obliterated by the storm.

Stumbling from the window, Charles sat dejectedly on the sagging hospitality mattress, a bottle of cheap tequila in one hand, and outmoded service revolver in the other.

On the nightstand lay divorce papers, recently served. In his opinion, the documents were an abomination, hard evidence his estranged wife was no longer willing to tolerate him. Their drift had been going on for years, until suddenly it seemed Raines could view their relationship from a distance, as frighteningly devastating as the snow that now slammed against the hotel window.

His wife, Suzie, was determined to ingest everything defined as community property in her ravenous maw. Her attorney listed every detail—the custody of the youngest child, a minor; the family Dodge; the Janesville property—even the heeler, Finn, had been included in the catalog of Suzie's mercenary complaint. Raines wasn't completely heartless. The dog's heart belonged to their son, Chucky.

The fight hadn't totally slipped through his fingers. He intended to exact retribution by killing himself.

A clause in the life insurance policy made no bones about a man owning his life. Once a policy was underwritten, a man signed over the value and manner of death to a corporation. The final gasp of Raines's melancholic existence would arrive in the gleeful moment a bullet tore a gaping loophole in the policy.

Along with his income as a state trooper, Suzie had dared to include the insurance policy in her list of settlement demands. As though her venal desires would supersede the expressed written guidelines of the Langsford Insurance Corporation.

He stared at the blank window through the filter of odd despair, prepared to take control by having the final word.

The remarkable fact was that he wanted to live.

He wanted to see his children, fish up at Eagle Lake, chase down speeders, and have raunchy sex with his buxom mistress. This session in the Lassen Peak Inn was meant to balance his wants with this single need, the dire appetite to destroy Suzie.

He stirred from his funk, and set the revolver and tequila onto the floor. Twisting from his position, he gingerly shoved aside the legal documents, and grasped a notebook lying beneath. He adjusted the bedside lamp, so he could read the scribble of his empirical reasoning.

Cheating on Suzie hadn't become a consideration until Raines realized he'd been spanking the monkey more than half the duration of their marriage. Suzie owned a litany of excuses, and a revolving door habit of inserting them into a pistol-voiced drawl guaranteed to make any man's dick limp. Her frigidity gave permission for Raines to snuggle with another woman.

* * * *

Charles's mistress was Sonia Anderson. She was employed by Lassen County as Highway Vermin Eliminator, the title a smokescreen to the true meaning of scraping animal carcasses off the road.

Sonia made the grade for this career by earning a master's degree in Physics from UC Berkeley, qualifying a modest thirty-five thousand dollar salary.

To honor of the title, Sonia shuttled around in a battered and fluid-stained 1986 Chevrolet Scottsdale owned by the county, outfitted with tarps, pitchforks, and shovels with various blades. She carried a sidearm to dispatch the occasional deer crippled by a speeding car or errant big-rig, jut a poor creature huddled in a roadside ditch bleating in pain, until Sonia shot its brains out.

Officer Raines first spotted Sonia on Interstate 395, while she was clearing a flattened jackrabbit from the pavement.

Raines parked the cruiser on the shoulder, and strolled up to the woman. Bent over a bloody mess swirling with flies, she was chipping off the sunbaked carcass from pavement a blade-length at a time.

There was a sultry quality about her, announced by tight jeans configured to her amazing curves. Her blond hair, creamy to the roots, maintained respectability in a thick, sinuous braid.

"Excuse me, ma'am," Officer Raines interceded, his dick instantly intrigued by her sensuality. "Need any help?"

She eyed him curiously from beneath a billed cap.

"Not one bit," she assured. She tossed a shovelful into a black plastic garbage bag containing nasty, mixed-media road kill. "Just doing my job."

He leaned over the bag, pulling at the lip to steal a glance at her trophies, and caught the edge of the shovel across the knuckles for his effort.

"Oh." She snorted. "Sorry." The hat shaded her face, but he swore her voice dripped with insincerity.

"Ouch." There was a gash across his knuckle, spotting the asphalt with blood.

"You silly, stupid man." She shoved a paper towel at him, fished from a pocket of her County-issue vest. "Even I, a woman, know enough to keep out of the way of a shovel."

"Yes, ma'am."

As he applied pressure to the wound, she chatted about the weather, his manly hands, and the terrible expense of gaining a master's degree simply to scrape crow-bait off the road.

He complimented her prowess with the shovel. "You do pretty well."

"Hey." She loaded the plastic bag and shovel back into the Scottsdale. "Come over here, and let me treat that thing."

She poured hydrogen peroxide into the cleft marked by the shovel, while he silently writhed.

"You're quite a man," she remarked about his failure to scream.

"Thanks."

While she layered on ointment, and topped the gash with a dressing, they made their introductions. He was conscious her hand was absent a wedding ring, and she was fully aware of his.

"I don't suppose you'd like to go eat somewhere," she posed.

"I suppose I would."

He followed her to a roadhouse, Pablo's Bar & Grill, where they ordered burgers. There, in the musty shadows, surrounded by the sounds of clinking beer bottles, and a bellyaching television, he ate the best meal of his life. They sat across from one another in a discreet booth while Sonia, having toed off her boot, brazenly rested a foot in his crotch.

He knew where this foreplay was heading, when after the meal Sonia scooted her foot into the clunky boot, and said quite casually, "I suppose this means you want to get laid."

He raised his brows in shock. They stuck in that position, all the way into Doyle, where Sonia rented a motel room in some sleepy, forgotten establishment, and lay naked on the double bed. Not until he'd been divested of his uniform, and pleasured the woman four times, did he realize just what he'd done.

"I like you, Charlie," she called him.

To Suzie, it had always been 'Cha'lz', pretentiously addressed.

"I like you too, Sonia."

He was dead gone on this woman, who seemed unabashedly receptive to his advances. He could have done her until the cows came home—and then some—while every night at home, he was more familiar with his right hand than his wife's vagina.

"I'm letting you know. I'm not interested in marriage," she told him, before they parted ways.

Good, he thought. *What a gift. Thank you, God.*

"But I have certain needs, and demand their fulfillment if you want to keep up our fucking arrangement. Consider yourself forewarned, Charlie."

* * * *

The affair had lasted two years, and not a furtive relationship. Just about everyone in the County knew about Charles and Sonia. Even Suzie was aware of his active indiscretion, though most of the time, she chose to ignore it.

She had only called him on it once, and that was at Christmas, six months into the liaison, when she'd busted him slipping out the door to drive over to Sonia's Westwood home for an illicit rendezvous.

"Just where do you think you're going?" she asked, standing in front of his Jeep, as though her crossed arms would bar his exit.

"Where do you think I'm going?" he countered.

"Better not be!" Her response implied proprietary interest in his physical activities.

"If I was getting it at home, I wouldn't have to go anywhere else," he pointed out, and he started the engine.

For a moment, he swore she wasn't going to budge, but she had processed his statement, apparently weighing the merits of either condoning his deceit, or fucking him.

The former won out, and she stepped aside. As he watched her diminish in the rearview mirror, her silhouette seemed to expand, with sharp, cutting angles, like the scales of a beast, or a frieze from religious demonology. The horns, a forked tongue, and red eyes—they all incorporated into Suzie's true appearance.

Though realized freedom to come and go as he chose was linked to a clock running on borrowed time, his soul was cheap recompense for sex.

* * * *

Charles and Suzie Raines had three children, conceived in the first six years of their marriage on a schedule that followed a breeding cycle of fifteen-month intervals.

Paranoia nagged Charles ever more critically than his own wife, though he was too stupid to follow intuition. By the tally, and Suzie's behavior, Charles reckoned his services were required in the marital bed during the peak of fertility. After she'd been impregnated, she exhibited no interest in sexual intercourse.

For a few years, he managed his carnal desires. He tried turning her over in the middle of the night while she was sleeping to get some wary ass—that worked a few times, but then Suzie started to wear pajamas. In the end, he rested upon the laurels of his right hand.

His career headed off his needs for a time. But it wasn't until the episode at the Shady Acres Motel in Doyle, that Charles suddenly realized what he'd been missing all along, adulation—not just the stroking of his cock, but of his vanity. He needed to be wanted in a sexual sense.

The eldest child, a son, was named Myron Henry Raines, after Suzie's beloved father, Myron Henry Jones, who hailed from Davenport, Iowa. Suzie's husband had taken a less than secondary importance in the marriage, reflected in the given name of a blameless child.

Fortunately, Myron Jones was long dead and interred permanently in Davenport, so there would be no retributive ass whipping in store for an adulterous son-in-law.

Myron Raines manifested the tongue of a slick talker. He could rid a schoolmate of loose change or lunchtime snack through the power of cajolery, rather than a feat of bullying. A slight child, and then a skinny man, he inherited his mother's fine features, and his father's detachment, so Myron could pick and choose just where to invest his emotions.

The middle child, a girl, was a dead-ringer for Charles—black hair and electric-blue eyes—which someday would bring the men crawling in on bloodied knees. Christened Portia Devigne, she was destined to grow into her Nordic genes and heft her Shakespearean legacy like a sword. Her figure grew into well-placed sinew and mighty breasts. Portia was ruthless behind the stone-cold eyes, though she reserved a special tenderness for her father.

When their third child was conceived, Charles lost most of his interest in mating with Suzie. He was immune to his wife's immaculate and healthful body, repulsed by her utilitarian sexuality that, despite Suzie's best efforts, aggravated Charles's impotence. In the end, she'd been forced to get him drunk to set the wheels in motion.

Within nine months, their third child—their last—was born.

In the hospital, while Suzie slept off the ordeal of childbirth, Charles submitted the birth record without her consent. When she awoke, and she'd realized too late she'd been duped, as Suzie held in her arms their second son, Charles Manson Raines.

Charles threw down the gauntlet. "Have him live up to that reputation."

"I'll never forgive you," she snarled at him, but his revenge had been accomplished with a clean conscience.

One of the specifications on Suzie's laundry list of dissolution demands was for Charles to restore the semblance of a reasonable name to their third child. After he shot himself in the mouth, and invalidated the life insurance policy, he wouldn't care either way, though he knew his dick would sorely miss Sonia.

* * * *

Charles Manson Raines, often referred to as 'Chucky M.' by his peers, had visited his father twice at the Lassen Peak Inn. He was sixteen, an athletic drummer, and deeply involved with a metal band out of Reno that had signed with an indie record label and was ready to tour the western United States.

Before Charles's bloodshot gaze, Chucky M. had proposed in the voice of a lawyer—a contrast to the homegrown body piercings and bootleg tattoos—that his personal future had been settled, and he was by no means agreeable to changing his name from the dubious moniker of Charles Manson.

"What about this band tour?" Charles asked, scratching his head. He wasn't so stupid that he couldn't grasp the recreational drug use that accompanied these excursions.

"It's cool, Dad. Don't worry. I just need the signature of one parent to go. And Mom won't do it."

Chucky M. knew his father had been his band's frenetic concerts. That look in Charles's eyes meant he was pondering whether Suzie's stress level would elevate a few more ticks if Chucky M were allowed on tour.

"Quick, give me the paper," said Charles, reaching with restless, wiggling fingers. "I'll sign this, and then I'll finish going through those other papers your mom sent me."

Chucky M., amused at how simple it was to manipulate his father, glanced at the wedge of the dissolution documents.

"A real throat-choker, eh, Dad?"

Charles shook his head grimly, and approved the tour slip with a flourish.

"So, what's this Mom says about you having a girlfriend?" Chucky M. asked, folding the paper into his wallet for safekeeping.

"It's true. I've been seeing someone."

"You know, Dad, you're a terrible husband," said Chucky M. judgmentally, and then he punched his father good-naturedly in the upper arm. "But one hell of a man."

This last meeting with his youngest son had taken place two days prior, which was, as Charles counted on his pocket calendar, a mere twenty-six days since his wife had thrown him out of the house.

* * * *

Charles had arrived home to discover his personal possessions trashed across the frost-killed patch of front lawn. His stomach sour with dread, he made a show of stomping his way into the house, where Suzie greeted him with her typical stance of folded arms and padlocked vagina.

She thrust a finger upward toward his eyes. "I know all about you."

He had just come off a day of hazards, and Suzie's weapon of choice, her anger, goaded him.

"You don't know shit," he hissed.

"You've got some whore you've been seeing," she claimed, substantiated by a pile of photographs snapped at Pablo's and The White Dog and the County Fair, among the many locations specific to his trysts with Sonia.

"Where'd you get these?" he asked, intrigued, going through them slowly, and remembering every luscious deed.

Suzie jabbed at a photograph of Charles and Sonia kissing passionately beneath the Heritage Oak in front of the Janesville Post Office.

"In public," she growled.

"Well, you wouldn't do that with me," he pointed out, "not even in our marital bed. And look, isn't she Goddamn hot?"

Suzie struck the photos from his grip with the flat of her hand.

"Get out, Cha'lz!" she screamed.

With a pause to gather his belongings from the lawn, he hightailed it for Susanville, but not before he'd made a point to scoop up the photographs, and shove them onto the front seat of the Jeep.

* * * *

Sonia liked Charles's room at the Lassen Peak Inn. She enjoyed the dip of the ancient mattress, and the window seat, where she could set herself naked on his willing lap while his head pounded the casement.

"You know, it isn't so bad, Charlie," she insisted. "I mean your kids are almost grown up, right?"

"One is, for sure." He referenced Myron, who, at age twenty, had landed a cushy job as a publicist in Las Vegas—without a college degree and by virtue of his persuasive demeanor—entertaining corporate bigwigs and the occasional touring rock star.

"No, two," he amended, remembering Portia, age eighteen, and down at UCLA since late August, courtesy of a women's softball scholarship.

168

"I'm trying to give you some perspective, that's all, Charlie. And your little one, Chucky is it?"

"Chucky *M.*," he corrected.

"He's got the ball rolling with Slasher Nails, so you needn't feel guilty about abandoning them."

"Who says I'm abandoning them?"

Sonia sat up nude in the bed. If he compared their time together stark or clothed, he would have to gauge he saw her jaybird-naked more often than dressed up.

She grasped the latest *Great Basin Register* from the niche in the bottom of the nightstand, where she'd tucked it after clearing it off his bathroom floor.

"Here it is. Apparently, Velma Harris interviewed your wife. Some drivel about cops not being able to keep their pants on."

Sure enough, a half-page was dedicated to unfaithful husbands. This Suzie R. of Janesville—*what effort had been made to hide her identity?* Charles wondered—stated that "cops are the worst type of men, too pushy due to their elevated testosterone, which not only propels them after crooks, but flimsy skirts, too."

VH: Is your husband a cop?

Suzie R: Of course, he has a woman on the side, and is quite willing to abandon his children.

"Hogwash!" Charles leaped out of the covers and paced the cold, worn carpet.

"Well, I know *I'm* not a side woman, Charlie." Sonia laughed. "I think ol' Suzie got it backward." She pulled off the sheets, revealing the entirety of her nude body. He was deeply distracted by her perky breasts. "Come on, Charlie, some medicine, huh?"

No more coaxing required, he stumbled across the room, and landed between her thighs.

* * * *

The Red Rock Tavern was located inside the first floor of the Lassen Peak Inn. During last year's renovation work, the tavern had been updated, small defects covered in fresh paint. Gentrification should have been extended to improve upon sagging mattresses and shabby carpeting.

Charles had expected high-class, pleased to discover a haven of comfortable furniture, quaint framed placards from post-Prohibition-era breweries, and the subtle odor of grilled meat. The spacious bar, beveled glass topped tables, and a parquet dance floor, where on Saturday evenings, a little jazz trio set up shop on the dance floor's edge, playing standards in the local tradition of Bluegrass twang.

Charles was attracted to the bar, which gathered the moths of middle-aged law-enforcement to its hickory-wood flame. Snow or shine, you could find California Highway Patrol or Sheriff's department or local police in their civvies, dithering away free time, before reluctantly returning to home and hearth.

Charles had gained some notoriety among his brethren.

"You're a lucky guy, Charles," was the common refrain. "You've got a warm room, and a nice piece waiting for you upstairs, just an elevator ride away."

The piece they implied had nothing to do with his gun.

One evening, Charles conferred with off-duty Susanville police officer Emmitt Dearly over a couple of draft beers. Dearly had recently married, and in the dim light of the bar, his wedding band shone as a reminder of Charles's matrimonial failure.

"How's married life?" Charles asked. His own ring lay on the top of the nightstand up in the hotel room, where it served as blind witness to the unremitting sexual encounters with Sonia.

"I won't complain." Dearly shrugged, a smile on the corner of his mouth.

"Honeymoon stage, right?" Charles grinned.

"Enough about me, what's your deal, Charles?"

"Not much, the kids are mostly grown, and I've been blessed with a litigiously frigid wife."

"Did you know that Sonia Anderson once studied to be a rocket scientist?"

Charles sipped his beer, aware that stupidity had begun to cast a pall across his vision like a cow on the slaughterhouse walk.

"Of course," he agreed, buying time while his head spun. "She has a degree, right?"

"Yeah, but what would a woman with such a background be doing scraping dead animals off the road?"

"She…" Charles searched for the answer, his mind working in froth while considering Sonia's higher intellect. "She likes the scenery."

When Charles parted ways with Emmitt, he returned to his room, and the bed occupied by Sonia, in her customary pose of informal nudity.

His eyes took in the woman quite differently, now that he was aware that her brain capacity exceeded whatever pulsed listlessly inside the cramped limits of his own skull. He suspected the blood rushing to his erection every time he was in her proximity tripled his perceived disability, and impaired much of his cognitive function.

"Charlie, I've been waiting for you." She patted the lumpy mattress beside the pocket of her warmth.

He teetered, caught between the need to initiate conversation, and the upwelling of lust that made speech impossible. But it was late, the beer impeded his good sense, and he displayed an awkward strip dance in his haste to join her.

Later, while she stretched like a languid tiger, he lay stunned by the sex and alcohol, and the strangling bulk of his seemingly insurmountable problems. He finally reached out and ran a hand down the silky curve of her back, and she leaped up, giggling like a bimbo.

"Charlie, you jokester!" She lost her smile at the depth of agony in his eyes. "Charlie." Settling back into the bedding and holding him close in a motherly fashion, she asked, "What's wrong, Charlie? Is this getting to you?"

"You're a genius," he accused.

"What have people been saying about me?" she demanded to know.

"I've heard that you were studying to be a rocket scientist," he blubbered.

"Oh, is that what's bothering you?" She sighed, shaking her head. "Charlie, I may be smart, but I'm just dumb enough to really enjoy you, do you understand?"

He nodded.

"So, what's the problem?"

He motioned to the legal papers still waffling on the nightstand.

"Look, just sign the papers, let it all go. What's that adage—render unto Caesar what is Caesar's. Only, I think in your case it's, give the passionless bitch her due."

Beneath the sum-and-substance of Sonia's words, Charles slept deeply.

* * * *

Up to the pivotal moment Charles was holding the cheap tequila and the thirty-eight. He placed them on the floor in order to gather up the notebook, which tallied the wretched minutiae of his marriage.

How can a man spend his life working toward perfecting his masturbation technique, while his marital intimacy and fidelity have crashed and burned?

The snow was slamming into the window, a virtual whiteout, and the thick walls of the hotel bravely repelled the cold.

The silence was ripped apart by the telephone ringing on the nightstand, pushed to the very edge by the heap of monstrous legal documents. Inhaling painfully, Charles Raines staggered to his feet. He tipped the tequila bottle over with one big toe, while the other foot shoved the gun beneath the bed.

"Hello?"

"Dad!" Chucky M., distraught, his teenaged rasp filled with urgency Charles had never encountered. "Dad, something happened to Mom!"

* * * *

171

Charles would hear the story repeatedly in the following days, regurgitated from the mouths of law enforcement and the press. His eldest children returned home, readying for a closed-casket funeral, once the coroner released the body.

On that night, when the Plumas Savings sign sang out eighteen degrees to the willful storm, Chucky M. had been pushing up the access road in his mother's four-wheel drive Dodge, bleary-eyed on return from Reno, when he noticed a peculiar glow shimmering through the steady, freezing downpour.

Upon approach, the rose-colored flare metamorphosed into a full-throated inferno, busily consuming his home. The cattle dog, Finn, ran circles around the blaze, barking furiously.

Despite the unreliable coverage of his cell phone, he managed a call to Janesville Fire & Rescue, but assistance was hampered by the blizzard, the late hour, and stored railroad cars blocking the main crossing.

While the falling snow hissed upon the leaping flames, facts indicated that Suzie Raines burned to a crisp inside her home on Duvet Lane in Janesville. The heat generated by the fire was so intense, that the antique wrought-iron bedstead melded with her charred remains.

'*Faulty kerosene line in the external furnace closet,*' stated the report of the field fire inspector.

The coroner initially ruled as an accidental death.

Chucky M., inconsolable—yet counting down the days to his band tour—had joined his father in the close quarters of the seedy room at the Lassen Peak Inn.

Up in the snow-blown hills of Janesville, the leavings of the Raines home scorched a rough perimeter of soot from a blackened midden. Long abandoned by forensics, Adam Bailey, the coroner, was allegedly studying what the remains of Suzie Raines, mere chips and ashes.

Sonia, it seemed, had flown the coop the moment Chucky M. demanded Charles's paternal attention. There were rumors, of course, that she had been seen scraping road kill, but neither had she clocked in at the County corporation yard, where the Scottsdale sat idle and cold. As far as Charles was concerned, their feckless physical affair had faded into the past.

Charles would stare down at his hand, with that old scar made by Sonia's shovel, all that he had to cling to, besides erotic memories. If not for Chucky M.'s presence, Charles might have returned to the rhythm of a former lover—his right hand.

* * * *

The telephone call came three days after the fire, very late. Charles had been gazing down listlessly at the icebound streets, while behind him in a hideaway bed Chucky M. snored like distant thunder.

"There seems to be a mistake here," said the coroner, Adam Bailey on the line.

That jitter in Bailey's voice expressed his nervous energy.

"What mistake? What are you talking about?" Charles was nearly too exhausted to care. All he wanted was Sonia. With Suzie gone, Charles had floated halfway to the carrot.

"The dental records," Bailey explained. "They didn't match your wife's." He took a deep breath, one to lean on, like a rock. "I took a chance, Officer Raines. I requested the dental records of Sonia Anderson, and do you know what? They match the burned corpse, Officer Raines. They. Match."

Afterward, staring down at a street empty of traffic, and pooled with the glow of the nearest signal lights, Charles grasped what he could of the macabre facts—the body kilned in the fire belonged to Sonia Anderson.

This meant Suzie Raines was clearly still alive to perform her witchery.

But what Charles Raines would frequently call to mind was the opinion of Sonia, when she held him while he sobbed in the sex-rumpled bed at the Lassen Peak Inn. The phrase repeated in his head in the most disturbing manner: "Give the passionless bitch her due."

Quite plainly Suzie Raines's evil had risen to power.

Chapter Ten
Live From Susanville

Kristina was in her senior year of high school, and no longer with the *Great Basin Register*. She'd taken a job with Lassen County College's radio station. The hick configuration, complete with a low-powered transmitter, expressed a fondness for agricultural phraseology, and country music.

Though her twelfth grade AP English teacher, Arlene Seldon, had urged Kristina to once again apply for the cyclical apprenticeship, the *Great Basin Register* was a distant memory now that she was earning real money.

Before the job at the college had dropped into her lap, she'd struck up an acquaintance with America Parker. They had very little in common, except for a connection to the Spotted Horse Ranch, and the Lassen Women's Quilting Society.

Shortly before Kristina's seventeenth birthday, and after she'd wrapped up her apprenticeship with the *Register*, America came to the ranch with her stepmother, Angeline Morse. Angeline was in the midst of writing another coffee-table memoir of small-town life, and had asked to photograph the quilting group's work in progress. While the women chatted and worked on patterns, Angeline shot photos of pliant hands and brightly colored fabric, and profiles of faces framed by brilliant, sun-filled windows.

America sat on the sidelines with Kristina, and observed.

"Do you ever sew with these ladies?" America asked.

"Rarely. It's an acquired taste, and a skill for patient people, though sometimes I'm asked to give input on a pattern."

"I can't sew either. I'm too cagey," America admitted, "but I like to watch Angeline at work. She's inspired me into a career as a photographer."

"Is that what you want to be? I mean, can you make a living."

"Sure, professionally speaking. I work as often as I can behind the camera."

"Are you going to college?"

"Yeah, at Columbia River College of the Arts, in Portland. This'll be my junior year. What about you?"

Kristina hesitated, wondering how to answer.

* * * *

With Jake Weatherby in mind, she had applied to UC Berkeley, Stanford, and UC San Francisco, but she had also sent an application to Berkshire University in Maryland, a noteworthy private journalism school. Berkshire was her preference—though it seemed traitorous to flee the opposite direction of Mr. Weatherby's present employment.

The loophole in their mutual, ancient promise had been the clause of no contact, and she had neither seen nor heard a peep from Mr. Weatherby since his departure months ago.

This was not to say that she didn't think about him. He was on her mind, either in the forefront or simmering on that figurative back burner all the time. The distractions had been enough to derail her from her junior prom at the end of the last school year, and from casual dating proposals by several of her male classmates, who had suddenly taken a keen interest in Kristina Sumner's confidence.

"Guys, they think you're uptight," Claremont Whitehead had mentioned to Kristina, in a chance conversation as they passed on Main Street, three weeks before her seventeenth birthday.

"I'm glad. That avoids any misunderstanding."

"No, you see, but they like you." He grinned to dispel his shyness in being frank with this girl. "I mean." And here, he shuffled his feet, embarrassed. "I like you, Kris."

He was wearing a pinch-front hat, coming off the rodeo at the Fair, all slick looking in Lee jeans and a button-front with Southwestern flair. The riding boots were scarred from jamming stirrups while flinging on the back of some flank-strapped bronc.

She thought he appeared dashing in a Susanville theme, and then happened to glance at the American flag on the Book Shelf's frontage. She pictured Jake Weatherby, and her throat closed up.

"I like you, Claremont," she said kindly. "Just not in that way."

No form of rejection can ease a young man's feelings, especially good ol' hot-blooded Claremont Whitehead.

"Suit yourself!" he'd snapped angrily. "I could get any girl."

Claremont's immaturity, and fast temper were revealing about his character. She knew his ego had been bruised, and she was relieved for her wise reply.

* * * *

With America Parker, Kristina had waffled, because she'd decided to stay true to herself.

"I'd like to go to Berkshire University. It's in Maryland," she explained to America. "I'm going to major in journalism."

"You're perfect for it. I've read your articles. Say, uh, I have a cousin who works up at KLCC."

"The college radio station?"

"Yeah, and she said they're looking for an idea for a show. Do you have any?" America's eyes were expectant, as though she instinctively knew Kristina would pop out some genius concept.

"Maybe," Kristina allowed, the gears of creativity already racing in her head.

"You should call her. Her name's Soleil Parker." America pulled a wallet from a back pocket—the tomboy definition of a girl without a purse—and found what she sought. She passed Kristina a business card.

Kristina studied the card. "This says she's a realtor."

"Sure, that's her better paying job. Well, you know, if and when property moves, right?" America winked at Kristina. "But she has a part-time job as the KLCC station manager, it's just that they're too cheap to spring for cards."

Kristina decided not to ask if the venture would involve financial compensation, assuming America's part in the transaction ended with the card. A thought occurred to her.

"Maybe your cousin's looking for a college student to fill the position."

"I wouldn't know, but what do you have to lose by asking?"

"Not a thing," Kristina agreed.

After mulling it over for a day, Kristina picked up the ranch telephone and called Soleil Parker.

"Kristina Sumner?" Soleil spoke with a smile in her voice. "Aren't you the girl who wrote those high-caliber articles for the *Register*?"

"I don't know about high-caliber, but I did work with the *Register* until just a few weeks ago." Kristina explained the apprenticeship program, and Soleil listened politely.

"I might hire you, Miss Sumner," said Soleil, already incorporating professionalism into the conversation. "Are you available for a one-on-one interview?"

Kristina said she was, and made an appointment with Soleil for the following morning at ten o'clock.

They met at Soleil's Uptown real estate office, occupying the first floor of an aged, granite slab office building on the corner of Main and North Streets. The cheerful space was painted cantaloupe-orange, and decorated with photographs of the sagebrush range, and included the time-honored deer head mount above the wall clock.

Kristina sat before Soleil's desk in the glass enclosure, and waited while Soleil was finishing up conversation with a client in a waiting area by the entry. The man was elderly, a sunburned rancher with a slight Basque lilt and knuckled, arthritic fingers. When Kristina had walked past him to Soleil's workspace, she noted he smelled of bourbon, and she felt her heart drop on the man's behalf.

Their conversation winding down, Kristina turned her attention to Soleil's desk, on which were two framed photographs. One was a female deputy, dressed in formal uniform of the Sheriff's Department. The other was a photo of Soleil standing with a man shorter by at least five inches. They leaned close like lovers, hands tightly clasped. The man wore a pinch-front hat, and sported the healthy tan of an outdoorsman. Conversely, Soleil was supple alabaster beside the sunbaked man, strangely complementing the couple.

The man departed, shuffling out into the heat of the day. Soleil strode back to her desk, and tapped the photo of the female deputy. "That's my sister, Cherry Parker. And I see you've met my husband, indirectly." The wheels of her chair squeaked sharply as she pulled up opposite Kristina.

"Your husband?" Kristina leaned in close. "Is he a rancher?"

Soleil nodded. "His name is Grady O. He works on a sheep ranch up near Madeline some distant childless Parker cousin gifted him half of." She smiled affectionately at the photograph. "It was an easy thing, really, because we're both Parkers, so I didn't have to adjust to, nor change my name."

"That sure does make it simple." Armed with that knowledge, she said, "Mrs. Parker, your cousin, America, mentioned to me that you've been looking for a programming idea for KLCC radio."

"That's right."

"How does a radio talk show sound to you?"

Soleil pursed her lips, considering.

"It's not innovative," Kristina continued. "Plenty of urban areas have talk shows, they're a dime-to-a-dozen, but I've never heard of one in this area outside of the syndicated broadcasts on KSUE. I think there's a need for dialogue, and a healthy exchange of opinion."

"There's an exchange all right, if you count the Swap Shop on KSUE. As for opinion, I really doubt that either Laura Ingraham or Sean Hannity want to know what you think, Ms. Sumner." She laughed, and then sighed softly. "It's a wild idea, and it just might work. Would you be willing to write me a proposal, and e-mail it to me?"

"I'm happy to contribute."

Soleil moved some files around, locating a W9 tax form she handed over to Kristina. "You'll need to complete this, so I can arrange to put you on payroll with the College district."

"Are you saying this is a paid position?"

Soleil waved her hand. "Yes, it is, and I wouldn't take advantage of your talents the way that Jonathan Barringer did. As far as I'm concerned, you deserved to be compensated from half of everyone's salary at that good-for-nothing excuse for journalism."

"I had a positive experience at the *Register*," Kristina maintained. "It was never going to be a job, it was only for the exposure."

Soleil studied Kristina's face. "I like that. You're not about to badmouth your previous so-called employer, even if you were only someone's errand girl—which isn't what I want from you here, Ms. Sumner. Your humility is a fine trait, young lady, and one that a prospective employer will embrace. Now." She tapped the W9 with a fingertip. "Fill out this income-tax form, and get it back to me as soon as possible. You can e-mail the signed form with your outline."

"When do I start, Mrs. Parker?"

"Today. At the risk of my presumption, you've already been hired."

"That's all? That's it?"

Soleil put her arms on her desk, and leaned forward. "I suppose I should have made it more difficult, right? In the future, after college, I imagine your job interviews will be nerve-wracking, but trust me when I tell you that I had you in mind for this all along, I just never thought I'd get you to actually inquire."

"Did you tell America Parker to ask on your behalf?"

"No, I simply mentioned the need. America's a smart cookie. She put together the rest of it, Miss Sumner." Soleil settled back in her chair. "So. What do you think you'll call this radio talk show?"

Kristina folded her hands. "Live, From Susanville."

That had occurred eight months ago, before Kristina's senior year at Susanville High. Now, her school year was nearly over, and she was astonished how time truly did fly.

* * * *

The program was broadcasted on Tuesdays and Thursdays, from seven to nine p.m., which fit around Kristina's homework load, and roused the interest of a community in need of intellectual stimulation.

During the shows, the assigned producer, Heath Call, a student at the college, sat in an adjacent booth, and directed the incoming telephone guests.

"Call Mr. Call, folks," was how Kristina designated the process of screening.

The subject matter was left to Soleil, who often delegated choice right back to Kristina.

"You're shrewd," was Soleil's reasoning. "You know what's right, and what the FCC won't allow."

Her words were echoes of Paul Sumner's characterization of his daughter's integrity, when he'd learned of her crush on Jake Weatherby.

That theme became the focus of an entire week—right and wrong; good and bad; holy and evil; and the vast gray plain between.

"Live, From Susanville, you're on the air with Kris Sumner."

Kristina had nominated herself as "Kris," which didn't own the childishness of Kristy, or the formality of Kristina. Kris was mature, and demanded respect.

And the reward—besides an accolade to her list of achievements—was that bimonthly paycheck. Kristina banked it wisely, because she'd received an acceptance letter from each of the colleges she'd applied to—Stanford, UCSF, Cal, and her preference, Berkshire University. She lived with the solemn expectation of footing the probable housing and related expenses she'd acquire in the coming months, and the job was a ticket to adulthood.

* * * *

The trial date for Calvin Simms had been set for August 11, 2008, nearly eighteen months after the commission of the crime. The Sumners were dealing with the stress, as both parents and their two minor sons were expected to testify at trial.

The Lassen County District Attorney had recommended Calvin Simms be charged with a seldom-used clause in the State criminal code. The law allowed for perpetrators of a crime to be prosecuted for first-degree murder of their accomplice, if the alleged conspirator had been killed by the victim while engaged in the act of deadly force in mounting a reasonable self-defense. The law basically meant the victim could kill an attacker, and the surviving criminal would bear the legal consequence.

Simms—faced with enough counts to put him away for a minimum of forty years before he could hope to even stand before the parole board for a hearing—had opted against the advice of counsel to plead not guilty.

The Lassen County District Attorney, Lucille Jennings, had offered Simms a plea deal. Aggravated by constant leg pains brought on by Mrs. Sumner's table turning attack, Calvin Simms had replied to the terms with a snarl and a curse.

"I ain't signin' nothin', God damn it," Simms growled.

"Your client is aware of the evidence we possess." Jennings addressed Simms' public defender, a knockabout by the name of Waylon Rice.

"Your evidence won't stand up in court, Lucille," Rice countered.

Lucille Jennings referred to her file, and the list for discovery.

"Several personal journals from both Simms brothers that reinforce racist viewpoints, and a handwritten outline of their plan to kill Katherine Sumner and her family, focusing upon the *Register* article's depiction of her painting, 'Amerika.'"

"Small details." Rice shrugged. His ridiculous repudiation of the glaring facts was as though hinting at personal mental illness, a perfect mindset for a small town criminal defense attorney.

"More like a manifesto of intent," Jennings parried. "We've got your Mr. Simms down cold, Mr. Rice. The jury won't have any choice but to convict."

Calvin Simms, mutely planted beside his lawyer, had been building up to an eruption during the conversation, and now, with his face red, he slammed his shackled fists onto the tabletop.

"Go fry in hell, bitch!" he'd hollered at D.A. Jennings, who called in security.

As a consequence for the defendant's nastiness, no other offers were put on the table.

"We need to go over the deposition transcripts," Jennings advised Kate Sumner, about four months before the trial, when Kate agreed to meet the D.A. in her office on a school day.

"Why? I've been truthful about everything."

"They're no doubt going to bring in the other killing," Lucy Jennings persisted. "Roger Barnhart Jr., in 1988, out at your ranch."

"Let them try. That was well over twenty years ago, and it was ruled justifiable self-defense."

"And they'll bring up the fact that your daughter Kristina killed Tucker Parker the year before the Simms' assault."

"Let them do it," Kate invited. "A jury negated the civil suit for wrongful death that Kurt and Patty Parker filed against my family." Kate referred to the parents of Tucker Parker. "That reinforced self-defense on Kristina's part."

"Kristina still used deadly force, Kate. It *will* be brought into this trial."

"I'm game. Look, Lucy, I'm Indian. Maybe I have a target written all over me. My children must have inherited that target."

"But Barnhart didn't try to kill you because you're Indian," Jennings pointed out. "He intended to kill you because his father was caught committing arson and first-degree murder in nineteen seventy-eight, and you were the one who impeded Barnhart Sr.'s getaway, and the reason he moldered in prison."

Kate only stared at the D.A., incredulous, though far from defeated.

"I checked it out, Kate, and that's what the defense will do. Any lawyer worth half a damn, they'll check out all parties and possibilities. You can bet that Waylon Rice will try to portray you as having a tendency to periodically commit murder, and that you teach this value to your children." She yanked a paper from a folder. "And what's this about Jacob Weatherby?"

"I wasn't aware we had killed Jacob Weatherby," said Kate sarcastically, yet without malice, and with such ease for her mouth having suddenly gone dry.

Lucy studied the file. "I see that the Lassen County Sheriff's Department surmised that Mr. Weatherby was having a statutory relationship with your daughter, Kristina, before and during the events that took place in Milford, at the McKinley Ranch."

"Are you forming a prosecutorial monologue for this trial, or for Terrence Hobart's trial, Ms. Jennings?"

"Kate, Jake Weatherby is supposed to come back to Susanville for Simms' trial. He submitted an application for a press pass into the courthouse. I'm simply trying to uncover as much factual evidence as I can, so we're not blasted by the defense."

"Jake Weatherby never did anything illegal with my daughter." Kate was unflinching.

"Are you *sure?*" Lucy asked.

Perhaps to preserve Lucy Jennings' faith in her, Kate dictated the course of events that ended in Weatherby leaving town in June of 2007.

"You told him that he might be welcome when Kristina is eighteen, but that he'd better stay away from her until then?"

"Yes."

"This, after he admitted to being in love with her?"

"I know Kristina, Lucy. I know her well."

"Did you know she was capable of killing a man?"

Kate smiled. "Yes, Lucy, I did."

Lucy Jennings inhaled, shaking her head. "These are the types of questions you might be asked, Kate. And that one would definitely count against you."

"It bothers me that a defense attorney would ask if my daughter were capable of killing, when she wasn't involved in the Simms case."

"It's about character. A defense attorney will establish your character, and elaborate on its extension to other members of your immediate family."

"Well, thank God the defense won't delve into my ancestry. They might find an Indian who killed a white man or two."

* * * *

But Kate's bravado had dissipated by the time she left the D.A.'s office and hurried over to Susanville High School, where she could meet with Kristina. Kate signed her daughter out of school for the day, and took her for a long drive and private conversation.

She told Kristina about the trial, and the probable return of Jake Weatherby to the area. Kate had no clue of her daughter's expression, as Kristina was staring out the passenger side window. Except for a slight hunch to Kristina's shoulders, she might have been asleep.

Kate pulled to the side of the road at Red Rock, off of I-395, less than thirty miles from Reno. In the backdrop of steep, sagebrush hills, the wound in the earth showed through in bright red and pale amber, fronted by twisted junipers and tussocks of shaggy native grasses, untouched by the mouths of cattle.

"Kris," she pleaded gently. "Please, tell me how you feel."

"I feel..." Kristina shrugged.

"You don't have to see him," Kate assured. "Not if you don't want to."

Kristina turned toward her mother, her face alight, not at all pained.

"But I *do* want to see Mr. Weatherby, Mom. Only, not this way, not at a trial about you and Dad and Charlie Kat and Dakota."

"Could you apply for a press pass?"

"I already did, Mom, weeks ago."

For Kate, the pieces clicked into place.

"That's why Lucy Jennings was asking about Jake Weatherby." Kate slapped her thigh. "She knew you and he would be in close proximity, and she wanted to reject Mr. Weatherby's application, if I indicated anything untoward had happened."

"But Mom, nothing happened. He's never even hugged me, never tried to touch me, never held my hand, or anything like that." She paused. "He's called me Kristina only twice, and the rest of the time, he referred to me as Miss Sumner."

"I like him more and more," Kate concluded. "Go ahead with the press pass thing, and bring him to the Ranch for supper, if need be."

Kristina spontaneously hugged Kate.

"I love you, Mom. I really do."

Kate patted her daughter's back. "I've always loved you, Kris. Long before you ever were."

* * * *

"Live, From Susanville, you're on the air with Kris Sumner."

"Kris, this is Theodore in Doyle, thanks for taking my call."

"What's on your mind, Theodore?"

"Well, I've been investigating all types of electronic voting machines, and the inherent failure they have, where someone can just go in and reprogram them."

Theodore went on to offer a web site where listeners could watch a film clip of an Internet journalist, as she hacked into the election computers of the Ohio Secretary of State.

"Thank you, Theodore, and hopefully the people of Lassen County will check it out."

She reached for a bottle of water to take the edge off of her tongue, after being involved in discussion for nearly two hours straight. Through the glass window, Heath was holding up a paper sign, his usual mode of contact, because of some strange aversion to the intercom system.

The paper read, "Daniel, Santa Cruz."

She scrambled for the microphone. "Our next caller is Daniel. Are you there, Daniel?"

"I'm here," Daniel confirmed.

"Where are you from, Daniel?" she asked, testing this young man, her elder brother.

"I hail from Santa Cruz, presently, but I grew up in Susanville."

"What's on your mind, Daniel? Do you have an opinion on electronic voting machines?"

"Yes, I do, I think that I have to agree with Theodore from Doyle, electronic voting machines are open to fraud and manipulation, and should be chucked until a better system can be created, one that voters can trust."

"Hand-counted paper ballots can be subject to fraud, too, Daniel."

"Yes, they can, but if each county registrar created a database contingent upon the serialized ballot, all voters could reconfirm their vote. It wouldn't be completely foolproof, but at least the voter could determine if their ballot stub matches their filed vote, and then odds of being totally disenfranchised would be far lower."

"Registrars would complain about the higher cost involved in maintaining the database."

"Yes, but just look at how the election process has already been cheapened by questionable maneuvering in both the two thousand, and the oh-four presidential elections. You can't put a price on the Constitution."

Kristina glanced at the clock—eight fifty-eight. Her time had run out.

"Thank you, Daniel from Santa Cruz, for that commentary. It was very educational. Folks, this is Kris Sumner. I'll be back on Thursday. Until then, keep asking the difficult questions. They're your roads to knowledge. Stay tuned for 'Country Lanes' with your D.J., Jervis Quill."

Heath Call made a killing motion with one finger telling her she was off the air. She removed her headset, and then picked up the telephone extension for discretion.

"Don't hang up, Kris," said her brother.

"I haven't."

"This is so cool, hearing you on the radio."

"I thought you might be in town. I mean, your call to the radio show and all."

"I'm at school. Apparently, the College put an audio feed of your show on their web site, so that's how I've been following it."

"It's nice to know I have at least one fan. When are you coming home?"

"In June, for your graduation. Did you get any acceptance letters?"

"Yeah, I received four, from Berkshire, Cal, Stanford and UCSF."

"That's excellent, Kris." Daniel finally broached the primary reason for his call. "Mom told me about Jake Weatherby, Kris. I hope you go to the college of your choice, instead of bending to some guy."

"Fact is, I'm considering taking the Berkshire acceptance."

"You should do it, then." He seemed supportive, but there was a tone beneath his words that raised a red flag.

"Besides, I don't know anything about Mr. Weatherby anymore," she said, and let that hang in the air.

* * * *

Daniel hesitated, because he had taken the initiative to confront Jake Weatherby on his own, driving from his coastal familiarity of Santa Cruz for nearly two hours, until he reached Oakland, where he went directly to the television station. He wondered how Weatherby would react to the tall, athletic young man who met him in the front lobby.

"You have your sister's eyes," was Jake's first comment.

Daniel had asked that Jake accompany him to lunch, with a shrewdness the older man couldn't refuse. Instead of catching a tight booth at one of the local eateries, Jake suggested that Daniel follow him home, which turned out to be a charming cottage in the Berkeley hills.

"That's better," Daniel had agreed. "Then we can talk, straightforward, like men."

Daniel took note of everything related to Jake Weatherby—the American flag on a pole in front of the cottage, complemented by the smaller, distinctively colored American Indian Movement banner. Daniel was Native and a liberal, but his first thought of Weatherby in regard to the AIM flag was *what a nutcase!*

The neatly swept yard was landscaped with native plants. The spare, yet comfortable interior of the little house was decorated with relics Jake had carried with him from Susanville, from a wooden bowl of beach rocks collected at Eagle Lake, to a pair of deer antlers mounted above the fireplace mantel.

Now, as he held the phone to his mouth and stared at his computer screen, Daniel allowed the disclosure.

"I went to see that Weatherby character myself," he blurted to his sister, who was rarely ever a fool.

* * * *

Kristina imagined the scene, her eldest brother, and his tireless excellence in just about everything he endeavored—faced with Jake Weatherby, a man more noted for using his journalistic slyness, and knack of good luck to hatch out a story.

"How did that go?" she asked, though, knowing her brother, the answer was a given.

"All right, until I mentioned your name."

"What happened then?"

"It was an inquisition of sorts, Kris."

* * * *

Jake had made omelets, and served out the food on a brick terrace at the rear of the cottage, where an enormous sycamore tree, gnarled and leafing out, had allowed for the midday sun to warm the damp backyard. While they ate, they spoke of everything unrelated to the Sumner family or to Susanville.

"Why my sister? Why Kristina?" Daniel had asked quite abruptly. "Is there something the matter with you that you have to entertain yourself with a sixteen-year-old girl?"

* * * *

"What did he say to that?" Kristina inquired, merely curious, not yet angry.

"He told me that he'd never entertained himself with you, but that he considered you intelligent, sensitive and honest, and sincerely cares for you."

* * * *

Following their short meal, Daniel had asked to use the bathroom, and once inside the small locked space, had quietly checked the medicine cabinet for evidence of female intrusion, along with every possible nook and cranny. There was none, and he was let down by the substantiation of Weatherby's integrity.

He had also canvassed Weatherby's dirty clothes hamper, dumping the entire contents of the wicker basket and sorting through.

Jake Weatherby had been waiting for Daniel in the living room, hands in the pockets of his slacks.

"Would you like to check my bedroom?" Weatherby asked, not in the least annoyed.

"Yeah, I would."

"While you're at it, I suggest you go over everything. It's a small house, and I have the time."

Daniel wasn't too proud of taking Weatherby up on his offer—rummaging through Weatherby's drawers and closet, while the owner of these personal effects stood aside patiently. Daniel hadn't the nerve to peruse the man's kitchen or the office that occupied the second bedroom, except to open the closet door, and verify its emptiness.

* * * *

"Did you?" Kristina paused to breathe deeply to stop her anger. "Did you look through *everything* he had?"

"Matter of fact, I did."

"Wow. I can't believe you did that."

"Really, Kris, he acted like he had nothing to hide. No traces of a woman, no long hair in the shower drain, no smelly soap, nothing. No panties in the hamper."

"Mr. Weatherby has no reason for dishonesty. That's why you couldn't find anything."

"I have nothing on him, Kris. Nothing. Though he did ask if Mom put me up to it."

"Well, *did* she?"

Daniel related the conversation he'd had with his mother, the evening before his bold foray to Oakland.

"Mom told me, 'Leave it be. I am not about to be involved in policing Jake Weatherby.'"

"Interesting. So it was all *your* doing."

"Yes, it was my initiative."

"What made you think you should make an ass of yourself, and interfere?" she demanded.

"Jesus, Kristina!"

Daniel had apparently forgotten his little sister wasn't complacent, nor was she a pawn for anyone's hidden agenda.

"It was a beautiful friendship, Daniel, and you made it seem like a dirty, foul thing, like Mr. Weatherby is this sinister pervert, and I'm an innocent."

"Well." He assumed a defensive tone. "Isn't it like that?"

"Not at all," she spoke, her voice stiff.

"There was this one thing, a photograph, blown up and framed, of a tree. It was the only thing hanging on his bedroom wall."

"So. What about it?" She was pissed at Daniel, though she knew she would eventually forgive him.

"And a poem. Yeah, a picture of a cottonwood tree in a nice wooden frame, with these eight lines printed on computer paper, stuck under the glass at the bottom."

"Can you quote me the words?"

"Not verbatim."

"Was part of the first phrase, 'Cottonwoods, arisen from water and earth'?"

"I guess, yeah, that sounds about right."

"You were out of line, Daniel, because that was a poem *I* wrote. It was supposed to be for English class last year, but I really meant it for Mr. Weatherby."

"So, what does that prove? That he likes your writing?"

"It proves, at least," she concluded, "that he's been thinking about me."

* * * *

The radio show advanced with "Special Guests," as Kristina dubbed the local characters she invited to join her on Live, From Susanville. They were chosen from public memory of controversial behavior, either past or present.

Her first guest was Police Chief Sam Pilger, who arrived at the station lot in a cruiser, and slid it delicately into a parking space marked "compact," while Kristina watched from the lobby. When she got him behind the microphone, one of her comments to get the phones ringing was his ability to handle the car.

"I didn't know a Crown Vic could fit in a compact slot," she said smugly. "Do you often make use of parking spaces that otherwise unremarkable citizenry would be liable to be ticketed for?"

"Of course I don't," Pilger snapped.

Marge from Susanville called in, and claimed, "Chief Sam likes to use the handicapped spaces while he's down at the Monseigneur Ransome Bingo Hall."

"Since when have I *ever* played Bingo?" Chief Pilger choked.

"I see your car there near Our Lady of Mercy, Mister Smarty Pants," Marge insisted. "Don't deny it."

"But I don't play Bingo." Chief Pilger was mystified.

Marge just cackled, and hung up.

"So, does your wife call you Sam or Samuel?" Kristina asked. "Or is it Chiefy?"

"It's Sam!" He seemed irritated. "My given name is Sam, not Samuel. If she called me Samuel, I might get to thinking she's mistaken me for somebody else."

"Then I guess Chiefy is out," Kris concluded.

There were many others, their stories taken from the pages of the *Register*.

Heath Call's elder cousin, Janelle, was featured by telephone link from her USC dorm room, where she was finishing out the semester. Janelle spoke of the eternal vigilance to one's family, and personal responsibility to the community.

Chief Pilger's wife, Aurora Campbell, was a guest, and with self-effacing charm, encouraged women to attain careers in niches traditionally belonging to men.

Kristina even managed to convince Wade and Sheila Clark, of the AlpineGlo, to render their experiences contributing to the youth in Lassen County—finding herself sorely tested to ignore the couple's inability to keep their hands off one another.

District Attorney Lucille Jennings was featured with the tale of a local woman's self-incrimination—how Suzie Raines, the estranged wife of CHP Officer Charles Raines, had killed her husband's mistress, and started a fire to cover the murder. Once the coroner discovered the body burned in the Raines' home actually belonged to Sonia Anderson, a County employee—and Officer Raines's mistress—it was only then that Suzie Raines's motives were investigated. An insurance investigator determined Mrs. Raines had changed the beneficiary on her half-million dollar life insurance policy from her husband, to the name of Tallulah Bankhead—a deceased actress famously noted for her extreme promiscuity—with an address in rural Cuernavaca, Mexico. The scam was realized, and a private bounty hunter, hired jointly by the life insurance carrier and the Lassen County District Attorney's office, traveled to Mexico to find Suzie Raines. She was ridiculously easy to locate, living openly under her legal name on an agave plantation—as the Mexican farmer's lover—uneventfully taken into custody, and extradited back to Lassen County for a murder trial.

This was perhaps the finest of Kristina's shows, though she considered herself a conduit for the truth, not the principal of public focus.

* * * *

On Friday, the thirteenth of June, the graduating class of 2008 lined up on the football field at Susanville High School for the commencement ceremony.

Sorted toward the straggling end of the class by virtue of her surname, Kristina was seated on a metal folding chair between Andrew Sinclair and Gwen Thomas. The chairs magnified the pleasant heat of the late afternoon, so by the time the graduation activities had begun, most of them were perspiring inside of their black acetate gowns.

Up in stepped bleachers, her family sat beneath the shade of several striped, oversized umbrellas, including her two siblings who had finished school for the summer, returning faithfully to the ranch, as the swallows do to Eagle Lake.

Kristina shared her ranch accommodations temporarily with Sara, a blessing after being apart for so long. All of their young lives had been spent in separate bedrooms, being the only female progeny of Kate Sumner. The boys had reveled in being stacked three deep in their spacious second floor rat's nest, but girls were different, team players in dire need of individual expression. Their tastes and preferences owned a polarity that suggested imminent culture shock, had one been forced to live with the other in a common space. Sara loved the color of vivid blue, and Native American motifs. Kristina drifted toward pastels, and wildflowers. Even their sleep patterns were opposites, as Kristina tended an insomniac's habit of writing into the wee hours, while Sara was generally useless after ten p.m.

But they had the rare fortune of having always been close, except for the period of time when Sara associated with that vile, murderous boyfriend, Chase Piper. The fact that Sara chose Joaquin Parker, and remained true to the young man, had inspired Kristina's own sense of fidelity in her memory of Jake Weatherby.

The sisters found plenty of points for disagreement during a conversation shortly after Sara returned from U.C. Davis.

"You're talking about a man almost thirty-four years old, Kris," Sara said. "A man doesn't fall for a minor, unless he's a pedophile."

"Look at me, Sara," Kristina demanded, receiving lengthy scrutiny from her sister." Kristina was built like their mother, short, slim and muscular, with the full-breasts of a mature woman. "Do I look like a child?"

"I suppose not," Sara said, with much reluctance.

"I haven't changed since I was fifteen," Kristina chided. "So, what makes you think that Mr. Weatherby is attracted to a child's physique?"

"I guess I was wrong about your body." Sara shrugged. "But you're still not eighteen."

"Do I act like a foolish teenager?"

"Not at all. I don't think you ever did, even when you were a kid. Mom used to say that you were born already grown up."

"No, Mom used to say that I was born an old woman."

"Same thing."

"I haven't been a child for a long time," Kristina insisted. "Not in my mind, anyway."

"I can see that," Sara gave in, though privately, some of her doubt remained.

* * * *

In the field, and over a crackling public address system, the school principal, Edwin Davies, began to announce the students' names alphabetically. According to rehearsal the day before, those called were required to walk quickly to the podium, shake Mr. Davies' hand, accept their diploma—and return to their scorching chair, to await the end of the ceremony.

Four chairs down from Kristina, Claremont Whitehead waited for the senior class finale, without looking at her once. After she'd turned him down, he'd been too bitter for mere friendship. He wore a walking cast on his right leg to heal a major fracture inflicted by a nasty throw from a wild horse that had been adopted from the BLM roundup corrals by Pyramid Lake. The horse had survived their brief battle for dominance without a scratch, though it made sure the boy knew who was boss. After tossing Claremont onto the dusty arena, its left rear hoof slammed down on the boy's tibia with a compressive force the strong bone couldn't handle. The injury defined the end to his Rodeoing for a while, a major setback for a young man determined to make bronc-riding his profession. Aside from the injury, his self-absorbed disappointment in Kristina's rejection was reflected in his sunburned face, and in the indifferent attitude of an entire school year.

The last time Kristina was a bystander in the bleachers was Ian Calhoun's graduation a year ago. They had remained friendly, as she felt indebted to Ian for distracting Tucker Parker that fateful day in the school auditorium. After commencement, Ian moved to Florida to act as caregiver for his mother's elderly parents. He and Kristina rarely corresponded, but would always be connected by the horror from their mutual past.

While she waited and listened for her name to be announced, Kristina scanned the crowd in the bleachers. She recognized her immediate family, and also the select friends of the Sumners—Charlie and Dove Foster, and their elementary-aged daughter, Hannah; and Sara's father, Victor White Owl, and his wife Lora.

There were numerous people whose names she had catalogued, defined by life in the boondocks, where, aside from the tradition of flying the American flag like patriotic lunatics, everyone seemed to be linked by the knowledge of name and family affiliation. You knew where people came from—whether they were descended from the era of the Emigration, or fresh meat hired as prison guards—and you knew in which neighborhood or subdivision they lived. Ultimately, the community became an enormous extended family, the unique character of a small town.

During this audit of the throng in the bleachers, Kristina recognized Mr. Weatherby, and felt a startling heat expand from her center, to match the searing warmth of the afternoon.

He was seated alone, between the Swift family (Uptown) and the Klings (Lake Leavitt). Under the shade of a wide-brimmed canvas hat, he gazed at her with immutable eyes. A distance that blurred everything except passing time separated them, and yet he was plain to see.

This sudden realization in Jake Weatherby's attendance, and Kristina very nearly missed responding to her name.

"Kris!" Gwen Thomas nudged her rudely with an elbow, waking Kristina from her trance.

"Huh?"

"Get up, he frigging called your name."

"Thanks." Kristina arose with composure, as though nothing had happened.

She went forward to shake Mr. Davies's hand, receive the standard rolled paper with its yellow silk ribbon. When she glanced up to the bleachers, there he was, watching her. He even raised one hand in a surreptitious thumb's-up salute, to which Kristina gave a welcoming nod, too nervous to smile.

But later, when the ceremony was complete, and she had located her family members, Mr. Weatherby was nowhere to be seen. She was letdown, though she hardly blamed him, as she wasn't yet eighteen. She imaged rushing into his arms, her open lips connecting with his mouth— well, enough of a scandal to warrant Mr. Weatherby's arrest.

* * * *

On a stifling hot Friday evening in early August, and while driving through the stacked-up traffic exiting the Bay Area, Jake Weatherby pondered on the meaning of life.

His used maroon Toyota Prius had been purchased complete with carpool stickers, and though perfectly legal to use the commuter lane, he received the occasional vicious honk or upraised middle finger for zooming through solo.

Behind him, on the rear passenger seat was a packed suitcase, along with his wheeled briefcase that bulged with the items of his professional occupation, including a laptop computer.

A carton wrapped in pretty, flowered paper lay next to his pile. Inside of the disguised carton was a wheeled briefcase which matched his own, a belated graduation present for Kristina Sumner. He had purchased it in May, and though he'd attended the ceremony—hauling ass on a busy Friday morning to sit on a sunbaked bleacher seat, packed in like a sardine in a can—he hadn't the nerve to actually pass the gift into her hands.

Once he saw her on the field, all of his latent questions had been answered, and fear was tangible. Ahead of Kristina's eighteenth birthday, Jake knew there was no way he could keep his hands to himself.

In the cargo compartment of the Prius was a laptop computer in its naked carton. He'd complicated matters by buying the Toshiba Satellite for her eighteenth birthday, a gift of extravagance, though Miss Sumner more than deserved it.

He knew to outside eyes, his love of a woman nearly half his age was ridiculous. A tenderness and rare beauty had expanded inside of him over the past eighteen months defined as a welcome encumbrance, hindering strange women on the prowl. They needed only to observe that expression in his eyes to interpret his preoccupation.

Yet, the sense of dignity in this love had carried him. Love possessed purity, a sweetness that sprang from the honesty of his friendship with Miss Sumner.

Who in the hell was he kidding?

He often spoke her name to the now-empty rooms in the Berkeley cottage. His personal effects had been packed and shipped to D.C., where he'd accepted a job with *The Washington Post.*

This was the final chapter of his foolish agony. Once he congratulated her new phase of life, he was heading east. His future had been hatched, and there was no turning back.

The date was August 8, 2008, and the highway descended into the furnace of the Central Valley, with its haze and urban sprawl. At one time, the Valley had been a haven of farms, but the disease of settlement and progress had infected rural communities, the dearth of personality reflected in the repetition of strip malls and hefty subdivisions.

He remembered Susanville, the slower pace and glaring incompetence. The American flag served as a reprise to the venerable history of Uptown; while on the outskirts, cattle grazed on the highway verge, and horses ran beneath a hammer-blow sun.

He would have stayed in Lassen County, despite the fact that his chunky and pathetic elder brother Carl would probably be ousted as Sheriff in this fall's election. During this contentiously one-sided campaign, Carl had been Kris Sumner's guest on Live, From Susanville. Kristina's tongue-in-cheek interview had only served to magnify Carl Weatherby's unfortunate idiocy, and secured Jake as the show's most committed enthusiast.

The only issue that worried Jake was Miss Sumner's family—not Mr. and Mrs. Sumner, but the older brother, Daniel. Daniel's surprise visit and rummaging through the Berkeley cottage had unnerved Jake. He had longed to tell Daniel how much he cared for Kristina, though it would be more likely to provoke rage, instead of understanding and tolerance. Therefore, all Jake could do was stand back and let the search play out. He'd had nothing to hide, including the depth of his feelings for Kristina.

His body and heart had been in unison, deprived of female companionship, and waiting in expectant joy for The Moment. He had been saved from any serious agony by focusing on his job, which left little time for him to embrace self-pity.

Still, within days, he would be gone from California for good. He had no intention of holding Miss Sumner to their ludicrous promise. He figured she was at the beginning of her life, while he had already tallied up a lot of mileage. She deserved a man who was fresh and new, not weighed with baggage of life's experiences.

* * * *

On Friday morning, Kristina drove into Susanville, and picked up her press pass at the front desk in the District Attorney's office. Signing into the logbook, she noted with some disappointment that there was no evidence that Jake Weatherby had picked up his pass. This gave her some unease, but she pushed it away, and walked bravely from the office, her mind processing a mental list she'd been steadily satisfying, before she left for college in two weeks.

She had decided to complete her enrollment at Berkshire University, despite the suggestions of Mr. Weatherby, who had indicated he in no way wanted to leverage his influence. Not as remotely expensive as Stanford's tuition, Berkshire's fees were nevertheless pricey.

The financial burden to her family had been alleviated by grants, scholarships, and financial aid from the American Indian Fund, because of her Quinault tribal registry. There had been only the course books out of pocket, ordered and waiting for Kristina to claim at Berkshire's Student Union.

Self-disciplined to a fault, she had gone on a hardcore shopping trip to Reno with her mother. While in Reno, they booked three round-trip airplane tickets to Baltimore, Maryland, with Kristina's ticket allowing for an open-ended return date, in the off chance that she wanted to come home on the next break.

The hometown of Berkshire University was Potawatomi Springs, closer to Washington D.C., though the University had required all incoming freshmen to fly into Baltimore. She and her parents were scheduled to meet a charter bus, along with all out of state freshmen arriving four days early to attend Orientation. Her personal effects would fit into a suitcase and a carry-on, except for her eMac computer and its peripherals, which her parents had proposed to ship by air.

Kristina expressed this regret. "I should have gotten a laptop."

"Christmas," Kate promised, as they were passing the Lake Leavitt subdivision, too far from Reno for a simple turnaround. "Hopefully, that bulky computer of yours will hold you until then."

"We could always look in Baltimore," Kristina suggested. "Keep the eMac here. Maybe the boys can use it."

Her mother had quickly agreed.

The sun beat upon Kristina's head, as she stood on the sidewalk in front of the D.A.'s office. A desiccating breeze blew up from the Honey Lake Valley, wrapping her in familiarity.

This would be one of a thousand incremental points of Lassen County she would miss. Having rarely been away from her family, she assumed homesickness would infect her painfully, though she was mentally prepared. She had also gone to the doctor for a round of immunizations, having read about meningitis running rampant through college populations.

She imagined her entire life spent upon a thinly populated island, the whole of Lassen County, isolated by geography, her immune system dictated by her experiences, suddenly thrust into the viral stew of students from all points of the map.

But, in spite of her apprehension, she carried an enthusiasm not dampened by uncertainty. She supposed that verve was a blessing—or a curse—of youth.

* * * *

In his cell at the County Jail, Calvin Simms was feeling ill, seated on a lower bunk, and hunched over to accommodate his height.

The sickness had started before Saturday morning's breakfast with an unsettled stomach, and continued with diarrhea, two bouts of vomiting, and a gathering pain in his left jaw.

At midday, shuttled with the other inmates to the cafeteria, Simms ate halfheartedly. Dinner was a carbon copy, with the queasiness increasing. Food was the high point of Simms's life, and to reject two straight meals should have attracted the attention of a C.O.

He attributed the symptoms to poor jailhouse victuals and a broken molar, the latter having lingered without repair for two years. State funding would have installed a crown, but as with most of his life's habit, procrastination was the rule. He would have asked to visit the clinic, but it was Saturday, and a nurse wasn't on duty until Monday morning.

He didn't intend to blame any of his physical discomfort on stress caused by the impending start to his trial, set for the morning of Monday, August eleventh, less than two days away. The very length of time's passage between the crime—the scheme of his deceased brother Robert—and the start of the trial, had caged him to County Jail for a year and a half—eighteen months of depositions, legal wrangling, changing lawyers, and court motions to dismiss due to poorly healed knee replacement surgeries.

He'd persuaded a lawyer to file a civil suit against Katherine McLain for the damage to his knees, which had prevented a large man such as Calvin Simms from jail yard exercise.

Judge McFarlin had taken a single glance at the suit, and thrown it out of court.

"I would have done the same, Mr. Simms, had your hands been around my throat, rather than involved in throttling Katherine Sumner," Judge McFarlin had seemed to feel obliged to comment.

"I object, Your Honor," said Hank McOwen, Simms's attorney for a civil case theoretically projected to net the lawyer several thousand dollars for contingent representation. "That 'throttling,' as you call it, is alleged. My client hasn't even been tried or convicted in criminal court."

After a warning to McOwen of contempt, Judge McFarlin summarily dismissed the suit as frivolous, which didn't ease Calvin Simms's mounting frustration and rage.

Simms had stewed in his crockpot of bad luck for eighteen interminable months, eaten away by the acid of a dismal future, and trapped inside of his impaired body, which contradicted twenty-nine years of life.

"Simms, quit fucking making that noise," his cellmate, Kelly Brooks, growled from the top bunk, as he attempted to sleep. "I can't fucking think."

Brooks was awaiting trial for stabbing a meth dealer to death at a bar in Calneva. His pairing up with Simms was an indication that the County flocked certain jailbirds together.

Calvin Simms lay like a stranded whale on the bunk, nausea clenching. Pain gripped not only the left jaw, but was complicated by a shooting pain in his left shoulder. He clutched the upright of the bed frame, and hauled himself into a sitting position again with some difficulty.

"Simms, shut the fuck up."

Brooks, his incarceration muddled by his commission of an armed robbery at the Gas 'N Shop in Susanville, en route to murdering the meth dealer, despised sharing cell space with this bloated slob, who wasn't too shy to lumber over to the head and take a crap at any time of the day or night, or to masturbate in plain sight.

Besides, Simms stank, shit or not, rising from the pores of the man like rot from a carcass. So, when Simms began to moan in earnest, and then make an odd bubbling rumble, Brooks decided to be proactive.

"Simms, ain't I told you enough times already?" Brooks yelled, leaping off the bunk, coiled up to strike the larger man with his feet.

Instead of the usual pale, blubbery visage of Calvin Simms, Brooks was faced with a pop-eyed, purple-faced man, jammed up against the bed frame, lips thick with a white froth of saliva.

"Shit!" Brooks swore. "What the fuck is going on? C.O.! I need a C.O. here! I need a C.O. right *now!*" he screamed at the top of his lungs.

* * * *

On Sunday, the Sumners drove to Our Lady of Mercy Catholic church in Susanville, a routine that required they awaken before dawn, leave by seven a.m., and endure the twenty-mile, one-way trip from the remote Spotted Horse Ranch.

Out of habit, they patronized Our Lady of Mercy. The fact that there were two Catholic churches within five miles of the Spotted Horse Ranch—in Westwood and Chester—might have defied good sense, had the Sumners not been partial to the benedictions of Our Lady of Mercy's pastor, Father Sanger.

This August morning should have been like any other, except that Kristina was going away to college on the twentieth, with Daniel and Sara to complete their exodus a week later. Even in the heavy shadow of tomorrow's court opener, the family clung together and followed routine, common roots of one tree. In this natural gravity, they could hope for a hint of normalcy in their otherwise strange lives.

Kristina had earlier assisted her youngest brother, Dakota, by reminding him how to iron his slacks. While she supervised Dakota in awkwardly handling this mundane chore, she thought, *we're charmed and cursed, and it takes the flair of being Sumner to negotiate the risks.*

On the road, they were quiet, unusual for people who usually sang songs, or debated issues, without an edgewise silence.

Paul sat behind the wheel, sensitive to his wife's distraction, their hands linked companionably. The beauty of the morning increased with the height of sun. In the rearview mirror, Paul could count the heads of their five children, connected by trauma and delight, and the simple view of a summer day.

In Susanville, they descended the grade, made the turn past the BPOE, the green GMC Yukon reflected in picture windows along Main Street. They had been part of the white Suburban for so long, that both Paul and Kate often sought it in parking lots after shopping, before they realized the minor slip of the mind.

The Half Moon café was open, already crawling with seekers of coffee and fellowship, and Ace's Donuts on the next block was balancing caffeine with sugar and shortening. The odors of frying and brewing mingled with the scent of pine trees and sagebrush, as Paul turned left onto North Federation Street.

On Arizona Street, the block immediate to Our Lady of Mercy, were large parking slots, mighty convenient in width for a town filled with SUVs and work trucks. Unlike suburban strip malls and parking structures, the lots and slips in Lassen County pandered to brawny vehicles, instead of discriminating against them. Paul pulled into a slot between a dinged blue Dodge Ram, and a Chevy Silverado with mud-caked wheels.

Kate caught a glimpse of a familiar woman standing on the red concrete church steps.

"Is that who I think it is?"

"Hmm?" Paul turned off the engine, and pocketed the keys. "Who is what?"

"There!" She pointed to District Attorney Lucille Jennings, who scanned the immigrant throng, while peering at her watch, and tapping one foot in obvious impatience.

"Is she a Catholic?" Paul asked, adjusting his glasses, and opening the door. Their offspring had already disembarked, and were making their way to the sidewalk.

"I don't think so," Kate said cautiously, getting out.

True to her wardrobe, Kate wore a pair of clean denim jeans and a button-front blouse, as far from a dress as she could possibly manage. Her loose hair, grown well past her waist, lent her a youthful flair.

Lucy Jennings had caught sight of the milling Sumner family, and called out, "Kate!"

For discretion, Paul told the children to wait for them inside of the church, and hold a space for them in a pew.

"What are you doing here?" Kate asked. "Is your conscience bothering you?"

"I tried to contact you at home, but I guessed you'd already left." Jennings nodded. "Before I drove all that way, I decided to wait for you here." She smiled broadly at Kate.

Kate seemed to sense, through the subtle relaxation of the worry lines on the D.A.'s face, something important had occurred, and she gripped Lucy's shoulder.

"Tell me, what's happened?"

"Calvin Simms had a fatal heart attack last night. Believe it or not, accompanied by a stroke."

"What?" Kate pressed a hand to her own chest. "Are you sure?"

"He couldn't have been very old," Paul commented.

"He was twenty nine," Lucy confirmed. "The EMTs that responded to County Jail couldn't revive Simms. He was transported to Lassen-Flagg, where he was pronounced around ten p.m. last night."

Kate folded her arms. "So, what does that mean?"

"There won't be a trial," Paul concluded, before Lucy could say it.

"I'll be in court tomorrow morning anyway," Lucy explained, "having the case dismissed due to the defendant becoming a decedent."

A weak attempt at a joke, but Kate flashed a smile.

"Don't get me wrong, Lucy," Kate said softly. "I vigorously support all life. Calvin Simms's death is as much a tragedy as his brother Robert's, and I'm a party to that tragedy. It's just that I'm relieved I won't have to show up in court to answer to my defense of a heinous crime against my family."

"The vultures would have tried to pick you apart," Lucy agreed.

Above them, the church bell in the tower began to ring its deep, resonant tone.

"We have to go. It's time for clemency." Kate hugged Lucy Jennings briefly. "Thank you, Lucille, for everything."

She walked up the red concrete steps, one hand in the crook of Paul Sumner's arm.

* * * *

D.A. Jennings, adrift on a beautiful Sunday morning, strolled over to her car. The county issue Crown Vic had drab steel-gray paint that weathered after five years of continuous duty, three of those dedicated to her predecessor.

She grasped the latch, and hesitated. The sun was beckoning, birds chirping in the shrubbery, and the air smelled of mountains and desert. Oddly inspired, she removed her hand from the door handle, and walked briskly toward Main Street.

One block south, and two blocks west, she crossed Main at a signal light, and headed toward the entrance of the Half Moon café. Patrons gathered at little tables along the sidewalk, where redwood planters spilled with blooming flowers and twining Boston ivy on lattice supports, lending color to stonework that glittered in the sharp morning light.

Inside, she stood in a short line, ordered a coffee and a croissant, and was about to find an empty chair, when she noticed a man entering the café, laptop case in hand.

She recognized Jacob Weatherby.

Standing with a steaming coffee and the paper bag of pastry, Lucy eyed him openly as he took his place in line. His face appeared freshly shaven, and his slightly wavy hair, thick and dark brown, fell neatly across his forehead. His attire, jeans and a long-sleeved cotton T-shirt, complemented the fit lines of his physique. He might have seemed ready for the world, except for a haunting sadness in his hazel eyes.

"I noticed that you haven't signed for your press pass yet, Mr. Weatherby," she said.

His eyes swung to her face. "Don't I know you? Because you seem awfully familiar to me, and it's obvious you know who I am."

"I'm Lucille Jennings, Mr. Weatherby."

"Ah." He smiled and nodded. "You're the D.A."

They shook hands, and she noted the firmness of his grip. Lucy responded with a grasp of steel the hallmark of a successful woman in a male-dominated field.

"Good to meet you, D.A. Jennings." He had moved to the front of the line. "The dark roast, Sammy, your largest size."

"Jake, Jake, Jake." Samantha Chambers grinned. "Have you come back to Susanville for good?" she asked, handing over his coffee, and receiving payment.

"No, I'm just passing through. I got a position with *The Washington Post*, so I'm off for D.C."

"Good luck, then," Samantha urged.

"Thanks."

Lucy perked up at the statement. "Going to D.C.? What about your business in Lassen County?"

Jake carried his coffee to the mixing counter, Lucy on his heels.

"Yes, that." He opened the lid and poured in sugar and a dollop of half & half. "Since Calvin Simms kicked the bucket, I guess I won't be staying very long."

"Where did you hear about that?"

"I have my connections."

He headed for a booth, set his computer case on the tabletop, and took a seat, motioning to the bench seat across from him.

"Care to join me?" he invited.

"Thank you." Lucy slid in, and set her coffee and bag upon the table. "What about those connections?"

"Ms. Jennings, in all due respect, a journalist never reveals his or her sources. I'm well aware of my Constitutional rights."

"I see."

"Besides, I have tools." He opened the computer case, and removed a hand-held police band radio. "And they're legal."

"If you knew, why didn't you tell the Sumners?"

"Because, that's your job, Ms. Jennings."

"You make yourself sound very upright, Mr. Weatherby."

"Not at all." He opened his laptop, and turned on the power. "I'm pretty slippery."

"Such as hiding the relationship you had with Kristina Sumner?"

His expression remained nonchalant.

"There was nothing to hide, Ms. Jennings. Miss Sumner and I worked together professionally. Anything outside of the *Register*, I'd categorize as friendship."

"Really? Mrs. Sumner told me that you admitted to being in love with her daughter."

"Very true, but I acted as a mentor, not a rapist."

"I see."

"I've never touched her, never held her hand, never embraced, even when I drove out to the ranch to say goodbye. And except for maybe a couple of slip-ups, I've never even used her first name, it was always professional, it was always 'Miss Sumner' for me."

"I see."

He seemed amused. "Is that your trade response, this 'I see?'"

Lucille Jennings was beginning to feel irritated.

"I don't quite understand, Mr. Weatherby, what a man of your age would see in a young girl."

"To be frank, Ms. Jennings, Miss Sumner is the kind of person who won't change very much in the coming years. Her ego and personality are both highly developed, as is her sense of morality. I noted a rare form in Miss Sumner, something beautiful, and both delicate and tenacious, which I know is a contradiction."

He removed his wallet from a back pocket, and pulled a slip of paper from its leather folds, which he passed across the table to D.A. Jennings.

"What's this?" she asked, unfolding the creased paper.

"Read it. Aloud."

"Cottonwoods, arisen from water and earth,
exuded the rank odor of death.
Their scent of spring and green rebirth,
belie my faltering, guilty breath.
That evil portrays a placid face,
and hides its killing, wicked side,
Beneath the brief and tender buds,
as flames consume my rage and pride."

Jake Weatherby pointed at the paper. "That entire paragraph describes Miss Sumner."

"I don't quite understand." Lucy slid the paper back to him, and he tucked it carefully into his wallet, and the safety of his back pocket.

"There's something unbearably sweet and enduring in those four lines. It speaks of maturity, and insight. When I first read what Miss Sumner had written, it floored me."

"I see." Lucy grimaced, chagrined at her own statement. "I didn't realize she'd written that when I read it. Yes, I agree with your assessment, Mr. Weatherby. But that still doesn't explain why you'd profess to being in love with a sixteen-year-old girl."

He tilted his head. "Isn't it more accurate to state that you're wondering why I wouldn't fall in love with an attractive, mature woman such as yourself, Ms. Jennings?"

She nodded. "Yes, privately, I suppose I *am* wondering that, Mr. Weatherby."

"Would you be able to reach inside of yourself and create those lines?"

She considered the question, and then shook her head. "No, it's not in me."

"That's why, Ms. Jennings. *That's* why."

"I'll be in court tomorrow," she told him, rising from the seat, with the bag of untouched croissant, and the partially finished coffee jammed into one hand.

"So will I, after I pick up the press pass early. I'll watch the dismissal, and then I'll be leaving Susanville. Or maybe I'll just leave town without attending the dismissal."

"Do you have to?"

"What?"

His eyes, she noted, were changeful in the light of the café, depending upon his emotions, and intensified by the color of his shirt. Though she had seen Jacob Weatherby several times before he moved from Susanville in 2007, court-related ships passing in the night, so to speak, she had never actually *looked* at him. The gist of the refrain of the poetry ran through her head, and she understood why he carried that expression in his gaze.

"I'm asking, Mr. Weatherby. Do you have to leave town right away?"

He shrugged. "I'm supposed to start my job in D.C. in ten days. I'm driving, so I figured I'd stop along the way, and kind of cruise through the states slowly."

"Kristina Sumner will be eighteen on Thursday," Lucy said softly.

"I know that." He seemed miserable. "I won't do it, Ms. Jennings."

"Won't do what, Mr. Weatherby?"

"I won't change the course of her life."

"Everyone we meet changes the course of our lives. We're not living in a vacuum. She very clearly changed your life, and as well, I believe her experience with you affected hers."

"I can't do it," he insisted.

She set aside the professional bearing of her office, and placed a hand on his shoulder. She remembered how it felt this morning when Kate Sumner had clutched her, that connectivity to humanity, and Lucy hoped she was conveying a similar emotion.

"Don't leave without seeing her," she said firmly. "*Don't.*"

He nodded, looking up at her, and then she removed her hand.

"Have a good rest of the day, Ms. Jennings."

"Yes, thank you, Mr. Weatherby, and please do the same."

As she left the café, the smell of the woods and the casual pace of the passing traffic lightened her somber mood.

* * * *

On the return to the Spotted Horse Ranch, with Kate at the wheel, Paul Sumner announced to the children the fact that Calvin Simms had passed away, and the court case was going to be officially dismissed by the District Attorney the following morning.

Kristina, seated on the middle bench seat beside Sara, felt tremendous relief escape. She sat close to a window, so she could watch the landscape which at once seemed so familiar, and yet, ever changing.

Now I can leave in peace, she thought, because she had been anxious for the emotional wellbeing of her family during the pressures of the trial. In part, she had wondered how her parents would be able to go with her to Maryland, had they been required to remain in Susanville.

She thought about her brothers, Charlie Kat and Dakota, who shared the seat with their elder brother Daniel. They were cheering and giving each other congratulatory high-fives. Kristina knew the singular disappointment for the two younger brothers was the lost opportunity to declare to the court how Calvin and Robert Simms had destroyed the security of their childhood.

Dakota had confided in Kristina his determination to explain his role in loading the handgun, and bringing it to Kate. Though the trauma of witnessing the literal explosion of Robert Simms' head repeated itself endlessly in his dreams—and occasionally during his waking hours—Kristina knew the edge of that horror had worn smooth. Acceptance, rather than paralyzing fear, had soothed the damage to his young psyche.

Kristina harbored the secret knowledge that she would be seated in the press box close to Mr. Weatherby. She entertained sensations of being in his presence, maybe the sound of his voice speaking her name, "Miss Sumner"—or, if he were so inclined, the uncustomary "Kristina"—and even their skin brushing in passing. These were but fantasies. She was pragmatic enough to recognize her mental deviation from reality.

"I'll go with you tomorrow, Kris," her father offered, throwing a cold bucket on her reverie.

She blinked, emerging from her thoughts. "Tomorrow?"

"Lucille Jennings is going to dismiss the charges formally, in court," Paul explained. "Your mother thought perhaps you could accompany me to the event." He studied her closely. "You do have a press pass."

"I do," she confirmed. "Yes, I'll go with you, Dad."

Later, at home, she handled the chores with her usual precision—washing breakfast dishes, sweeping the walkway, and folding two loads of laundry—all the while thinking about Mr. Weatherby with the daring of someone not quite experienced past the boundary of virginity.

She had been raised around open sexual activity between animals. Her parents were horse breeders, and were matter-of-fact about the passionate nature of mating between their herd of brood mares and the hot-blooded feral stallion, consummated in pasture breeding.

For Kristina, reproduction had served as an awakening, and wonderment. The horses' sexual union was both ardent and intense, mares and stallion equally sharing in the come-hither process. She would catch herself wondering if humans were as vigorous in the act—though, according to the school district's clinical description of human sexuality, mating was nothing more than a seeding process.

Media coverage was quite a different subject, portraying the lust and fanfare of passion. Her favored reading genre was as far removed from Romance as the sun is from the earth. But it was not to say that Kristina hadn't read a Romance novel at any point in her life. Her school friend, Stacey Corcoran, had passed a particularly racy book along to Kristina, entitled "Satan's Fury," repugnant and arousing, and Kristina hadn't the nerve to finish it. Feeling guilty, she hid it beneath her mattress, like a young man with a porn magazine.

Imagining herself as the heroine, and Mr. Weatherby as the raging lover, was ridiculous in her mind. The conversational language of the horny lovers in "Satan's Fury" had left Kristina feeling appalled, and even slightly annoyed.

Added to the bizarre prose, was the impediment of she and Mr. Weatherby never having passed the formality in the usage of one another's first names. She couldn't imagine saying, in the midst of lovemaking, "Oh, Mr. Weatherby," much less, hearing him whisper, "Miss Sumner, my love."

Compounding that was the concept that her only measure of human sexuality was seeing horses mating. If people were as noisy and boisterous as a stud and a brood mare—or as swiftly to the point—she was in for a lifetime of disappointment. Strangely, if she pictured Mr. Weatherby as the stallion, and she as the mare, she would lie awake, and want it to happen exactly that way.

She knew her body by touch and feel, and had masturbated quietly in the darkness of her private room, but had never allowed another's hand to offer the sensation that ultimately led to sexual climax. She had difficulty in imagining giving this secret to somebody else, even to a man she cared about. Since Tucker Parker's death, Kristina was so accustomed to building up a wall as a means of emotional survival that it was almost impossible to break down the barrier that kept her safe.

Life was just so frustrating.

I am still a virgin, she would think, knowing the jewel in being, but wishing she had moves, that she wasn't such a sexual clodhopper, that she could be a brazen lover with him when the time was right.

"Hold onto it, Kristina," her sister, Sara, had urged. "Give it up to someone you love."

"Did you?" Kristina had asked directly, her brows raised, though Sara's sneaking blush said it all.

"You know Joaquin," Sara said softly. "He has my gift."

But there was an essence between Kristina and Mr. Weatherby she often imagined, which transcended lust. She used it to soften the restlessness thoughts of lying with him invoked.

She would remember their conversations, his radiant declaration in loving her, the admiration she experienced in his gaze. These were qualities she often noticed in her own parents, undying love, which bonded two partners to keep their fire burning.

* * * *

On Monday morning, the grounds of the Lassen County courthouse were crawling with people—lawyers, the print and television media, and common folk. There were more cases being heard on this day than the Simms issue, but it was evident that at least among the press community, Calvin Simms's death was a monumental letdown to the potential journalistic frenzy a long, drawn-out trial would have afforded.

Kristina and her father walked slowly from their parking spot on South Greeno Street, kitty-corner to Mission Street, where the stately courthouse stood.

The elms surrounding the grounds were emerald in the early heat of the August morning. Beds of pansies and impatiens colored what would otherwise be a vast expanse of barren earth edged with native lava stone. Rose bushes bloomed in deep red or bright yellow, depending upon the type, and a band-tailed pigeon called from its hiding place in an elm.

She saw Jake Weatherby well before he spotted her. Noting his attire, she was glad she had chosen to wear the business suit, a wool-blend cool enough for the heat of the Honey Lake Valley, and classy enough to use in a professional forum. The black fitted blazer and a knee-length skirt complemented the athletic shape of her calves. She had intended to use the outfit in her press capacity, along with the striped blouse and low-heeled black pumps. With her long hair pinned up, the outfit lent Kristina Sumner the veneer of maturity.

He had been walking along the concrete pathway at the top of the garden aimlessly, even appearing a bit dispirited, but when he saw her, his face came alight. His eyes caught her and held, and without hesitation, he began to walk toward her briskly.

"Kristina, isn't that Mr. Weatherby?" Paul asked, without pointing.

"Yes, Dad," she said, feeling breathless. "I believe it is."

"Mr. Sumner," said Mr. Weatherby. "Miss Sumner."

She could swear his voice changed when he mentioned her name.

Paul moved forward to shake Jake Weatherby's hand. "Jake, how are you?"

"Fine, just fine." Mr. Weatherby grinned. "And you?"

"Great." Paul motioned to his daughter, which was completely unnecessary. "I'll give the two of you a moment." He headed toward the steps of the courthouse.

"Miss Sumner," said Mr. Weatherby. He wore a dark blue suit, which brought out that color in his eyes. "I've really missed you."

She held out her hand. "I've missed you too."

They shook for a bit longer than Kristina had ever been subject to shaking someone's hand. When they were done, he simply kept holding her hand, but then, she didn't mind, as her fingers shaped to his.

"I have so much to tell you," he began. "This has been the longest eighteen months of my life, and now it's almost past."

"It doesn't feel like it's been almost a year and a half," she agreed. "It could've all happened just yesterday."

"Well, that's positive, don't you think?"

"And better, because I'll be eighteen on Thursday, Mr. Weatherby."

"I know." He nodded. "I've never stopped thinking about you."

She caught a hint of deep sadness in his gaze. "There's more, and it isn't good, is it?"

"I won't be here on Thursday, Kristina," he said painfully, his voice filled with unshed tears.

"That's number three."

"What is?"

"The third time you've said my name."

"No, I've said it many more than three times."

The truth tumbled out as he recalled his time in the Bay Area. He described the house in Berkeley, the American flag—and the AIM banner—for what else would a reactionary-turned-liberal hang in tribute to his Native beloved? The empty rooms he wandered, speaking her first name. The interminable months without her, and the paper he carried in his wallet.

"What paper?" she asked.

Releasing her hand, he dug it out of his wallet, her poem of the cottonwoods, age-softened and creased. She was happy enough to know he carried it. She folded and returned the paper, and noted how reverently he tucked it away.

"Daniel told me all about his visit," she confessed.

"I had hoped he would."

"I figured...I supposed that everything would change. You'd find someone like Tammy Hart, and you'd have a life. I never expected anything else, Mr. Weatherby. I'd hoped, but I never expected."

"Why would I go out and find someone else, when I'm in love with you?"

This silenced her for a moment. The sun was in his eyes, and when he spoke, he squinted like a boy, yet he was a man, and in the honesty of his words, any doubt she carried fled.

"How can you say you're going away, after telling me something like that?"

She could hear the pleading tone to her voice, but she didn't care.

He nodded, and looked away, as though he was on the verge of losing his poise. When he turned back to her, his eyes were bright.

"You go to college, Kristina," he said, taking her hand again. "Soak up higher education, learn everything you can, and when you're famous, when you've achieved your career goals, I'll be around somewhere, keeping track of your progress."

"What you're saying, what you just said—"

"I won't destroy your chances, Kristina, for making something important out of your life. I've passed that point myself, but you have a brilliant future."

"Why can't I have you there, too? What makes it so impossible?"

"I make it impossible," he admitted. "My ethics do."

"I could make a case about the incompatibility of love and ethics, but then, you're the attorney."

"And you're the poet, Kristina. Love and ethics are one in the same."

"Why does life have to be *so* difficult?"

"No, it's easy. Falling in love with you, actually, was very easy."

"Then, remember me, will you, Jake?" she asked, her voice almost a whisper, the first time she'd spoken his name. Every ounce of her felt the pain of speaking his name.

"I'll never forget you, Kristina. You're on my mind every day." He saw her father at the top of the slope. "Your dad's waiting for you." He released her hand.

"For what it's worth, I meant to tell you that time at the Ranch, before you went away, that I love you too, Jake."

She was going to cry before this was over. The pain was agonizing, worse than any novel could suppose.

He opened his arms, and hugged her close, no indecency, just the virtue of his feelings. The sensation was so emotionally painful that it crushed any threat of impropriety.

"I'm not staying for the dismissal," he told her, when he released her. Paul Sumner was returning, but slowly, so they could finish their conversation. "I left some packages with Gladys Reed at the Book Shelf for safekeeping. They're for you, and she knows all about them."

"It would be childish for me to beg, I know it." Her voice felt strained, and it was becoming difficult to speak. "So, I won't." She touched his arm. "If you decide to change your mind about Thursday—"

"I'm sorry, Kristina, I can't, I simply...can't."

"Then, I hope to see you again, Jake."

She kissed him on the cheek. Her caress was unexpected, and he brought his hand to the place her lips had brushed, then reached out and touched her face with trembling fingers.

To delay the tears, she turned, and began to walk swiftly toward her father. Behind her, she could hear the footsteps as Jake Weatherby hurried down the concrete pathway, toward his car and escape.

But D.A. Lucille Jennings hadn't yet entered the courthouse, and waylaid Kristina before she could reach her father.

"Kristina." Ms. Jennings grasped her hand.

"Yes?" The teary-eyed anguish on Kristina's face said it all.

"I'm so sorry," said Lucy. "I gather that you spoke with Mr. Weatherby."

"Yes, but I'm all right," Kristina lied, though at least that made it easier to make it through a conversation with Ms. Jennings.

"I'm not sure what Mr. Weatherby conveyed, Kristina, but when we spoke, he seemed reluctant to alter your life, that you have so many options waiting for you, and he didn't wish to become an impediment to your future."

"I understand that."

"When I had this conversation with him, he thought it was better that he went straight to D.C. as soon as possible, no waiting for the dismissal, which is just a formality at this point."

Despite rising numbness, Kristina heard something that triggered a flare of excitement.

"Did you say D.C.? As in Washington D.C.?"

"Yes, didn't he tell you? He got a job with *The Washington Post*. He's supposed to be there in about ten days."

Now Kristina was grinning like an idiot, but she didn't care. Far down the street, she could see that Jake Weatherby had ducked into a maroon Prius, and was driving away slowly, hunched painfully over the steering wheel.

"No, he must have forgotten." She laughed involuntarily. "Did I tell you that my parents are taking me to the university? We're flying out of Reno on the twentieth."

"Neither mentioned it, but I suppose they would have, if there had been a trial." She glanced at her watch, antsy, as the time was eight forty-five a.m., and Judge Beck's court started at nine o'clock sharp. "Where are you going to school?"

"I'm enrolled at Berkshire University, it's in Maryland."

"Congratulations, Kris," said Lucille Jennings. "I'm certain you'll be successful with everything you aim to accomplish."

Kristina took a deep breath. "Thank you," she replied, while in her mind sang the sweet refrain: *Berkshire University is only ninety miles from Washington D.C.*

The beloved vista of the Honey Lake Valley seemed to echo her thoughts, as she climbed the slope to join her father.

About the Author

A California native, Karen Kennedy Samoranos has a deep and abiding love for the Golden State, reflected in the settings of her books. She believes in love at first sight, undying passion, and the rare balance of two souls in sync. As an author, all of these elements are a constant theme of her work. By day, she and her husband are committed to a music education business that forwards the cause of live jazz stage performance for children, ages 4 through 18. Family is the ultimate fulfillment—the author has four adult children, and six young grandchildren.

Made in the USA
Columbia, SC
29 May 2020

98612017R00120